W9-BCK-409

CHELSEA GIRLS

ALSO BY EILEEN MYLES

Snowflake/different streets (2012)

Inferno (a poet's novel) (2010)

The Importance of Being Iceland: Travel Essays in Art (2009)

Sorry, Tree (2007)

Tow (with drawings by artist Larry C. Collins) (2005)

Skies (2001)

On My Way (2001)

Cool for You (2000)

School of Fish (1997)

Maxfield Parrish: Early & New Poems (1995)

The New Fuck You: Adventures in Lesbian Reading (with Liz Kotz) (1995)

Not Me (1991)

1969 (1989)

Bread and Water: Stories (1988)

Sappho's Boat: Poems (1982)

A Fresh Young Voice from the Plains (1981)

Polar Ode (with Anne Waldman) (1979)

The Irony of the Leash (1978)

CHELSEA GIRLS

EILEEN MYLES

An Imprint of HarperCollins*Publishers*

CHELSEA GIRLS. Copyright © 1994 by Eileen Myles. All rights reserved. Printed in the United States of America. No part of this book may be used or reproduced in any manner whatsoever without written permission except in the case of brief quotations embodied in critical articles and review. For information address HarperCollins Publishers, 195 Broadway, New York, NY 10007.

HarperCollins books may be purchased for educational, business, or sales promotional use. For information please e-mail the Special Markets Department at SPsales@harpercollins.com.

A paperback edition of this book was originally published in 1994 by Black Sparrow Press.

FIRST ECCO PAPERBACK EDITION PUBLISHED 2015.

Library of Congress Cataloging-in-Publication Data

Myles Eileen.
    Chelsea girls / Eileen Myles
        p.   cm
    ISBN 0-87685-933-3 (cloth trade): $25.00. — ISBN 0-87685-934-1 (signed cloth) : $35.00. — ISBN 0-87685-932-5 (pbk.) : $13.00
        1. City and town life—New York (N.Y.)—Fiction.   2. Young women—New York (N.Y.)—Fiction.   3. Lesbians—New York (N.Y.)—Fiction.   4. Chelsea (New York, N.Y.)—Fiction.   I. Title.
        PS3563.Y498C45   1994
        813'.54—dc22
94-9895

ISBN 978-0-06-239466-8

16 17 18 19 OV/RRD 10 9 8 7 6 5

FOR TED MYLES

CONTENTS

Bath, Maine   1

The Kid   13

Merry Christmas, Dr. Beagle   19

Light Warrior   25

Bread and Water   29

My Scar   47

Everybody Would Go Play Cards at Eddie and Nonie's   49

The Goodbye Tapes   55

Robin   63

Madras   75

1969   101

February 13, 1982   121

Violence Towards Women   133

Toys R Us   139

Neuromancer   147

Dog Damage   151

My Couple   153

Mary Dolan: a History   165

Popponesset   181

Marshfield   187

My Father's Alcoholism   191

21, 22, 23 . . .   209

Quietude   215

Robert Mapplethorpe Picture   221

Leslie   229

Epilogue   237

Jealousy   241

Chelsea Girls   253

CHELSEA GIRLS

BATH, MAINE

I really had no damn business there. I mean, why am I living with my ex-girlfriend and her new girlfriend, and *her* ex-girlfriend. How could that possibly be comfortable. I could be writing this from a jail cell. Funny, huh? Ted and Alice, before I left, said: "Out of the frying pan and into the fire, Eileen." I didn't know what else I could do. I flew, yes I did, up to Portland and Judy and Chris picked me up there. I was so ripped on the plane. Elinor had given me some of that crystal, one good line, and I had a handful of Tom's pills. He had stayed at my place the night before. I was writing these poems up in the air, really stupid ones all over those cocktail napkins they give you. God, they were awful. About vitamins and stuff. I was off cigarettes which always made me particularly insane and I had those red beads on, when did they break, I remember them breaking in Maine—well, the two of them picked me up—I remember we went right into a bar—I think I remember having a shrimp salad sandwich and beers, and Chris was already drinking icy Margaritas. The place had all lobsters up and traps and all. Then we got back in Judy's car. That night we all went to the gay bar in Augusta. Oh god, that night. We were all speeding, and drunk, and it was real hot. All the men were taking their shirts off and dancing. We got mad. We wanted to take our shirts off. So we did. Everyone thought it was great. Except the manager and a couple of fag bartenders. Put 'em on. The men don't have to put their shirts on. Just get out. You can't be in this bar with your shirts off. Put your shirts on and get out. We did. But first we took our pants off and walked out. Chris threw a beer bottle at them too. She always had a lot of style. This is just three years ago.

After that everything went pretty much the same way. The night I was all amorous in the back seat of Judy's car with Darragh, her ex-girlfriend, we were actually out looking for Chris who had left us because she was looking for someone else, a man. Naturally, we were all smashed. Chris had been picked up by the cops for whatever the Maine initials were for operating under the influence. Understand, this was common practice to get arrested. We worked at this mill and every morning, or pretty close, someone had been arrested for speeding, drunken driving, had an accident, got in a fight. This is baseball hat and truck country. I loved it. The men were all men, and we were all lesbians, and everyone loved to get smashed. After work we'd sit on this big green lawn and Casey, the boss, would put down case after case of Bud Light and Labatt's and we'd just get crazy. Sheila was a problem. She was this big blonde girl, and she was Casey's girlfriend and she was really interested in the fact that me and Christine were lesbians. Now, I am a sucker for paternalism, I love having a boss who's a young good old boy, and when his girlfriend seems to want to go the other way, fascinating as it seems, and I do want to be the one she's wild about, nonetheless, I try and turn the other way.

Chris stopped drinking after the arrest night. She still had to go to court, it was a small mess. I loved her not drinking, she just got prettier and prettier, all glowing, and she got rid of that bloat she was getting from beer. I have never seen it make as much difference as it did with her. Also it was a relief. One night I was in bed with Judy and she came at me with a crowbar. I'm going to re-shape your head, asshole. What a frightening moment. I could see the shadow of her head, hand and crowbar against a strong light from behind. See, I had actually been up for a week the month before and had thought it was just like Valhalla. You know, it was just like paradise. Judy has this house in the middle of all this land in Maine, and out back are sheep bah-ing, and she had dogs, one a black lab named Myles, and there's little kittens, and hens out back, and a rooster, and fresh eggs and beautiful breakfasts with fried potatoes and tia maria in our coffee in bed. The first night I was up that time me and Chris were instantly back in love once we got drunk, and were out in a hallway, kissing each other, and saying: what about Judy. So the three of us were in their big bed—I just happily climbed right on top of Judy. Christine didn't like that—I wasn't supposed to get so into it. It was *smash*, battles, right from the start—though only one major eruption that week—Chris had gone out running, leaving Judy and me in bed and when she came back something was going on that—"How come you never fucking do that to me, Judy!" Judy would soon get hers. Christine was an emotional tyrant. Her and I had lived together for a couple of years in New York, before she came to Maine, and it took watching the movements of her and Judy's relationship to see just how demanding and impossible she was. I myself was a good-natured cloud, which would float by and steal things, and wait for praise. I could never understand why life just didn't feel substantial enough. I was sitting on your couch, or we were drinking your whiskey in my apartment. Now, let's go out, I'd say. Do you have any money. I'm broke tonight. I'm really sorry.

One night after work we all went drinking in Bath, Maine. "We" meant me, and Chris who was breaking out that night, figured it was okay, Sheila wanted to go out with us, and we had to go home and pick up Judy. I guess they all were going to play that night, they had a guy in Bath they played with, Mr. Michael, some kind of architect with a loft. All of Judy's friends were professionals pretending to be artists. Pretty disgusting, yet they had the stuff: lofts, the cars, houses etc. They are the mommies and daddies. Usually they're so insipid and have nothing to say, but you get to be fabulous, for a while. For me, they're like jobs.

I don't think Judy was overwhelmed with love for me. I think I was there to be neutralized. You know, Christine would get drunk and call me. Or, she'd just talk about me all the time. Okay, let's get this icon and get her on my farm. Things would happen like one night Judy had her whole collection of mangy men over: Ron, the lumber man, who she was always going "clamming" with tomorrow, or who was the little weasel who knew all about, what, electricity or something. They were all anti-intellectual types who were dying to fuck Judy and she kept them around for, I don't know, entertainment, and certainly real help, and I think she thought of them as colorful, possibly admirable. They made her think she was countrified. She was a consultant to an environmental outfit, she would go and look at fish factories and come back drunk. Previously, she had been a broker in San Francisco. Now she's some kind of film person in Boston. Judy looks right. And she'll never stop telling you about what kind of good girls' school she dropped out of. Her mother's a drunk. She's one of those women who despises her mother and is just like her.

So Judy said to Chris once, riding in her car, I just don't see where Eileen gets off thinking she has the last word on truth. That's what she said. What's funny is I picture her car saying it. You know, one of those shots where the white Datsun is wobbling through the narrow windy roads of mid-coastal Maine and the car says: ". . . thinking she has the last word on truth." Fuck you, Judy.

I remember standing in the back of the truck that fateful night drinking a Bud Light and thinking: this is not going to be perfect—about the night, it looked too perfect—going with the girls to Bath. Judy and Chris would play with Michael, Judy on bass, Christine on rhythm, Michael on lead. Sheila and me roving through the local bars, sounds okay, but—what?

What I was trying to say about Judy and her gross men was that she'd have these smelly horny guys come over—that night we made a pitcher of strawberry daquiris with Mount Gay which I was currently binging on, and once drunk Chris passed a slip of paper to Judy which I later learned said, I want to eat you—how Christine paid her rent, and the two went giggling stumbling off, leaving me to be game warden to her charming friends. This is why I had been invited to Maine. These guys talked real slow—stopped after each phrase for your girl-reaction. The best I could do was an occasional *heh*. After a while I just stared at my feet.

At work we dipped in these small—or sometimes fairly large—wooden frames into vats of stain. Their destination was the cheap carnivals, and beach towns of America. Those mirrors that say Grateful Dead, or NY Yankees. After dipping the frames into vats of stain and lining them up in rows of twenty on the sticks overhead, bundling them, and putting the plastic tape around each bundle and stacking them in the truck to Chicago or wherever, at the end of the day I'd be covered from head to foot with brown stain, Dickensian-looking I thought. I usually didn't bother to get the stuff off before I got drunk. With me sloppy has always been good, meant sexy.

But this night we were using this "glup"—it was tan, looked like bacon fat, and seemed to come in Mason jars, but the people I knew bought it in quantity. We were really going out, so we had to take the spots off. That's what I usually looked like: a dalmatian. I just think dogs are the cutest beings, and the most perfect. Sheila seemed to be getting bombed on the vodka, cape codders we called them. I remember taking showers, having a drink going and a beer going, being way up there and wondering if maybe tonight I wouldn't have to come down.

The light looked translucent, just pearly, as we drove into Bath with plenty of beers in the car. I really missed drugs. All we ever had was this shitty homegrown pot. David was coming up at the end of the month and I was begging him to bring heroin. It was beginning to seem preferable to getting drunk. I mean, if you were going to get really drunk, you could just achieve the same state in a much less messy manner by snorting some stuff. I liked it. But the last time I got some we got beat.

We parked out in front of Michael's, and Sheila decided she needed to lay down in the loft. See, we worked really hard, starting at about six, so some nights you had no tolerance at all. So I went up for a minute, sort of remember a big yellow bathroom, and an extremely pleasant loft that Michael had "done a lot of work on," those people are so boring. I was glad to be going off on my own.

The bars in Bath were like the bars everywhere, except with that New England distrust, no one talks to you. I whipped out my notebook, but I couldn't even communicate with myself. I was drinking vodka and grapefruit. I had on a white teeshirt with FATS WALLER on the front. I ate a lot of peanuts. Next bar I switched to tequila. What could happen. I sat at like this long coffee table, kind of Gothic looking, ancient S & M, with a big candle. I didn't want anyone to come near me. The place looked kind of "datey," like it was attached to a restaurant. The clientele was sunburned and clean, like vacationers. Was I feeling better? In the last place when I had nothing to say in my notebook I began to write the words from the jukebox

And only love
can break
your heart

So try to make sure
right from
the start . . .

It made me suspicious. I had willed that I really was not still in love with Chris, I had decided to be a dispassionate viewer, it would be a pleasure not to care. What if I didn't know what I felt anymore? I probably had never known what I felt. I only liked getting drunk and being in love. If I wasn't either one of those things, I simply needed my rent, cigarettes, and coffee, simple enough. I really liked the life of the poet.

In barged Sheila and Chris. Judy's an asshole, Chris goes. What are you drinking, Margaritas? Yay, let's get four, I think they're slow. Then we were all in the bathroom, unrolling toilet paper all over the place, and kissing each other. Judy and Michael showed up just as we were getting thrown out. At the next bar we seemed to be standing in line watching something, but I can't remember what it was. The order you stood in was very important, so I wanted to go outside.

I think I was sitting on the curb when the cops came. Everything occurred very fast in some grey soup.

The cop was trying to pull Chris out of the front seat of Judy's car. Chris was hanging on to Judy's hair who was holding the steering wheel tightly. Previously, they were wrestling for the car keys. Drunk out of her mind, naturally, Chris wanted to drive. I guess I still do love her. She is a trophy to anger and intolerance with brown curly hair. She was always like my little sister I wanted to be as bad as. So she was bashing Judy's head against that thing the stick shift comes out of, and maybe she would've gotten the keys if the cop hadn't come along. I figured it wasn't my fight. See, I come from an alcoholic household, and resultingly kind of don't react to violence. I think it terrifies me, but I am so drawn to it. I never hit anyone, but I would love to kill a lot of people

It's okay I tell the cop, as he moves through the grey soup, towards the white car. As the story goes, he said *Stop* into the car window and Chris punched him in the face. God, I love her. So that's when he started pulling her out.

Like a famous tackle I performed on a boy in sixth grade, the last tomboy gesture of pre-adolescence, I do not remember getting off the ground, I only remember sailing through the air, leaping on the cop's back, getting my arms around his neck to choke him, or flip him, or something. On my float towards him I saw something. The girl god, or the dog god, or the dead drunken daddy god, all the gods that protect me in my living did not spur me to reach for the one thing I saw as I flew to his big blue cop shoulders. The gun!

No, I just landed up around the shoulders, and so fast I was way over there, on the sidewalk with my head smashed down, and MACE in my eyes, it stung, and there were tons of them now, cops, a holocaust, and yet handcuffs, too. I was a freedom fighter of some kind. I've been in handcuffs a couple of times. Handcuffs make me wild.

They were trying to take my picture down at the station, and of course I wouldn't stop making googly eyes, sticking my tongue out, spitting on the floor. They were not going to have an attractive prison picture of me. There was a fat woman guard I really had it in for. You are a traitor to women, you're a dyke, hey you big bulldyke, look at you, you bitch, you trai-tor, you like to suck cunt don't you? I guess I started this in the squad car on the way to the jail—which wasn't far—the police station was right across the street from where Judy's white car was parked. All through my denunciation of this woman I continued to spit on the floor. Also my Fats Waller teeshirt had ridden up around my shoulders so I whipped it off and started screaming police brutality, police brutality.

Eileen, shut up, said Chris. All in all, Christine believed I started this, had started the whole thing. This is where she really became a little creep. She didn't know it was a cop, that was her story. I did know it was a gun and was glad I didn't go for it. And, in my heart I know the moment of my flight towards the blue shoulders of the law, I was flying for Chris, did love her, and was saving her from the professional medi-ocrity of white Datsuns, I was releasing her from bourgeoise captivity, maybe bringing her home to the scrubby plains of my drunk art and love. Oh, Chris!

Well, she didn't appreciate it, the little bitch, why wouldn't I shut up, I was just making things so much worse.

Also, my real moment in the police station in Bath, Maine was when I lifted my sword and revealed to them that I was a poet.

I'm a poet, you fools, you asshole *cops*! Poet has always meant to me saint or hero, the dancing character on the stained-glass window of my soul, the hand lifting slowly through time, the whirr that records my material against strong light, gosh, why I live. It's the channel this ex-catholic took when getting down on her knees didn't keep anyone alive, or help the dead stay dead. I was a devout child, but my prayers were ritualistic insurance, and a real list of dead people—God, take care of grandma, grandpa—it became so long it was unfeasible, by about age eleven, or twelve, so I began to keep a diary and sat under the light of the hall stairs and recorded what I ate that day, and who I thought hated me, and who I loved, and how I won. The poem got born in jobs, when I realized I wouldn't win, wasn't in fact, even present. So I began to take up residence in my poems, saw my life as a loser's, hence poetic.

Okay, okay, so you're a poet, let's hear a poem. I don't *know* my poems I proffered, snobbishly, being baldly attached to the page. I hold the poem, the sacred document. Oh, alright. This was like martyrdom, baptism by fire, by blood.

It's called: "Roast Chicken."

I hesitated, stumbled, and forgot a lot, and they mocked me, but I got it out. And, nothing happened.

Sometimes . . .

Roast Chicken!

Okay, okay, "Roast Chicken."

Sometimes . . .

Some poet, she doesn't even know her poem.

> Sometimes
> in the middle
> of the night
> I think about
> holding you

in your beautiful
tan

I think about
in your beautiful
tan . . .

    I blew it. They weren't listening anymore. I had failed. So
what. The test of blood was on.

Sometimes
in the middle
of the night.
I think about
holding you
in your
beautiful tan
wishing you
were
all of mine
and I
was only
yours.

    Finished. "Oh, no," said Chris, when she asked what poem
I was yelling at them. "Oh, no," she cringed, "not that one."

THE KID

I came home from school one day in the 7th grade with a punish task in my head fresh from Giovanna's fat white face, "Eileen Myles, 500 times, I will not talk in the corridors." I can remember my feet that day getting heavier than usual on the gray slate steps of St. Agnes School. We were on the third floor by then. It had taken us seven years to get there. Once to the top, you were out. For some of us, that just meant across the street.

So I came home that day too intent to even be pissed off. Kathy Marshall was having a party that night, boys were invited to come late, so it was a boy girl party I could go to—the party starting off all girls so I think I could go.

She wasn't listening to me that day when I was telling her what my punish task was all about. Watch your father while I go hang clothes, will you? Will you set up the card table in the parlor. It was another "watching Dad" job. I already had a pile of paper, white with blue lines and I would do my punish task in ball point. Pencil wore down too fast and you had to keep sharpening the pencil. Sometimes it was fun letting it get all flat, and pointed in different ways, running your pencil into the ground. Once I wore out a ball-point, a Lindy pen, writing the Constitution 7 times. I loved seeing a pen die, rather than losing it, like usual. Or someone clipping it in school.

The card table was smooth like old paper. Sometimes I put my face against it and rubbed. Once Mom caught me and called my name in that scarey way, like something you were doing was really sick. Anything we did that didn't look normal, that's what I felt scared her the most. She wanted everything to look good all the time. Because she was an orphan.

The card table was so brown and it was an old painting of a country house with trees and maybe people with a straw hat and a dog. It was so easy not to think of it as a painting but more like a rug, where it has things but you don't think of it as a picture. You only look at it if you get stuck like in church. There I counted everything, it was my prayer. I knew how many little holes were in the round ceiling that looked like light came down from a tube, and I knew the scrolley designs very well. Though they made me sick I would still go around them like a little car. Then I even doubled back to make sure. It was my job. In mass on Sunday I kept the church there by crawling along the designs. Otherwise it would all go away and I'd be alone.

Dad lay on the couch in front of me in his grey plaid shirt. I liked that shirt, he turned the cuffs up to his elbow and he had black hairs on his arms, and a wedding ring, and when he did anything he held his cigarette up to his lips, thought, and then spoke. He looks great against a tree smoking. Or else in the window of his car.

Dad, as you lay there sleeping, I can feel the bristles on your face, and I can feel the hair on the back of your hand and I can see your slippers on the couch which was funny, because you usually wore those white mailman socks which the doctor said were more healthy.

Dad, the worst time ever with you was when Mary McClusky was over and you had your red lumberjack shirt on and you were lying down and you had those awful headaches which kept pounding and made you always look like you were going to cry, and you put your two fingers to your lips—were you talking on the phone lying down or were you watching a movie on teevee. You couldn't talk and you kept making that two-fingered gesture even though I felt like it wasn't what you wanted I knelt down and kissed you in front of Mary which was hard because she is such a tomboy. "No, God damn it, a cigarette." "She kissed him," Mary laughed. Myles kissed him, she laughed all the way down Swan Place as if I wasn't there. I know you got angry because of your headache, Dad, but I felt like such an asshole. I think I just wanted to kiss you in front of Mary because you were lying there sick.

The day you died I think I even knew it was going to happen. I felt like I was in church. In front of you: Eileen, watch your father, like I did all the time. When I saw what was happening I knew it was right and I always wanted to watch someone die, and those sounds that meant more and more, and I knew exactly what was happening but I still stayed there, even kept writing to be sure that it was really happening. This can't be a lie. I didn't want to tell anyone; I wanted to be alone with you when it happened because it was like you were mine all along and it was my job to stay there and see, and *then* let everyone know.

I hated all the rest of the stuff, the way I got ignored, and I was there. Didn't anyone ever tell anyone that I was there when it happened because I was your kid? People going to Terry, well, now you're the little man of the family. Father McGinty asking Bridgie to do her tables for him while the whole house was crying except me. What was I, invisible. Well, from now on I would be. If they think I am a kid, I will be a kid forever. They made me wear lady clothes to the wake. Black velvet bow on my head and a royal blue straight wool skirt, and squash heels. Yuck. I winked when we filed out of the church the morning of the funeral. I saw my friends in the last row of the church and I winked at them, and Franny told me later, they all cried at that.

I wish I was in school the day they said over the loud speakers, "Prayers are requested for the father of Terrence, Eileen and Bridget Myles. He died last Thursday. They won't be in school today." Everyone in the room will have to think about me and the kids who hate me won't know what to do. What can they do? Sit there and hate me because my father's dead. Ha. Scoff on them. Especially boys.

All the boys who I love and think I'm a jerk and the girls who think they're too good for me will die. They can't say a word. When I came in everyone acted the same and I hated it so much. I had to act different. I acted real serious and got real cheap. I acted like I couldn't do anything anymore because we were poor.

We weren't but I decided I would act that way. It made me

sad, and I decided that was a new way I could be. Nothing made me feel. Everything was quiet. Mom was funny, Terry was mean, Bridgie would just crawl up on my mother a lot. I acted like a kid. I would be a beatnik, I would make everyone so sad and be so cool. Loads of laughs, Eileen.

MERRY CHRISTMAS,
DR. BEAGLE

There's a place I don't go anymore. Get on the "F" anywhere, take it, bells ringing and all, air-conditioning in the summer, out to Roosevelt Avenue, there you change to the number seven train, old clanky, interior dry as bone, people grim, canned— to the very end of the line, Main Street, Flushing. Come up, into the street, Alexander's, finally pass the intersection into the area of small brick buildings, down a couple of concrete steps, note the security system warning on his dark red door, step in to the bright nightmare of Dr. Beagle's office. Sign. Sign your name on the clipboard. Eileen Dolan. I chose this name eight years ago on my first trip to the doctor's because of my best estranged friend who had that last name. She's a nurse, her husband's a doctor, they would abhor this action, using her retired moniker as the key to my life of endless mornings. Wake up. Again and again. Turquoise pills that break neatly because of the indented line across their circumference. Made for breaking, made for sharing. Alice loved those halves a lot. I made some friendships that way. Hello. Would you like a good pill? I love these. Salty, then just behind the tongue those little glands go blinng at the familiar taste. Wheeee. Not the strongest pills, or the roughest, or the smoothest, but just the prettiest, my blue pills. I got 84 each month for seven years. At first I'd sell you ten, I'd give you six, I'd pay back the money I owed you by letting you have sixteen free, acid from Ann in exchange. Eventually times got hard and I sold them all to Harry at the Strand. Nervously bounding down the stairs to the basement. Hi. Two wry grins, and boomp back up the stairs to the street, free. Or one more stop.

Ellen was Sherryl's friend, in medical school, Ellen did a lot of speed. I was fifteen pounds heavier than her, I was perfect. She borrowed a car and we drove down the BQE to the doctor's the first day, eight years ago. I had no interest, really, not doing drugs, just drinking a lot as always. I agreed to take fifteen anyhow from that first lot, I took one hesitantly. It wasn't so great. It just made me a little different, nervous, not hungry—yogurt was fine. Coffee and cigarettes were sweeter I noticed and . . . xeroxing at work was a joy! Flash, flash flash, I loved watching the sheets kick out of the machine, I began to time it with a little twist of my hip, bend my knee. I loved the exquisite calm of xeroxing. I had a notebook where I put my thoughts. Dry Imager. That was the name of a small poem I wrote around that time.

I was going to Alice's workshop on Fridays and I would give her a few in the bar afterwards to make her like me and she did. Eventually she liked me anyway but now at least she liked me. I drank bourbon with my blue pills and one night I fell down in Phebe's on this combination and another time I fell down in the Locale. It was really embarrassing. A) I was with a bunch of older writers who were allowing me to hang out with them and I was doing well and B) the bartender rushed over and put ice on my nose, I believe, as if I were a dog, and I realized I knew him. I had waitressed at the last bar he worked in. I was such a drunk. It showed.

In my real lofty voice I want to tell you this is a sentimental journey I don't take anymore—at least since last March and I realize I have taken this trip with more regularity than any other action repeated in my life in the ten years I've lived in New York. The trip to Dr. Beagle's was home. The waiting was excruciating. You never saw a good looking person in Dr. Beagle's office. Or even cute. Big thighs in jeans. Just big immense thighs. Since this was all going on in Queens everything was synthetic. Blouses, purses, shoes, paintings on the wall, vinyl chairs, my name—I couldn't believe these people were real. "Sargent," the nurse behind the desk would call. A fat lady would get up. Sargent, the nurse would repeat, handing "Sargent" her card. *Eileen Dolan* I was called next. Hi, I said dryly. I felt tiny. What's that little bitch doing up there I felt the collective angry fat in the room aiming at me. "Now, we want to get into a bikini this summer," the worm beamed at me, "so, Miss Dolan, we're going to have to work a little harder. Watch the breads," very slowly he spoke, "no, *sweets,*" he flirted, "and I'm sure . . ." he heaved the time-worn card into a stack of others ". . . we'll see some *progress,*" he dinged the bell for the next cow to come in through the door, "next month." What a cynical bastard I thought to myself, dropping the tinkling container of pills into my bag. I was usually unscrewing the lid in his hallway, slipping the two into my jean pocket.

I stopped in the Barn-hill pub to wash them down. And wait. Early days had me "getting off" someplace between Queens and Manhattan on the "F." I'd be looking out over the blackening sky of industrial Queens, and boom the flatness of a pane of glass would come over my feelings, all smoothed down and graphic. I could look at them. As pieces of business. There. And often a good solution would come to mind. I'd marry this guy or go to New Hampshire this summer. Leave New York when I was thirty. I must. To have any integrity at all. Good. Settled, now what can I do tonight?

But, I don't know, I suppose it was the introduction of a companion to my ritual. As all rituals are, it was private. Maybe I'd stop at the donut shop on the right side of Roosevelt Ave. as I was heading to the train. It was the most synthetic donut shop. The sandwiches were served . . . old women, a few clean men, me, smoking a cigarette with coffee. Perfectly slipping my plastic lighter in and out of the correct pocket, controlling my change, just nervously shifting things before the descent into the subway again and the big shift, into the speedy weekend. This coffee shop was merely a discipline.

"Let's go in there and get a beer!" suggested Christine. No, I always go to the coffee shop up there . . . "What do you do that for! I'm getting a beer. C'mon."

It was very dark inside, a classic brown bar. Old New York. Young guys after work, older guys, guys who really lived there, cheap cold beer, good jukebox. We'd stay there for one, two three beers. Make friends. Get drinks bought. Eventually be on the train, the empty Main Street Flushing. That late in the day, no one's going into Manhattan. I am. I've got a tall can of Schlitz and I'm even smoking on the train. I'm around 30, I'm with my girlfriend. Everything's okay. I'm full of poems.

That was the Barn-hill pub. Very dutch, to my mind. Certain experiences are like cigars, which I have never smoked. Certain experiences are like being around cigars. Accepting that about where you are. Everyone wanted to see me on Fridays. Lucy and Greg. Lucy. I'd go down to Prescott's where she was bartending and I'd hand hers over. Did you take one yet? she'd ask. Lucy had caught the habit in childhood. A doctor's daughter. Yeah.

How many? I signed two. Big deal all of this but I felt like a dealer. Around Ted's funeral I was cabbing downtown from the Strand, smoking a Marlboro in my favorite striped shirt. It was a gorgeous sunny day, my best friend had just died and I was getting Alice some pills, one last trip, and I felt great. I was heading late to work. Work was Irving Trust, paper department facing the green statue of Trinity Church, working was counting credits and debits, doing this and watching the statue, drinking coffee, smoking, doing that. I was told it was the kind of job you did to get better. Everyone around me looked worse than anyone I'd ever had around me before. But for the cab ride down I was a cocaine dealer. It just happened like that. I forgot Ted, the job, that I was merely buying pills, blue pills for 35 dollars and selling them for 100 and getting drunk on the profit one night. I forgot that and this is what my trip was all about. Go someplace out of your life, come back new, bring it around and make a little money. Clean your apartment. Write some.

LIGHT WARRIOR

My name means Light Warrior when you bring it home to the present day through Latin and Gaelic. I am a significant person, maybe a saint, or larger than life. I hear that you judge a saint by her whole personality, not just her work. I'm beginning to see my work as my shadows, less and less necessary, done with less and less care. I see my existence as similar to that of a sundial's when I simply stand, and slowly the notion of movement is suggesting itself to my consciousness and action is also appropriate in the realm of the saint, the character who begins her life in the windows of a church, in the religious air of her own imagination until history lines up with her nature, and the path becomes clear—the storms of identity erupt and implode and gather again and one of life's soldiers realizes her whole basis for living has changed and now she is impelled forward in a new film. I had thought I lived in a world of darkness and confusion and I was the single, glowing and true thing. I sought only the companions who would confirm this interpretation of the mystery that shrouded my life. I couldn't move from there, nor would I have chosen to do so. I was in classrooms and offices, bars, hospitals, state schools for the incurable, and I briefly flickered with a ray of hopefulness, yet as a cab driver I continually drove to these places bound to break down and so the hope for change, and the desire for an environment where I could become helpful was always quickly extinguished and I imagined it was the way the world was, or the way I was.

Like many others I became an artist. I choose not to dwell on that cultural accident. Let's say I have always been brilliant in the realm of play.

In neighborhood games I always crashed right through the lines of kids' hands. As the light fell in the suburban summer night I was a winner. They would call "3" and myself and another kid would feint and lunge in the middle for some object on the ground and it had to be grabbed and brought back to a team without the player having been sullied, and it was true—I had not been touched by my opponent.

There was something scummy about adolescence, it wasn't sex, it was how I hated myself when I was confused, how loathsome the act of waiting for something was. But when I was very young I had a mission, it was clear. A girl in school wanted to borrow my Joan of Arc comic book and I replied I would have to ask my father which struck everyone as an odd reply.

My oddness, my embarrassment also confirmed my specialness. My father had entrusted me with a Junior Classics comic book about Joan of Arc, the first woman I aspired to be. It was an instruction manual, and if the girl, Joan Salinger, had sidled over to me in the school yard and said, "Let me have it, Eileen—Light Warrior," I would have silently passed her the honor.

I have waited all my life for permission. I feel it growing in my breast. A war is storming and it is behind me and I am moving my forces into light.

BREAD AND WATER

A roll from the bakery at sixth street with flecks of garlic on the top and a giant glass of ice cold water. A batch of broken merits which Claudia left on the table in the bar last night. Two knives on the table—one for slicing one for buttering. Ever since Christmas we've had a lot of butter around here. Christine buys the lightly salted sticks and I like breakstone's sweet whipped butter better in the tub. I like the fact that the tubs are waxy. Chris comes in and we talk about our delirious days. She forgot to ask for the money for the pills last night so she had to pay Elinor twelve dollars for every-body. She had a hot dog for lunch because she saw all these people walking around with briefcases eating hot dogs so she thought that's what I need! She said her hot dog was so good she wants to keep eating them all day. That's what her eyes look like. Jim woke me up and invited me Sunday to Staten Island for dinner. 115 Stuyvesant Place. I put on my jeans and kept lying in my bed laughing about last night—drinking lots of coffee and smoking lots of cigarettes. I went out on the fire escape and took pictures of the virgin and the mop and the trees behind the fire escape black and then I held out the camera and took a picture of myself. I went to St. Mark's Place and tried to get the film processed. That'll be two dollars deposit. Um. Joe she doesn't have two bucks can we forego it. He looks up and down at me and my coat and says no. I ask the guy for a little bag so I won't screw up my film. He looks at me like I'm crazy and I stick the little bag in my pocket and I go out the door. Even at the xerox place I was told they couldn't do two-sided copying. Then he said come back at four. Maybe I can. Chris, goes out and comes in with some campbell's tomato soup and marlboros. You can do them both at the same time. I keep thinking in my mind for about a half hour *Merchard, Merchard.* Finally I call her that. We lick each other's navels, I smell her crotch and smell blood. She tells me she's got a crammer in herself. That's what the girls in Libertyville high school called tampons. I call the xerox place and he tells me he just did it. Chris I don't want to go out at all. Do you want to come walk around with me. My mind does but my body doesn't. Staple stuff go to the post office—is she a lesbian—she says she'll put the stuff in their PO box. She says don't make such a big deal out of it with her eyes when I thank you too hard. It's cold I'm walking over there. He's painting the place and she's in Brooklyn has a workshop tonight. I say Eileen was here and the guy painting the kitchen looks curious. A relative I think. Cutting into the village MacDougal street no Sullivan. Missed kettle of fish maybe googies no Village Corner on the way home. Dark becks ale. I guess I am too tired to do anything now. But cigarettes will go and thirst will come and I'm hungry could go to workshop and ask Barbara for some money but she always loans me money. Easy. I hate to be so legal but. We decide to move to California and become Froggi and Carrot-Face. Wimminsong—some lesbian culture identity who knows. I live in a commune in San Diego and my name is Froggi Wimminsong. Nah. Stuck dried tomato soup in an old bowl and I'm hungry. A glass piggy sitting on the desk and totally empty. Eileen Froggi Wimminsong. Look it's twenty-five past seven. This night. I want a teevee and a pizza. A six-pack. Everyone's sitting down at their seats at the workshop now. Mostly people I know. Me and Merchard have stayed home because we are weary and Merchard is reading seth material in a pink and black ski sweater and an afghan surrounds her. It is gold rust and plastic turquoise. On the wall is a funny polka-dot umbrella hat. I want a rich visitor. Please me. I do a little fart and Merchard seems to like it. It's one of those nights where I've got to be strange and gross rather than pizza and television. I've already laid on top of Merchard for a while but then she couldn't cough. Across first avenue a red burning liquor sign cuts through the blackness of my black window and the wavering trees. Merchard clears her throat. Heat's coming up in the building a big bang goes outside and sets off a dog barking which sets off something I can't hear. For extrinsic reasons I should've gone to this reading—to get six dollars to give Bob a book. Last night I went to a reading and gave Barbara twelve forks and Chris four pills and Michael gave me a magazine and Kate who I missed gave Christine books for both of us. If these things aren't moving around I hardly see the point in going anywhere. I called Kate at two A.M. to tell her how much I liked the book but she was asleep and not ready to re-adjust. Merchard is still clearing her throat. Though the heat's coming up it feels that my upper legs are getting cold. I need some paper anyway so walking into the kitchen I decide to move. I start heating up some coffee and eye the brownulated sugar to put that in too. Hurry hurry I'm hungry and cold. The thing wrong with the night if you stay in is all you have is sounds and changing temperatures— for instance I just put a reddish orange plaid flannel shirt on which I stole from Jimmy Schuyler because it was getting chilly out by the window and now I'm hearing a police car wheeeoo wheeeoo but that's all you get at night if you stay in. Puff a hiss of heat is coming in the room, footsteps over my head voices coughing—now that's not much. Or I could mention Merchard softly turning her pages.

Thing is I want to go neither outside nor inside tonight. Talk about how *I* feel or all that. Today I was thinking that though I felt pretty fried from last night and making everyone who saw me suspicious I still felt good—in my body and frisky, I liked my ideas—watching things as they go. I thought it would keep being that way but here it is night and everything's different. I just started doing this thing between remembering and imagining. Last night I'm taking what happened and unspooling each look into a conversation or really playing each conversation as they really were. I saw him chugging down something that looked like pills and I had already downed two but wanted more so I came over. He only had one lousy one he said but I said I'll take that. He didn't like giving it to me either it was out of shortage of pills or how he was feeling towards me that I think. But I'm going on to a more genial conversation with him now where he's saying Eileen who could say no to you. Yeah, that's how I feel—smiling. I never say no to anybody—Susan told me in the bar last week that that was a fault. Directionless. I tried to tell her that I just never care and once in a while I do and then I change places and start saying yes to everything over there. That's all it's like. But I plan to get him something so I can keep asking him for stuff. It's like people who want to "get" sex. Is that possible. In periods of normally perverse and abundant sexuality I never think of getting sex. It's nice too since nobody knows where your strings are. I don't actually think money is a string. You just want it need it.

Please. Cats do not walk on the pink table. After I've cleaned it. I can eat my hot dogs on a dirty table but once it's clean no cat shall walk upon it. A mug of cold water a steaming yellow mug of dark brown coffee a smoking cigarette. I'd like to talk about the hot dog. There were two. This is the third day I've started off with a couple of dogs in a roll. Tuesday a gigantic roll, mustard and onions. And Merchard was there of course eating her own two. Wednesday I sliced mine and put them in a roll along with mayonnaise, onions, tomatoes and tabasco sauce. Delicious. And Merchard was eating her own two and quite disgusted by mine. Yesterday we left the bag of rolls out on the table all afternoon and in early evening I place them in the fridge. This morning I eat my hot dogs simple: sliced in a round stale roll with simply mustard. Merchard is out applying for a job and anyway there were only two dogs left in the pack. A stale roll is terrible. I ate it dutifully mostly in spite of the milky and painful state I'm in. Got roaring drunk last night. Maybe roaring is too loud. I was quietly stinking—was somewhat making out with a guy and a woman in the bar and otherwise it was pretty silent. With my mouth drooping. Merchard told me of it. It's funny—my evening began after the meeting. Alice and I had a couple of quick bourbons in the bar and she told me about bisexual personal ads she read in the voice while looking for an apartment. As she left the bar she told me she was drunk. I think I went on to take those as clues as to how my evening should go. Now I'm kind of torn—should I go on the wagon or something? I rub my hand across my face and it feels slimy and bumpy. But I've been through revulsion before. I should clean this place but I haven't the energy. Coffee grounds and cat litter on the floor. Plaster from the ceiling white falling on this table. I think what money there is left is with Merchard. In the pocket of the jacket she's wearing now I wore last night. I've got this new teal blue maine jacket with grey knit cuffs and collar which Merchard wore last night. I tell her she doesn't look that great in it. I think she knows it's not out of possessiveness I say that but how I see things. Susan loaned me the jacket for four months. I had always admired it on her. I went over to her new apartment one evening and we drank cranberry juice and vodka and she showed me her clothes and I told her which ones I liked. Somehow she was determined that I should come away with a jacket. Her mother wore the jacket in her youth. Really it's the kind of jacket you wear in photographs building a snowman in your backyard with your brother in 1954. And even then it was a handmedown. I tend to wear a lot of clothes like that. Also clothes I see my father wearing in photographs from the forties. Or even the thirties. Chinos white teeshirts. It's funny last night I had nightmares about my dad. Haven't had those for years. I think I will go on the wagon for a while. At least till Tuesday when we have dinner with Michael. Now I wonder if the mailman came. Bringing me money from a poor artist fund. Started by a rich artist. The joke is I'm not an artist but you can't get money without a category. Merchard puts the blue jacket on and asks me how it looks and I say not for those people. Wear the suede. I meant not for any people. She looks too much like she's building a snowman. Merchard either looks very classic or very young. Hasn't the mail come yet? She looks great in black shirts and she wears lipstick easily and looks dramatic. I love Merchard and think she's beautiful. It's funny the night before last she got quite bombed. We take turns. For months Merchard did not get her period. I got two. Now I'm late as hell and Merchard keeps perfect time. Yesterday we put ten dollars down on a teevee. A massive black RCA from the fifties. Another old family photograph. One night last week we sat in bed and I showed her every one. She liked the one with some Alan Shepherd rocket blasting off on an old-fashioned teevee with a glazed madonna planter on the top. It was such a serious picture when it was taken—historical and all but now it looks funny and quaint. Camp's aunt. Merchard comes in. She got the job. It's on Pearl Street. The mailman did come and nothing in our box. Perhaps they know I'm not an artist. Merchard has to wear black pants white shirt and a black bow tie. She was introduced to one of the waiters there—Christine this is peter pan. They're going to be friends. What if they know I'm not an artist. Shit. Yesterday at the meeting the vote was neck and neck—I hold this final vote in my hand—we drew our breaths—and he won. Groan I did out loud I may not be an artist but I am a poor sport. I want to see us win. I mean I like him too but she should win. Oh well. I like drinking bourbon in the bar with Alice. I asked her for a pill and she gave me one of those speckled oblongs. Later on I was taking two thousand milligrams of vitamin C and I noticed how similar the pills were. C is white but equally oblong. And I get to take two and get to take them whenever I want saying that I do have some or I do have some money. Usually I steal vitamins. I tuck them inside my suede jacket or I slip them in the pocket of my dirty white jacket. Once I had a bag of grapes and stood there munching them in the drugstore and dropped in a bottle of Es when the woman at the cosmetic counter turned. Thievery is a split second art and that's why I love it. It's like being a comedian to be a thief. And also it's being able to turn any situation to advantage. I had a lousy time at George Plimpton's party so I stole a brown hat and a green and yellow preppy scarf. I jumped in a cab and headed down to the Duchess to meet Rose. I know I made a great entrance in that getup and the brown hat wound up on Rose's head. I think she's lost it. Months later I learned from Rae that the hat belonged to Michael Braziller. It was pretty expensive and he was quite pissed. Luckily he knows neither me nor Rose and probably never will unless we become South American or Yugoslavian male poets. It always comes around but nobody knows about it. Last night we left the bar and went across the street to get a pizza. The place was packed and we turned to leave and as she stepped out the door Chris said grab the ten. Right off a check. I did and we got our pizza take out and brought it to a bar. Christine said a couple of guys were making weird lustful remarks about our pizza. How they wanted some. Now I call that pretty fucking strange. I just asked Merchard if she'd like to split that beer in the fridge. She said no go ahead you have it. But I can't. It would make me an alcoholic. You've got to fight fire with fire. That's why I will never really go on the wagon. Then I'd be an alcoholic. Or an ex-alcoholic. Ugly Ugly Ugly. I would like to be an ex-smoker. They just look cleaner and their skin's so nice and they seem so happy. So what if they can't think anymore. I can't talk when I stop smoking. My sentences come out screwed up and gasping and I'm always breathing heavy and spitting. What a beast.

The mailman came today when we were asleep. Yesterday we sat around with the door a crack open and he never arrived. The day before Philip gave me a pink slip that he found in his mailbox. A new mailman and a real fuckup. It said I should go to Cooper Square Station to pick it up. No box was checked on the slip to say what it was. I knew what it was and it would solve Merchard and I's financial crisis immediately. No one could find anything addressed to "Eileen Myles" at the inquiry window. I understood. Undoubtedly it was what I was waiting for. Merchard got dressed early this morning, around noon, and trotted down to our box. Thousands of things but not what we needed. We lay in bed weeping and mock weeping and groaning and then harmonizing our groans. We get very funny on the verge of I don't know what. The other evening outside the post office Merchard suggested we cash in our chips. I agreed. We proceeded to El Centro. We had a dollar thirty five and four cigarettes. We sat in a booth in the back where there was no possibility of anyone offering us a friendly drink. Three guys lay sleeping in their own booths. The short fat tough bartender said things to them like fungoo hell will freeze over before you've spent ten bucks in here and they snarled at her and got up reeling towards the front. We had our two little watery drafts had tipped her the rest of the money except for a nickel. We would quit everything after this beer. Become glowing entities Merchard suggested. We sipped and discussed Sanpaku. Merchard's brother had told her about it years ago in Illinois. He spent a week drawing down his eyes and saying what do you think Chris? Do you think I look Sanpaku? Then we walked slow as hell to 27th Street. Rose and Andy were eating things out of bowls and swallowing pills to help them digest. Andy went out and bought a six of becks and Chris and I drank and smoked Barbara's kents all through the meeting. A fruitful one. Chassler drove us home and I told him I liked his haircut when I got out. We slept deeply once we realized there was no one who would give us credit or loan us money.

Yesterday was the day we waited and waited and the mailman never came. I guess they know I'm not an artist. The phone company called and said we'd be turned off Monday. I put on a grey hooded smock and pencilled some whiskers and a moustache on my face and curled up on the bed. Every time Merchard spoke and elicited a response I felt pained. The sound of my own voice broke my haze each time. The phone rang and a woman told me to come take a test Monday for a job. I looked at myself in the mirror and washed my face and started thinking. Merchard and I threw ourselves down on the bed and raised our arms in the air harmonizing our animal sounds directing them to the goddess's ears. I realized I could get back our ten dollar deposit on the giant black RCA we really wanted. We bombed down to St. Mark's Place and I showed the guy my slip and asked for our ten dollars back. He tried to throw us out of the store—five people have tried to buy that teevee but I was saving it for you so you can't get your money back—Get out of here! I pleaded, tried to reason called him a bastard and he awkwardly called me a bastard back. Somehow only males are called bastards. He was a large black guy who was really getting fed up. Get out of my store, now. *No.* I want my money back. I jumped in anger in this weird characteristic way I have since a child. I look like an angry frog. You can jump your ass off but you're not going to get your money back. You've got to give it to me. We're hungry. We won't have any dinner tonight. Nothing. You've got this store with all these teevees. You don't need my ten dollars. You're just doing it for spite. I didn't do it on purpose to you. I'd rather have that teevee. I love that teevee. But tonight I'm so broke I can't eat. Everytime he said get out I said no. I've never used this tactic before. Finally he peeled a wrinkly ten off a small wad of bills—Here, now get out. I was so worked up as we headed down St. Mark's Place. Merchard was patting me on the back and we turned into the deli on first ave and sixth street and bought two six packs of tuborg gold in bottles and a pack of marlboros. We felt so much better drinking and smoking and seeing a future and then the buzzer rang and it was Tim and we gave him a beer and the three of us looked at the cameras and the film and the way this apartment is laid out and wondered what kind of movie we were going to make.

By nine o'clock we had finished filming and Christine had blood all over her shirt and thousands of beer bottles sat on the table and cigarette butts and wires and lights were looping in and out of everything. The scene with the hand going toward the phone and then the cleaver and the squirt of blood was great. Or when I fell back from being stabbed I think and really hit Tim's nose so both of us looked pretty pained and Merchard thought it shot well. We were gleaming and pleased but no cigarettes were left so we went out in the rain and bought some and headed to the St. Mark's Bar and Grille to show Tim what a great place it was but it was a drag. I called Tom and Richard to borrow money but they weren't home. We thought it over a while. Chris came back from the bathroom excited that it was a quarter of eleven and Alice's workshop would be out and all drinking at El Centro. Tim was looking for pills and Chris and I just wanted someone to buy us drinks. The place was empty. So was the Ukrainian place. Actually it was packed but with wrong people. We wound up standing inside the 5th street deli trying to think of someone to call. Or we had one idea but no one had the nerve to call her. I asked Tim for a dollar and went to the deli and bought a box of lorna doones. They made us sick and we decided to spend the rest of the weekend starving not smoking not drinking and taking advantage of our situation by cleaning out. She fell asleep pretty quickly—I started to but as I was falling heard her voice go Eileen are you in there? It scared the shit out of me. I was either out of my body or Chris was talking to me from inside her dream. I touched her to reassure us and she barely woke and I told her I had a nightmare and she put her arm around me and fell back to sleep. I felt safer now so I could explore the situation. Every time I closed my eyes lights started flashing colors were reeling and I could almost make pictures out of them. One window was too bright and the closed one was full of ominous shadows. I felt I was flipping out. Then I remembered about a year ago when Joe and Tom were making a movie here and the place felt spooked afterwards. Like movies leave ghosts or spirits plus the sensation of watching or being watched doesn't stop when the film runs out.

First I shut the door across the window. It's cold. I'm shivering. But then I open it. I don't like to lose the light. The windows are so dirty and spotted. Outside looks like an old-fashioned painting. I don't like paintings but this one. The christmas interview is sitting on the table. Carter Calls To Arms. To Russia With Hate. He asked me if I'd be home at one so I called him collect at twenty past. Said we'd meet at 5th and second ave. Walked into the vicious bodega. Two women from there beat Christine up. Two months I'd walk in there drunk buy some marlboros say you hate women. You do. Once the ugly one raised a baseball bat from behind the counter. Go ahead. All these guys were standing around. We stared at each other for a moment. Then I left.

We walked into the bodega last night at one thirty and he went for the freezer pulled out two red and white sixes of bud in cans. I love men. If we're going to *drink*, we're going *to drink*. Big solid hand going for two sixes putting them down on the counter picking up the bag and going out the door. Stayed up till about five. We've got Susan's teevee for a week. Talking watching Joe Franklin move termite celebrities around seats asking asshole questions never wondering what the answer might be. Still a dream of mine to be on a talk show. Couldn't you be on because you always wanted to be a guest. Still I'd need an agent to do my explaining. So nice to see them yesterday. Big floppy house all their paintings like messy Gertrude Stein. Smoking his chesterfields drinking her beers we go out & get more of everything. A conversation always unfinished. The Truman Capote piece I was telling you about is in this red and green interview. We were watching teevee some old movie we didn't see but kept flickering while we talked. How everything's equal since I've been fucked over worse by women than men almost more because it hurts more. A woman uses you because you let her in so naturally never expected it's just chess. I've learned so much. Women per se. Men per se. Everything feels equal. Trust per se. You walk away thinking what a great man what a great woman. How really nice they are. In or by itself; intrinsically. No such thing. You make a hole in the weave if you expect anything to be something through and through. There. I've gotten to explain it. You look at people. They look at you. Sure. It's like have you been a catholic. Someone wants you to be a machine or else they think its just a passing phase. Lesbian per se. For their benefit I should be a mannequin—no, I never think of fucking men—they're never cute I think they smell, etc. Then you don't talk to them and it gets worse like nobody's real. I mean I am a dyke per se but unless I squelch all my ambiguities—be like a guy who won't admit another guy is cute or he'd be a faggot—Oh, no. Well I don't care. I just intend to carry on. I'm not going to worry about my persuasions or everyone's intentions—I know *just how* real I am. Honestly. Money in the bank.

The phone's half off, the power's going off tomorrow. I am unemployed. So is Merchard. I owe the woman in the bakery 4.65. I'll have to be flirty when I come back. I owe Mario across the street 3.59. I owe Vince upstairs two bucks. I owe Bruce next door 10. Philip downstairs 5. Greg 5. Rose 25. Andy 5. Richard 5. Ted Greenwald 5. Vicki 15. Helene 100. Gertie 150. Susan 110. Didi a dollar. Lots of dollars, so many dollars I can't remember. So many dentists (2) and of course the Harvard Coop—thirty dollars. I woke up with no tampax—blood streaming through my jeans so I took them off and I'm walking around like a giant thirty year old baby woman with an olive green towel between my legs. Fell back to sleep that way with my diaper on. Merchard goes down and gets the mail. A rebate check from the Harvard Coop for 2.41. Breakfast! Tampax! I pack my jeans with toilet paper and the two of us stroll to the check cashing place. The guy shakes his head at my teeny endowment. Deducts his and I get 2.01. I shake my head. Merchard suggests we go to the "Certified" on second avenue where we can get everything and probably steal. It turns out to be "Associated" but what the fuck's the difference so I don't point it out. Cram tampax down my jeans. Buy some eggs. Merchard's got a taste for ham she says so we try schacht's. Too dear. Spanish place on sixth and first has cheap ham. Two rolls at the bakery. Forty cents. We've got sixteen cents left. Heat up the rest of the coffee. I do the eggs, she does the ham. Everything's great, sun streaming onto our roaring breakfast, butter salt pepper everything being wolfed down by two lesbians per se while the cat countlessly assaults the trash bag and Merchard hurls her across the room. Once or twice. We let the cat—Little Andy—lick our dishes on the floor. The coffee's all gone. We'd love another pot. And also I suggest a big tall glass of good orange juice. She agrees. Would you like a glass of ice water. OK, I'm washing the glasses, setting them up. Dropping cubes into the tall ice tea glass and the shorter broader beer mug. I set them out. We're sitting in the sun, drinking our water. I'm smoking, Merchard's talking about really quitting today. I should too I proffer since I have no idea where the next pack is coming from. But I love to smoke. She'll probably quit—at least for a while. Ulle hasn't called yet. Merchard's going to do it today since I'm gushing blood and want to stay home and be cozy and warm. If Ulle hasn't called by now—it's quarter to three. So we lose $15. Start planning the other afternoon. She goes to the refrigerator and pulls out a couple of beers. A six wound up left from last night. Our future. The phone rings. Merchard's chugging her beer—I'm going to be late, I'm going to be late. Do you think I should have another beer. Maybe she should bring a couple—Ulle'd like one. Would that be cool? No, don't do it. So I go to get one right now. There. Pop. That's all times falling into each other. Merchard's still putting on her brown leather gloves, I mean Chris. She's looking English French American *lesbian*, not dyke. There's a difference, at least right now. I'm looking at her standing there, looking at her in her orange construction boots and everything else dark. I'm really adoring her as she's leaving and by the second she's getting more and more beautiful look at her eyes all green and golden brown and gigantic and these unreal lashes. Two are caught between her nose and her eyes are just sitting there and you know how people who really love you or who you irritate are always coming over and picking something off you. Well I can't even tell her I like those two lashes just where they are. Her entirety goes out the door. Eileen's entirety is lying on the couch watching teevee, waiting for them to turn us off.

MY SCAR

I've got a scar on the inside of my left knee which looks a little like a dog, or a scorpion.

As you went up the street where I lived as a kid there was a large field just past the Dingwell's house. The field held tall reedy grass and grasshoppers, bees, hornets, balls you lost last summer, skunk cabbage, a few milk duds, forsythia bushes (if you count the inclines that went up to Uncle Phil's house) and of course, broken glass.

I was playing tag with Ruthy Delay and I don't know who else, and I leaned, running, towards her to tag her and fell, knee-first, into the tall grass, into Ah—the round base of a bottle of Walker's orange tonic. Why I know it was orange I can't explain, but the round base and one tooth of glass came jabbing up from it, into the fleshy inner part of my left knee.

Ah, ah, ah, I said, hop-limping toward the front of the field, near the street and I fell down to look at it. It was deep and blue, you could see the veins, no blood poured from it. It was just an open flap of flesh on my knee. You're going to have to have stitches. Stitches! I had heard about stitches. It seemed all the Delays had stitches and my brother Terry from his appendix operation had stitches.—

My mother—I think—drove me to Symmes hospital. I had to wait an age. Finally they had me on the operating table. They put these metal clamps on my knee. Are you going to use those, and I'm not going to get stitches I asked. Don't look, just hold my hand the nurse said as they were sewing up my knee. In the next operating room a man was howling and blubbering. I saw him in the waiting room. He had a crew cut. He was howling and blubbering because he got his toes caught in an electric lawn mower. You were very brave, Eileen, you didn't cry. A little girl, the nurse said, and did you hear that other one, she said referring to the skin-head. Ah-who, Ah-who-ah, Ah-who-ah, he went. I could hear him. And he was why I didn't cry.

EVERYBODY WOULD GO PLAY CARDS AT EDDIE AND NONIE'S

Eddie Martin was an interesting case. He was Scotch, or a wasp. He went to a prep school called Kent Hill, he was in the navy which wasn't as manly as the army. He worked in Murray's stationery which was nothing special except he always thought he was the cat's ass. He golfed. They had an incredible collection of music boxes and hummels. He was my sister's godfather and she really scored since he was the kind of godfather who really shelled out the money. Come to think of it, godparents are always single people or whoever had no kids and this is how they would get attached to one. Bridgie got Eddie Martin and Aunt Florence. Terry got Aunt Anne and Uncle Ed. How obvious. But Eddie dug Bridgie and it was perfect since she was the baby and precious also. During the 30s and 40s they were Ed and Nora— Ed Martin and Nora Donnellan. By the 50s they were Eddie and Nonie. By the 60s they were no one. They were ditched by the family. Nonie was the accountant at the family drug store. It wasn't quite the family's—it was Franny O'Neil's, and he was the Donnellan's uncle, Aunt Minnie being his mother, I think, Susie's sister. Well, Franny owned the drug store though I can't imagine where he got the money, and Tim, for example, worked at the Ford factory putting in windows and when Ford shut down Tim went and worked at the drug store. With his brother Pat (the singer), Kaiser (big ears) and Nonie (Nora), the sister, married to Ed Martin. She had great legs and big tits. What a body, my mother said, but she always thought she was fat. That's why she started taking those diet pills, why she turned into such an alcoholic. Nobody ever wondered why they always had so much money. They had that beautiful spaniel named Muffy or something, and when Muffy died they got a stuffed animal that looked like Muffy, and it sat on their rug and eventually they gave it to my sister.

Eddie just worked at Murray's, no big shit, he was just this skinny little balding guy, but Nonie worked too, so there was no reason why anyone should have wondered why they had so much money. Every Saturday everybody would go play cards at Eddie and Nonie's. On the wall in their apartment were pictures of a boy and a girl, two profiles, both blonds. The girl looked like a girl, her hair in a little knot piled up on her head. They boy was beautiful, looked like a boy and a girl, no romantic loose strands, like the girl, but simply all falling down his head like an archer in the forest, like Peter Pan. Their house smelled so good and clean like a perfect cookie. I was scared to touch their music boxes, but actually I didn't care about them. Everyone would go—Oh, look at the music box—you turn it like this and it plays! You'd always see the bottom of it, where it came from, how it worked. And they'd always die from over-winding—jewelers fixed them. You could have those things if you didn't have kids.

But Nonie embezzled. That was the thing. All those years she was juggling the books. I don't know who really cared, I suppose it was just that they had it so fucking easy. No kids, everyone over on Saturday nights, being the grand hosts, all the time stealing. It wasn't like Franny O'Neil wasn't a son-of-a-bitch. They all hated him—all his nephews working for him, overtime and everything, no paid holidays. He was a cheap bastard and he took advantage of you because you were family and needed a job and had a family. Maybe nobody knew what to do.

I was nineteen and I was working at the Holiday Inn on Mass. Ave. in Cambridge. During our break time all the chamber maids, young and old, would go into an empty room and drink coffee. The older ones would smoke. I remember a couple who were roommates who ate peanut butter crackers, cokes, smoked, and talked about guys. I was into my body that year. I just looked at everyone and ate a plum or a pear and looked at everyone. There was Nonie.

Talk about long in the tooth—she looked like a vampire. I felt really dumb. I said, "Aren't you Nonie Donnellan?" No one ever called her "Martin." "I'm Eileen Myles—*you know*." She went, "Oh, my god," looked like she was going to cry. She was so fucking ugly, skinny, scabs all over her legs, her eyes were like this, like a rabbit. I had been hearing about Eddie all those years. Murray's had fired him—drinking, though he had been so uppity all those years, he was a salesman, a stationery store, but he acted like a manager. I imagine the drinking just pissed them off. Then we heard that Eddie dug graves, state jobs, we had a lot of family connections, they're all a bunch of drunks. Eddie in a toll booth on 128. Delivering liquor for Martinetti's. She goes Oh my God how old are you now—I can remember when you were—she looked at another woman. They were all the pint on the cart types—some fat, some skinny. Oh, and how's your mother, how's Gen? God, and Ted's been gone for so long, and Bridgie—?

You know it wasn't like they were cut off totally—my Aunt Anne, well, she wasn't a Donnellan but she was always a good Samaritan, and she would have them over once in a while. We'd never go. My mother'd go—Ed was bad, but she was worse—she'd always get all weepy over someone that died, or something, some memory. I don't know, it just makes me sick. Oh, oh, "alligator tears," cry for me, don't say you're sorry.

So, they were found dead in their apartment after the weekend and nobody saw Ed come out for work for a few days. Apparently he had come home with their weekend order. He was laying down the Hiram Walker, or the Old Thompson on the kitchen counter in clear sight of Nonie who was sitting on the couch when he fell, having a heart attack. Nonie was already so drunk she couldn't move or get up and help him or make a phone call. She just sat there helpless and watched him die. She didn't die for two more days, they said. She died of malnutrition, and she didn't even get up for a bottle of booze, their weekend order was sitting there intact on the kitchen counter with skinny little

Eddie lying on the floor underneath and Nonie across the way on the couch, staring at him. My Aunt Anne said you can't believe how filthy their place was, the walls were brown with tobacco smoke and filth, you can't imagine. And Nora was always so meticulous, and Eddie Martin, of course he always had class.

THE GOODBYE TAPES

"You're twenty-five? I'm thirty-four." You looked so great sitting on your grey couch. I couldn't figure out who you were. You moved to New York in 1980. You wore Blondie teeshirts in Texas and Patti Smith gave you taco chips one night. She was in a car and you looked at her and she said, "Here," and gave them to you. *Great!* Right before me you had this boyfriend who wore all leather and shaved his head and placed a leather cap on it. The night I figured out I loved you he was playing at a club and everyone was all crowding around, standing on things to see him and his band. You were standing up on a platform, alone, watching him. I was down here looking up at you like you were on a pedestal. It looked so calm, the spectacle of your watching. It was so incredible, you weren't excited at all. You had a drink straw in one hand and you were tapping it in the palm of the other. You were looking like a beautiful waitress who was waiting for her party to leave so she could get her tip. I didn't even know he was your boyfriend then. I just knew I had to leave fast because you were so important to me. You were a monument of calm.

You told me you weren't really his type. You said all his

girlfriends were those "trendy girls." Weren't you one of them? I really thought you were. I loved to tell my other friends the story of your life. I became you. I wanted to make your story mine. I ran along the East River with Andrea. "She's from Texas!" I screamed, pant-pant. God she comes from this wild family . . . guns and everything. OK . . . she's incredible. She . . . when she was in high school she had this coke-dealer boyfriend. He was around forty—(So am I!) She'd stay out all night with him—he'd give her coke so she could stay awake in school—incredible—well eventually her parents found out—I'm such an asshole, I shouldn't be telling you this stuff—and her father's not even her father—her own father's a drunk—but this guy pulls a gun on the boyfriend and says Are you going to marry her? So they decide to get married. He goes away—is going to come back in two weeks and get her. He's out of town looking at some land. Anyway a month passes. She figures he'll call her—she bumps into a friend of his. Larry's dead. Had a heart attack. Anyhow . . .

I couldn't stop talking about her. She told me her stories. We'd lie in the soft green grass down in the baseball field near the East River and I thought this is the most vulnerable woman I have ever met in my life. I am being entrusted with a treasure. She'd always precede her really wild stories with, "And I've never told anyone this before." My tongue was hanging out.

She worked in this Mexican restaurant. A trendy one on Second Avenue. I liked it best when I'd pass by on my bicycle and see her in the outdoor cafe. It was just a little fence and some tables. I thought of her as in "her corral." She seemed safe there. I'd go and visit her at work but my own feelings of homophobia came luxuriously splashing up in my face. It was like a railroad restaurant and there she'd be laughing with the cooks or the other waitpeople and here I'd be at the doorway, the dyke girlfriend. I always swore I'd never do it again but it was like a drug. I couldn't stay away.

I liked it best when she came over to my place after work. Absolute best if I was asleep. It'd be two or four o'clock and someplace in the depths of dream and darkness I'd hear the drill of my buzzer. Blahh. She had keys, I had given her keys but she liked to do it this way. It was that kind of love. I'd get up open the door, put on one light and crawl back into bed. The deep smell of fried food would crawl into bed with me. Cold skin, greasy smell. I loved it. You know how you're always half hungry while in bed. Well this was like sleeping with a meal, a big fried meal, you have your arms around it. Other nights she'd insist on turning all the lights on. It was different having a girlfriend who didn't consider herself a lesbian—or one who was always considering whether she was one or not. She was just so straight. She wore a black slip. She'd pull off her dress, and she'd have this black slip on. She saw herself as very sexy. She was sexy. There was no question about it.

She'd be taking her makeup off. Very carefully. Other times I'd be watching her put it on. It reminded me of sitting on my mother's bed watching her put her lipstick on to go to church. This woman was going waitressing. It's funny the year we fell in love I had just begun a job as a director of a small poet's organization. Amazing the things they give you when you stop getting drunk. It was a flexible job but still I was kind of responsible. If she wanted to have sex before she went to work on Friday nights I'd jump on my bike and head over to 12th Street. "I was thinking maybe I'd want a Korean salad too." Okay. "Do you think you'll want some of that Orangina for later!" I don't know where I'll be later. "I was thinking maybe you'd want to stay at my place tonight." "Well think about it. But maybe you should get it anyway."

There were pictures in my files at work that I'm not in, not really important pictures, but I know I'm not in them because I had lunch with you and never came back. I'm saying this because I'm proud of it. You were where I was that year. I was hiding behind your every wish. Yesterday I dropped a letter in a mailbox on University Place. It ended Please don't write. Love Eileen. I know you don't even like Paris.

I never met a person who liked to work so much. I asked you about it. You said, "I'm patriotic." You wore a sleeveless USA teeshirt. You had big white arms, strong but not skinny. You wore a whole bunch of "off" teeshirts that summer. You had a couple of Adidas teeshirts. I don't get it, I said. You said it's a joke. You kind of shrugged. "I have this funny kind of sense of humor." It was the exact same shrug you made a split second before you kissed me on the night we became lovers. Colombo was on teevee and we were sitting on a rolled up exercise mat on the floor. The look on your face, my favorite look was here goes. It looked like the smallest decision, like a boat slightly turning but now absolutely going in that direction. I was fixed.

Every night that first summer we'd go out after your work and we'd have to find a place for you to eat—we were feeding you. I couldn't even understand this thing about eating at night. I had no money. I hadn't started working yet. So I was just an accomplice. It was a left-over from drinking days when I'd go with friends into restaurants. I'd drink a beer while they ate. I would only eat in a restaurant if you had very clearly offered to take me. Anyhow after work we waltzed in there and everyone goes, Hi, Hi, saying your name. But you must be trendy, I'm thinking, you know all these kids with hairdos who hang out in restaurants. I couldn't figure out what we were doing together. You picked me. I didn't even know I thought women like you were sexy. I merely read the delicate coding as heterosexual. Not-available. You said I made being a lesbian look all right. You said you went to dyke bars in Houston. They were kind of motorcycle DA-looking then. It was a pathetic bar with big velvet portraits of clowns on the wall. See, but that's typical. Who could forget the glittering faded skyline of Manhattan scratched on the wall of the Duchess. Over the bar was a checkerboard pattern made out of mirrors and that fake snow, you know like thick dried soapflakes. I picture some Mafia guys making really ugly things they'd guess the dykes would find pretty.

My stories never seemed as interesting as yours. What was it? There was this curious detachment in your voice—referring to an ex-lover: "But he had gotten a new girlfriend by now . . . so . . ." "Well, did you feel bad," I'd ask. "I felt terrible." I could see a tiny, tiny hint of "terrible" in the distance of your pale blue eyes, but that was all. The whole process of your life seemed to be a kind of soft plotting, like moving across a graph which was time, or the world. Once you admitted that you wanted to be a painter, and that explained the trips to Europe. There you met a rich young Swiss guy, a sculptor, and you lived with him for a while. You lived in a medieval stone house in Italy and you drank a lot of wine and cooked for everyone, and there were a lot of people who lived in that house. He had a pet name for you and you told it to me and it'd inadvertently slip out, I'd call you that at moments and you'd flash a look at me like "Don't." You had a friend, a woman, and she lived next door to the stone house and eventually she started having an affair with your boyfriend, so you left. I think you came to New York, then.

When you first moved to Paris, that was last summer, I began to look on the streets and in the restaurants for the girl you were when you first came to town. I wanted to meet you before I knew you, I guess I just wanted to watch. You had told me about each one of your boyfriends, what kind of sex you had and usually you met them at one of your waitressing jobs, at the Odessa, at Kiev. I know what it was—I wanted to be gone, not you. See it's just me and the boyfriends and the restaurants now. We give each other these funny looks and the new girls who just came to town make me sad.

I was telling Bill how I felt today and Bill is one of your old friends. I can't take it anymore. I've just got to get out. I keep thinking I have a girlfriend in Paris, but who knows. I can't just keep waiting. And you know, it's no different than it ever was. I mean, we were lovers for two years and she could never decide if she was a lesbian or not. Bill laughed really hard: "She's not!"

I went out to a cafe, in the East Village, on 9th Street—the one you go in when you don't want to see anybody. I opened my notebook and wrote this all down. This is my daily island life. I end it with you talking to a "person" in Paris. I imagine you reducing me to story form:

"I was a waitress, then I started working in film—I was involved with a woman for those two years, yeah, but she was special, she was a poet . . ."

Well, for once I can smile and I feel really free.

ROBIN

Rightaway I'd like to separate this Robin from all Robins you or I have ever known. This Robin I am about to tell you about is not someone that any of us know. She is somebody I found and I would like to tell her secret.

I call her Robin because she is red and black and angular and resembles a bird in her speed and in her cruelty. I fell in love with her briefly, last year. I'm just not in love with her anymore but there's this residue.

She was sort of a famous junkie, which I thought was pretty exotic, never having been particularly involved with heroin, having had a taste here and there—I was at an art event a couple of years ago and a friend dragged me to the dinner afterwards and Robin entertained our end of the table with a story about how she had been busted for dealing dope, but instead of going to jail she informed on somebody else. She knew that she would die in jail, she knew she couldn't take it. I was appalled and thrilled by her coldness. She spoke carefully, slowly, halting, choosing her words . . . how is it that junkies talk, very ornate, piercing and hollow and obviously this girl was a prince. A dead one. She smelled of flowers, she smiled at me when she got up to leave. I'm so glad you're here she said intensely like I was the only soul in the room, or a soul who had a soul like hers.

I knew Robin had a girlfriend. Historically, they were kind of merged. My friends who used to do heroin said Robin 'n Babe as if it were one word. Babe played in a band, played till all the band members were so strung out that they were no band. By then Robin 'n Babe were an item so they teamed up and Robin sold drugs and Babe did them and they held sort of an elite junkie salon for a few years. Robin knew everyone in New York. Everyone on that trendy glamour junkie circuit. She wanted to write, had been doing so for years. In notebooks, in between experiences I guess. I think I had what Robin wanted and vice versa.

One day I was in her apartment and I found myself touching her leg. Her apartment was nice. Actually it was Babe's. It was hard to unravel where one stopped and the other began—It was Babe's bombed-out junkie rock star haven and Robin moved in when Babe kicked Lulu, the old girlfriend, out. Lulu died of AIDS. She wound up hooking on 3rd Avenue after they kicked her out of the band because she was so bad. The lives of drunks and druggies is such a treacherous moral landscape with avalanches and peaks and nasty pitfalls. Robin moved in and cleaned house, eventually at some point of successful drug dealing had extensive carpentry work done, the apartment had modernesque divides, shelves for aeons of rock star clothes and shoes, millions of records and Robin's little dealing room lined with scales and books. There she sat with her extraordinary stark white-face, a weirdly shaped skull, kind of cubist and long, with raven-ish black hair. I adored her because she was a masque. This, combined with her sensibility, literary and scrupulous, made her essentially Aquarian to me, an endless revolving door.

Just before I put my hand on her leg I had asked about her and Babe. I was making an honest woman of myself. We're roommates she said in her voice that was of the air, tentative yet treacherous. Actually, she leaned forward stretching her arms down to her pointed toes. "I don't really know. We don't really talk about it. Babe is not disposed to discuss anything so abstract as our relationship. She is not . . . " She sighed, thinking the better of continuing. "I don't know what she's doing." "Honesty," her face telegraphed. Robin had a deep morality of which she never spoke, but she communicated its breadth and its depth, by her protective pauses. You knew she was a good person because she held back at moments of deepest revelation. She did not spill, and I always felt that to push her a bit would be sloppy and expose my own lack of a system of conduct.

So I put my hand on this woman who smelled so good. Her fragrance was coming my way. When we smell a per-son's perfume we think that we're smelling their essence, their identity somehow. The body has to be there for the perfume to stick to, but when they're gone it's the perfume that we know. I've forgotten its name. I asked her once.

Some kind of sexy thirties jazz was on the stereo. I knew I was in her house now, not Babe's. The design was hers, but the ornaments were Babe's. Babe's paintings and the guitars and record collection. She had made a home for Babe, kind of a mother or a wife. I found that so hot to discover an ex-heroin dealer in the middle of the art world who was really a good woman, once I told her that—I couldn't believe how hokey it sounded and by her silence I knew she was horrified. I bet she wanted to break the silence of our affair just to tell Babe some of the stupid things I said.

Okay well if this is all right I put my hand on her leg. It seemed seductive enough. I'm really attracted to you I said. The feeling is mutual she replied. Soon we were half-dancing half making out in the middle of the room and it was really hot, I mean she had a hard desperate mouth, her hands were up my shirt and I was feeling her ass. All my instincts were on target in the particular way I felt like a bow and arrow nocked, then release.

Soon we were on the bed, ripping our pants off and this was when I began to feel in the middle of their relationship because you knew you were going wild in the precise same place where a couple woke each morning and looked at that painting, Babe's.

I think this is going to be a problem she said. She got up and sat on the chair, lit up a cigarette. A move I regard as "womanning" me—I've felt it before. It's the gesture of a torn, or badly married, man.

Well, are you going to tell Babe. Yes, I'm quite certain we are due to have a conversation about this, among other things. She bit each syllable as she spoke. Robin had to go to work, she was a cook, a neat transformation for a dealer, though actually she was a cook first, that's how she started dealing drugs. Cooking in all of Ricky Mountain's restaurants. Even sold him the drugs he'd OD'd on legend says, though Robin says it's not true. And she was the one who told me the legend. Someone else got him those. It was weird she said to have your boss coming in the kitchen to buy from you. They always came to me, she said of her connections. It was never something I decided to do. They knew I could help them, she said.

So she went to work, pretty wonderful, all vulnerable and pink. The pretty Robin. One of many. I guess I went home. I went running down in the park by the East River. I needed to stretch out my feelings that were really making me crazy and all furled & unfurled.

We had a date the next day at 4. I don't know how I tolerated my home, I think I was working or something, some piece of writing, but I stopped at three to let feeling build, and then it was 4:15, 4:30 I was out of my mind. Quarter of 5 she called. Where are you! Well I'm out doing a few errands. It took a little longer than I thought. Are you coming over? *Well* I had *thought* I would *still* do *that*, but it is pretty late. She was almost needling me off the phone. Yeah, c'mon I said. Up the stairs came this angry woman who I sometimes thought resembled Elizabeth Taylor or Keith Richards and sometimes when she was really nice, Donovan. Frozen and mean in a white jacket coming up my steps. Hello, I said, holding the door. I was no longer in fun-affair with vulnerable married woman. In one day that was already over. She sat in her white jacket on the small orange couch. Do you want a drink? I had automatically stored exactly what she had served me from her refrigerator the day before. I was glad she said no because I would have been ashamed to reveal what a copy-cat I was.

Raspberry Soho Cola. Your furniture is not very comfortable she said.

I feel nervous I confided nervously teetering over the counter that faced the itchy couch. "*Why* do *you* feel nervous, would it make you feel better to tell me?" These quiet utterances thundered like the I Ching. What a jerk I am. I never wanted to go to hell, but I thought I could date the devil. "I feel funny." Do you want to go up on the roof I asked. No I don't. Why would I want to go up on the roof? This is awful. I have invited a wolf into my home. I went over and started knocking into, touching, kissing the wolf. It was the only thing I could think of doing. C'mere get up I huskily growled. Where are we going she whispered. Tamed. Over there. I pointed at the bed. My goal from the day before was to get our clothes completely off, that kind of sex. I was trying to get her shoes off, to be sort of sexy/servile but I was so awkward she pulled her weird green 70s rock star boot back to herself and started untying. Behold the skinny body I loved. I was revolted but addicted.

Momentarily, she acted as if she intended to really ravage me, but it was a phoney growl. She didn't know how. I must fuck Robin. That was my job. She had the largest . . . cunt, vagina I have ever stuck my finger in. It was big red and needy. I stuck two three fingers in and fucked her and fucked her. I've always received complaints that I was rough but I felt like I could have been shoving a stick up this woman, a branch. Her ass was up in the air, it was April and the trees were still pretty bare and I looked through the black rusty cross-hatched window gates of my East Village apartment and I felt detached and I fucked and fucked her with my hand, and twisting her nipples. She moaned and growled with pleasure. Such a woman, I have never met such a horny animal nor have I ever so distinctly serviced a woman before. Do you want my fist inside you. Anything she shrieked, anything.

So this is my late winter stolen landscape. Robin's hungry butt bobbing in front of my window next to my desk where I write. I felt my home, myself, violated by this animal. I couldn't stop. This must be what faggots do. The inside of her pussy was hot and warm, it did, it did feel like a live animal. I put my fingertip to her butt-hole but there didn't seem to be any magic there. I was getting bored. Wanna come up on me. I wanted to be underneath—her pussy on my mouth. Sure, anything. I had no way of framing her true repertoire with these kind of replies. I suspected she had done everything in the past, or on the other hand maybe she was a liar.

Here it comes, the salty hairy organ, the slippery wet thing with a hard pearly center, jammed in my face. I started licking and sucking like crazy. I am wild for the sensation of having my face covered and dominated, almost smothered by a cunt. She was happy. It all seemed one to her, then a great groan and buckets of wet acrid fluid flooded into my mouth, splashing down my cheeks and onto my pillow. Initially I surmised she had come in some new way, but it was pee and now I had drank it for the first time. I swallowed some, but then no I don't really want to drink piss. I wiped the edges of my mouth and then kissed her. I think she said I'm sorry but grinned at me wiping my face. Do you have any music she said. Take a look—the tapes are on the refrigerator. I lay on the bed, fascinated by the acrid taste of piss, yet horrified at the inadequacies of my tape collection. Da, *duh-duh*, Da, *duh-duh* came the opening notes of "Kimberly" and Robin walked naked across the length of my apartment like she was the real Patti Smith.

I think we tried to cram more into her pussy for a while after that and she gave my lips a quick swipe with her mouth, but I really suspected that was not her cup of tea. Because she was not a lesbian, nothing like that.

Do you have a towel? Actually I didn't. Or I didn't have a clean towel and I didn't want to give her mine, out of a desire not to insult one of us. Finally I gave her a facecloth. I guess a towel's a towel. I didn't know what was going on. I've got to meet my girlfriend she explained. Today she had a girlfriend. A blow to the stomach, received in silence of course. I'm going out too I said. Well then come on, come with me to meet her. I did something in the kitchen sink, brushed my teeth, but I was feeling demolished.

Outside I unlocked my bike—"No, you know . . . I'm just going to ride off." She gave me a giant devil grin. Thanks she jeered. What am I going to do I thought as I rode off. There were millions of other ways to get laid but I chose this one. She called me a couple of days later. I explained how rotten I felt. I would never want to cause you pain she assured me. I felt mildly cauterized but Ouch. Actually what kept running through my mind was that an alley cat had run in and pissed all over my apartment. I went to see her at work on Saturday. She wore a mustard colored shirt. She was beautiful. She resembled Donovan. She was sulking in the sunlight. She had to start cooking. Come back later she said as she went in. I bumped into her that night at a party. I ignored her. She looked angry and flipped out. Babe was there. I feel like committing suicide a friend of mine confided to Babe. I feel like committing homicide Babe replied. I left town, stayed with Mary, David's sister at the beach.

Robin started calling me a few weeks later. I didn't return the calls and then I did. I felt strong. I was over her. She called me from work. Come see me she begged. I'm going to a memorial service I told her. But I haven't eaten yet. Come here she said. She made me the most delicious burritos. Fabulous. I could taste them all through the service, a room full of old friends of a man I hardly knew. I knew his lover. I liked him a lot. I hugged Roberto and left. Outside the church I unlocked my bike thinking about Robin. I got home and the phone rang. I must be crazy she said but I'm working a double shift but I can't stop thinking about you. Can I come over. She walked into my arms as she closed the door. It was the most delicious sex, her fingers jabbing inside of me so far up, I just felt I had grown so much larger inside just to accommodate her touch, just to take that woman inside of my stomach. I can't believe I'm going back to work now. I went to an opening and just smirked and felt so well fucked and aching.

It went like that, rattle-trap like a bad machine for many months. I told her I didn't want to see her anymore. I told her I just wanted to see her for coffee. We fucked, and I regretted it. The sex seemed to get wilder and wilder and in the midst of it she'd say: I hope you've gotten over your desire to call this a relationship. I hope you've gotten over your desire to publicize this.

About a year later I'm watching leaves drop off the branches of some different trees and the leaves landing among the branches themselves. I can't really remember exactly what she said or anything quite like it. I only know in the midst of passion she would always betray me like pleasure was a hook she used to throw me. I was just a poor fish. She didn't want me, she didn't want anyone to know about us, least of all Babe. She would invite me over to sleep in her home when Babe spent weekends on Fire Island and she'd call Babe and ask her if she was warm enough, and take her time and chuckle and have her relationship in front of me.

Once I woke up in the middle of the morning, maybe five, after dawn, it was blue and Robin was asleep and I lay there looking at Babe's painting. It got truer and truer to me, I thought it was pretty good. Two little fiery creatures, little crayons of color, one connected to something below the frame of the painting—really anchored and attached and the other, brighter, was floating in space. The anchored one, obviously Robin, was giving the other, Babe, a tongue lashing. Babe danced, immune, and yet it was a child's painting, a defiant work. A slap against her Mom. The reality of lying in their bed in the middle of their life looking at their relationship was more than I could bear. I had to move on—there may have been a little more but not much.

They lived in Soho. The first time I met Robin for sex we went to Rizzoli's. Then we saw some art. Big dark paintings that looked like designer sheets. We picked up sandwiches— mine was tuna, and we carried them home. I guess I don't regret not stopping at the sandwich. Once we did just have lunch and she told me about going all the way to Thailand to cop. And she snorted all the profits, her and Babe. Then someone passed the window of the restaurant that we both knew and she practically ducked. Later when I accused her of ducking she denied it. She carried drugs on the airplane up that massive pussy.

Once after we stopped fucking we had a small honeymoon. I went to visit her and it was late afternoon and it started to rain. It got darker, naturally, and she showed me in great detail her room. She had an extensive postcard collection, mostly from Italy and the Far East. My therapist said she was prob ably a classic narcissist and she couldn't love, not me anyhow but she collected people too. She was not an artist. This is one way I have of hurting her. She showed me an odd fan that looked like a globe. She knew where you could get hundreds of these at one time, they were intended for bankers—some place where you couldn't rustle the papers too much. I guess it kept her room cool when she dealt. All the rest of these fans were destroyed and now there were only a few and she had one of them here in her room. The titles of her books in her shelves didn't impress me. You could tell she still had her college books. I'm always shocked at what people haven't lost. There were pictures on her bulletin board of her and Babe going to one of Babe's gigs. Babe had weird makeup on and a cape, Robin just looked cool. She was. If I've ever met a cool woman in my life Robin was her.

Later she led me out to a round table in her front room and she told me about her early religious training and she went to Hebrew school. She was showing me her favorite spiritual book in the world something by Martin Buber. She read it very slowly, the smallest bite at a time, sometimes just a sentence. She had her head bent over that book and she looked like the sweetest Jewish boy, head bent in prayer. I fell in love with her again. I like the smell and taste of women's bodies. Sometimes I'm sure that's what I'm living for. But as for Robin I would like to make her drink piss. I know a boy who did it in high school. Somebody offered him twenty bucks to drink it the story goes. Did he drink it? Yes. I was about fifteen when I heard that story. His name was Frosty, he was from Lexington, and was the lead singer from a band that played all the local dances doing covers of the Rolling Stones. His big song was "I'm Alright." He would stoop down at the foot of the stage and his lip would curl up and it was heavenly. He was our Rolling Stone. I was amazed when I heard he drank piss. It was a new kind of spirituality I had begun to hear about. Humiliation. But this anger it has brought me makes me think I've done it wrong. She went to California for a week, rented a red car and discovered it was me she loved now. Not Babe. Too late. Now I sit in this incredible silence. I don't know why.

MADRAS

Mike Mullane's Madras shirt was navy blue and lime green. It was faded because he wore it a lot and he was one of the first ones to have one which the fading definitely proved. He had a dusty blue Vespa and long eyelashes, astonishingly long. He must've worked outside because he always had a sunburn. Mike was red and very friendly for a cute guy. He may have been limited, in fact as I think of it he was dumb. Nothing he ever said filled you with any kind of feeling at all. Actually there was something a little sleazy about him. He had a girl-friend Carol who hearkened to greaser days, by her style. At the time I didn't understand about sex so I thought your date provided a clue as to your deeper identity. Mike had none, he had those long lashes and that shirt. And he was a nice guy.

My own Madras shirt was maroon with a peter pan collar and three-quarter length sleeves that you had to roll. Under the dark Madras plaid was a second pattern, or a first, sort of oriental looking like mechanical dolls marching in chain for-mations down the length of my shirt. As the summer passed and my shirt hung on the line, naturally it faded and the maroon became a dull muted red and the chains became more evident and pronounced. Actually I liked it better. The two became a kind of paisley.* Busy at almost the same level, the plaid and the chains intersecting at points. This is the moment when people gained interest in my shirt. More accurately, the Hawkeses. If there ever were a pair of gatekeepers to the culture of Madras and all that was powerful in 1964 in Arlington it was Barbara and Mary Ann Hawkes. Arlington was a place of translation where who you were or what you did in Somerville or Cambridge, darker towns, had little to do with how you could shine in sunny Arlington. If a family's income enabled them to live up towards Morningside that was fine. It was where you lived, not how you got the money to live there. What I'm saying in a roundabout way is that the Hawkeses' father owned a bar, the Sunset Cafe, right over the Cambridge line. I was shocked when I learned that. It was so, kind of dirty, to earn your living that way and the Hawkeses were so important. People like my uncle, even my father could've drank at the Sunset Cafe. It was right there over the line at the MTA car barns. Probably a lot of bus drivers drank there. And Mr. Hawkes was tremendously fat. I just didn't understand where the power came from. Once I drove past the Sunset Cafe with my mother. The Hawkeses own *that*, I gasped at what seemed to be an old brown bar with a dingy sign. Yep, said my mother and I bet he does pretty damn good. A bar is nothing to sneeze at.

My mother and I were on our way to Gilchrist's Basement in Porter Square. Going down the dirty stairs that

* In India, where paisley was invented, they call it "mango," referring to the shapes that make up the pattern.

CHELSEA GIRLS

reminded me of the subway, the peanut smell of Woolworth's came along with us. There never was a reason to go into Woolworth's. We had one in Arlington, there was nothing in Woolworth's at all, yet the smells of these bigger, older ones were fantastic. They were for older greasier people and I envied them what they had. Behind glass under a warm light were cashews. Next to them, cold and complicated, were mixed nuts.

Gilchrist's Basement was something my mother and I agreed on. Shopping was. Both of us could spend hours rifling through piles of shirts or bathing suits looking for a name brand. Actually I'm not really sure my mother did it too, but she applauded the habit in me, she admired my patience and my energy. It's Madras, I explained to her when I found my special shirt. Only 2.99 I suggested. It's awfully dark, she commented, opening her purse. But I know what you mean, I've heard of Madras.

My father had died a couple of years before and one of the odd results of his departure was that someone my mother knew, someone who had more money than us had taken to giving us their used clothes. I don't know—take a look my mother said, thrusting the bag at me. That shirt is Ship 'n Shore. Before that I don't think I really knew about clothes. I understood them in terms of uniforms because I went to Catholic schools and also I understood them in terms of codes because in junior high I was trying to be a greaser, or as we called it, a rat. That meant tight black pants, black pointed bow-knot shoes, teased hair bursting out of a tight kerchief and a raincoat, unbuttoned, closed by a hand across your chest, holding books. The raincoat was lifted slightly off your shoulders like a mink stole and you tried to wiggle when you walked.

Times had changed, however, and so had the definition of cool. Now it was something called collegiate, or that was one of the available fashion strains. The widest possible explanation of this look was that you had money. Those who were best at the look did have money, or were thieves. You learned to steal topcoats out of J. Press in Harvard Square, Filene's in Belmont or Ann Taylor's or Casual Corners if you were a girl. I was and I stole. But stealing's another topic and we'll get to that later.

What I started to understand by the way my mother said Ship 'n Shore, the way she also said "Evan Picone" reading the label of the black pants Aunt Florence had given me one year for Christmas, was that the way that these same names also turned up in *Seventeen* magazine and *Mademoiselle* was no coincidence. It was not unrelated to how Skippy peanut butter or Welch's grape jelly were preferable to the supermarket's own discount brand, Ann Page. My mother wouldn't budge on those kind of shopping issues and in a way I agreed. Food didn't show. But clothes did and so did name brands: Villager, John Meyer of Norwich, Lady Bug. These indicated that you would probably go to college, drive a sports car, have a career and go to Europe at some point.

There was so much hope in clothes. We all wore teeshirts, regatta shirts actually that bore the names of colleges. Harvard was very popular. A nice maroon regatta shirt that faded into a reddy pink that looked good with a tan and seersucker or Madras shorts. Or cutoff jeans. There was a particular jean look one summer that was truly explosive. You shook bleach all over the front of your jeans. You bleached the front piece of your hair. There was a moment in which you could also wear a tiki. The beach boy surfer look was in the air at that time. It led people to wrap strips of rawhide around their wrists—one summer it carried a specific message. Don't let Hampton Beach go commercial. Other rawhide uses included ripping open the front of your sweatshirt (dark colors only—no white or grey) and if there was one, tearing off the hood and then stitching rawhide from one side of the gap to the other. This could be really sexy—in fact you had to be sexy to pull it off. It was the kind of thing you might labor on for hours in your bedroom and then be unable to go out of the house in it.

I encountered Paula Fuchs inside her house in Marshfield and I will never forget her—anything she said or did. She wore a workshirt, she was the first person I knew to wear one. She went to Bard College in New York where Bob Dylan often hung out, she said, and she knew what many of the lines in his songs actually meant. For example strike another match girl start anew was about marijuana, pot. On the back of Paula Fuchs' workshirt was the word "Oligarchy." It meant rule by a few which was some sort of problem at Bard College that Paula Fuchs was objecting to. As soon as that summer was over I ran to Woolworth's in Arlington Center and bought a cotton workshirt. I ripped the collar off mine because by then we were all doing that.

Life was a big parade in those days. Looking back on it, it

seems so patriotic. We wore tennis sweaters, and penny loafers (with Madras in the slots) and boat shoes and low Keds and bold striped teeshirts, for instance cranberry and navy blue or just black and white. Everybody had beatle haircuts, Sassoon or long hair like a folksinger. It was just before hippy and everything seemed to go. Yet it seemed so defended too. You'd get in your assembled coded wardrobe like a bright little tank. I have a photograph of myself at the New York World's Fair. I'm standing with my family in front of a futuristic fountain and I'm wearing patch Madras Bermuda shorts, a Boston College regatta shirt, penny loafers and the front of my hair is this really ugly blonde. But I would prance out of the house that way, stop for a cigarette about five minutes from my house and then proceed to Butterick's a local ice cream hangout with an immense parking lot. There the surfers and the bikers and the beatles and the preps would converge and loiter with an eventual goal of getting drunk or high and going dancing or having sex, or a little of all of it. There were many Volkswagens around. And one of the Hawkeses' girlfriends, Cherryl, had a green MG. Whoever was her boyfriend got to drive it.

When I was a kid I used to drive up to Butterick's with my family on summer nights. It was the local creamery and their ice cream was the best. There was one flavor, walnut fudge, I adored. It was very rich, the fudginess of it, and the walnuts were big. I would get a perfect cup of it. No cone to alter anything. I would sit in the car with my family and eat it till there was a small amount of dark chocolate liquid lining the bottom rim of the cup. I would try and scrape it up with a wooden spoon. But it was over. Then we'd watch the teenagers. Butterick's had a big green hill with an American flag at the top of it. The teenagers would all sit around it on the grass. It was a beautiful sight on a summer night to see all these big kids out alone. To be there as a group on the grass laughing and hugging each other. By the time I hung out at Butterick's the parking lot had been enlarged. The hill was gone.

I would order my cup of walnut fudge at the window, turn and walk back slowly towards the thing I was now part of. Maybe I was the only patriotic person there. The past was my country. It remained, unchanging, in the future. The flag was gone, but I had a Madras regatta shirt. I had a laminated Madras parka. By the time it got cold it was CPOS and pea jackets and loafers that went up around your ankles. It was tight white levis. It was corduroy jeans and wide wale corduroy pants in metallic hues. It was beatle boots. It was saddle shoes.

It was pretty tense, being nothing but your uniform. I remember being drunk in the back of a car in Arlington making out with someone named Glen Hobart who later died in Vietnam. We were heading towards a dance. We both wore Madras shirts.

Michael Camerlingo, the most handsome boy who graduated from Arlington High in 1965 rode around in a Volkswagen all the time with another guy named Connie Duggan and everyone joked that they were probably queer. They were both so goodlooking and seemed to prefer each other's company over anyone else's. Michael also got killed in Vietnam.

There were dances in Boston and there were dances on the South Shore of Massachusetts. The one in Boston was called T & C or Town and Country. It was in Mattapan a tough part of Dorchester bordering on Roxbury which was black. The hall it took place in was some old Jewish hall. There were two big tablets with Hebrew written on them hanging over the stage. The ceiling was covered with wax and when it got real hot it would drip on our heads. I was fifteen. We used to dance in these big circles. Usually one couple dancing. You'd cut in on them. So you had to be good and you had to be drunk. All the people on the outside of the circle would clap their hands and wave them in the air. We'd do splits and then flip around in the opposite direction and then jump up. If you were a girl in a skirt you would pull up your skirt as you were splitting down. It looked OK. Fights broke out continually. Mostly boys, and then everyone would jump in. You could just feel the room suddenly shift that way and then everyone was running. You'd see boys you knew with blood running from their noses, sometimes crying. A lot of these boys were jocks, mostly hockey players, that was the status sport, in fact that's how I think the word got around about these dances. Oh you should go to T & C. Who played there? Barry & the Remains. The Lost. Moulty & the Barbarians. The Turtles. Boys would dance together too. It was a macho thing. Or they would sing a song. I know you. Don't want me. I know you. Don't love me any more—ore—ore—you fucking whore.

One night two girls appeared on the scene. In the middle of the night, older girls, I bet at least twenty, maybe more. They had big full woman bodies. They looked strong. Their clothes were tight, faded jeans, workshirts, one wore handtooled leather suspenders, the other a wide brown leather belt. They seemed to be from Harvard Square. They danced together, they seemed to see nothing but each other, but it also seemed clear they had envisioned themselves as a spectacle. One had long blonde hair, the other I think her hair was up and held there with a piece of leather and a pick. There was an incredible authority about these women, almost a figurine, so marvelous. Twisting and turning, their bodies, their hips and their shoulders in relationship to one another. There was such an austere passion and a concentration. It had to be the result of a decision. Maybe they were taking drugs. All the boys turned immediately towards them and I was convinced they would not allow the boys to cut in, but they did, they allowed the boys to dance with both of them, they seemed greatly amused by it, occasionally giving each other some kind of eye, remaining connected.

A girl I know, Janey Coyne, got gang-banged outside of T & C. There were always girls puking and falling down and passed out in the ladies room. I remember Janey being a fucked up mess and she wore a ton of makeup. One night she left the place and got in a car with a bunch of guys she knew. Or she knew one of them. So they all fucked her. That was the last I saw of Janey for a long time. Lots of girls were whores. There were the blow job girls from Cambridge. I met them later in a part time job. I think I even said, Oh are you the blow job girls from Cambridge. That station wagon. I didn't think there was anything wrong with it. I mean, I remembered their car.

Anyhow, here's how a night would go. You'd put on your outfit and you'd go up to Butterick's. You'd see your friends. Now boys had cars, girls didn't. So you'd beg and beg for a ride. Some of us were younger sisters of the boys. Which was good and bad. Often they'd say no. And you'd get on the bus. This is the slow way. You'd take the bus to Lechmere—oh first you'd buy cokes, large vanilla cokes from Butterick's. And you'd put out your thumb on the Southeast Expressway and once you got a ride you'd ask them to buy for you. Half pints of Bacardi's. Pour it in the coke. Glug. Glug. You'd go to the Rex. You'd go to the Surf. These were big dances. What was funny was that these places were big band dance halls from the 30s and the 40s. Our parents had gone there. We were going to see the McCoys. Sonny & Cher. So you'd get there. The entrance to the Surf Nantasket was fifty or so brightly lit stairs with a cop at the top. We'd be drunk Catholic girls trying to walk straight. That was the joke. Tootsie heard Eileen Tracey saying the Hail Mary so Tootsie started laughing and that's why she didn't get in.

My friends often got thrown out. Ollie pulling her skirt over her head, just standing in the middle of the dance floor. Ollie don't do that. I can do anything I fucking want, Eileen Myles. Then a cop grabbed her. Tootsie, who knew I had only pretended to drink cough medicine with her in the bathroom—she saw me spit it in the toilet—Tootsie was on her knees at the Surf praying to Jesus when one of the McCoys threw his stick up in the air during a drum solo and it hit Tootsie on the head and she kept praying, thanks to the cough medicine—she didn't notice, so she got thrown out. I never got thrown out. I couldn't afford to because my father had died of alcoholism only recently so I couldn't get in trouble because it would break my mother's heart.

So I could only get finger-fucked and steal. All the boys

wanted handjobs. Like Gus, who was particularly cute, in fact I looked like him. That was a joke. They called me Gus too. He had a tan and a Vespa and rawhide around his neck and once at a beach party—we'd go to these huge duney beaches—Crane's up in Ipswich. I was wearing a navy blue regatta shirt with a cranberry trim, bleached cutoffs and Keds and I had something wrong with my foot. I had this big Ace bandage on it. But Gussie said c'mon and grabbed me by the hand and he had two sixteen oz. cans of Colt so we went over a dune and maybe talked for a moment and then he gave me one of those big plunger kisses but it actually felt pretty good and I was kind of drunk and he put his hand under the top of my bathing suit and that felt good too—it was so bright, all the white dunes and it was really hot with the sun beating—I don't know I just wondered how far I'd go and then he put my hand on his crotch. I liked how warm it felt, all kind of big and bulging. I actually really wanted to do it, but I knew what a pig Gus was. I had seen him driving into Butterick's on his Vespa yelling, "Handjob!"

Both Tootsie and I worked in Filene's Basement. Tootsie I can't do that. She got me the job. Yes you can. Just try it. Say Mr. DiMaggio, remember me? I'm back. He never remembers anyone. They won't find your files upstairs. So maybe they lost them. Say you worked during Christmas.

As I look back on it Mr. DiMaggio was a hunky man. Really kind of sexy. Slow and suspicious and macho. There's no way on earth he wouldn't have remembered every girl who ever worked in Filene's Basement. Tootsie's advice was perfect but for the absolutely opposite reason. You worked here before huh. Who told you to say that. He flicked a piece of paper on his desk. Donna La Bert. I guess we could probably use another friend of La Bert's around here he said to an imaginary audience. There was one fat woman with frizzy red hair filing but she could hardly be construed as listening. DiMaggio was sexy. He was kind of a sullen flirt. Everyone who worked in Filene's Basement was sexy. Well of course not everyone but lots of people. Everyone who worked there comported themselves as if they had a secret. That's why you worked in that crazy place. Miss Quealey undoubtedly was a lesbian. She lived with her mother. She had great legs. She lifted her eyes real slow when you explained you were late and she totally looked at you and you stood there in her gaze realizing, I am cute.

So here I am in Filene's Basement, La Bert's friend, with my cash drawer in a population that included black stock clerks from Roxbury and white Irish high school girls in maroon uniforms from Dorchester, named Cathy, tough, all of them, and Grace the salesclerk with her second husband, the cook, a bore, but not as bad as the first, the drunk. Filene's Basement was also extremely Jewish, there were women with beehives and big glasses and quite a few concentration camp tattoos on these women's arms. And they were angry. It was a strange place to work when you were in high school and had a hangover. I'd show up in the basement office, sick as a dog, they'd give me my money and tell me what department to go to. Toots said they'd probably use me as a "contingent" and that's what they did. A "transient" you mean. That sounded right to me plus I had read *Grapes of Wrath*. Okay don't believe me said Toots. I'm a transient I told the frizzy red headed woman in the office. A what she asked, raising her glasses. The floor of Filene's Basement was filled with square wooden counters, covered with carefully laid out sweaters, gloves, blouses, etc. You would stand in the center of your square, with your cash drawer now firmly ensconced in the register, folding. There would be a tall wooden sign on your counter with a peach colored cardboard announcement: Misses designer sweaters, $8.95. There were entrances directly into Filene's Basement from the subway. Once you had passed through the subway turnstile, you couldn't turn back and before 9 o'clock the doors of the basement hadn't opened. The women were packed in that tiny alcove, waiting, trying to read the signs. You were in your square, folding. Then it happened: Bong-Bong, Bong-Bong. Four recorded bells would chime over the sound system, would throb and echo through the maze of counters up and down both floors of the store. They'd pour in then, the shoppers. Mostly female, mostly white, the black shoppers all looked like young beautiful models, and the Asian women came in pairs to look at shoes. Then there was a significant population of gypsies and drag queens who loved to try on floor length gowns. Both of these populations were said to be major thieves, but mostly the detectives just liked to watch them, I think. There was a plainclothes detective who everybody in Boston who ever shopped in Filene's Basement knew was a cop. She was maybe forty, wore a brown turban, glasses, a grey raincoat, a big Filene's Basement shopping bag. The gongs continued throughout the selling day too, off and on. Tootsie told me they were codes for the detectives in Filene's

Basement, or maybe for this one woman in a turban. Moving her in not-so-secret secrecy around the store, like the Coast Guard or something else that's public, but does nothing, just cruising around.

The Rexicana Ballroom was in Marshfield, Mass., where coincidentally my family used to go each summer. So I had intimate access to the Rex as early as age 14. I saw the sensation of Chickie Gomes, a black guy with a gold tooth, a shiny green shirt, the front emblazoned with vertical stripes of a second contrasting color which resounded in the squared-off trim—kind of a jac-shirt and followed up by shiny pants with flared bottoms and pointed shoes. He dressed like a real Negro, satisfying my conception of what that looked like in 1964. There being no blacks in Arlington, my experience was limited to who I saw on the subway when I went in town. For me, Boston's inner city black reality corresponded to some other time in history. The Ink Spots or something, or of course James Brown. Immediately following the first few organ notes of the Midnight Hour Tootsie would hop into the elite circle of dancers that was crowned by Chickie Gomes. Even at her absolute drunkest she had the maximum grace and tension and carelessness that made a great dancer. Toots! Everyone loved her and she was always fearless about getting in with the black kids who lived in Marshfield. I didn't know black people lived here. Yes, my friend Lynn, a townie, told me, there's lots of them. They live in shacks.

At the Rex people would get speechlessly drunk. I remember people white-faced, people dancing who were never seen dancing before or afterwards in their lives. One night a couple of kids got killed, having piled into a trunk for a ride home from the Rex. The car got rear-ended.

My own worst disaster story had to do with the seduction of a boy named Gene Malloy. He went to Matignon, a neighboring Catholic school. People kept telling me Gene was an asshole. I liked his kind of overdeveloped upper lip. The area above the lip. He looked like kind of a monkey, something I would have drawn. He was unbelievably self-conscious, referred to his clothes which was odd in a boy. Yeah, got my stompers on he said, referring to some kind of shoes. All set for the Rex, he said tensely. Signs of tension in others relieved me. I guess I thought I could get Gene. He wound up liking one of my friends, that happened a lot. But in that era, one night driving down the Southeast Expressway in the drunken twilight of a half pint of rum on Saturday night I wore a raspberry heather cable knit sweater (a little warm for the summer but so what. Being inappropriately overdressed was no crime among the collegiate working class) floral peter pan collar shirt and rolled up white jean shorts. I must've worn some kind of Keds, something to butch it up, but it was very white and clean and pristine but then I had to pee. I was drunk and I was begging them to stop. They pulled over and I jumped one of those heavy wires attached to white markers and down into the deep green along the expressway towards some tall grass and whoops I was lying in a-a pool, a pond, some quicksand, dark brown with mosquitoes swimming in it. I was all wet and covered with mud and I clutched for blades of grass, weeds along the edge of the water and they were coming out in my hand so I started saying an Act of Contrition—Oh my

God I am heartly sorry . . . Leena, get up laughed Lynne. And Lynne Marshall hovered over me and it became clear I was lying in a few inches of water. I was just lying flat in it where I fell. We stopped at a gas station and tried to wash the front of my clothes, all of them, my face. Somebody gave me their shirt I think. A sweatshirt, but I really stunk. I smelled like a swamp. It seemed I got Gene that night. We were both drunk and we were making out. Swampy became a nickname briefly. Where'd he go? Not such a good school.

There was a boy who was positively Arabic looking. His name was something mundane, like William. Dark hair, skin, blue eyes, perfect sharp features, I think it was rumored that he was a model. He wore a maroon sweatshirt and it said nothing and it was perfect for him. There was a little bit of leather on his wrists, old. More than a message it reeked of sentiment. It seemed like the boys he travelled with were a gang of dogs and he was the head dog. Because of his handsomeness, because of his quietness. He wasn't unfriendly. He just didn't care. It was like these boys all had a secret. I saw them coming down the sea wall one day, in an obscure side of town. They stopped because we the girls knew them. But they wouldn't get involved. They moved on and I had a sense that this was the thing to value, that beautiful visual strangeness.

I loved Tootsie's face. Thin with pointed features, thick long eye lashes, jet black hair with big bangs. Pale, her cheeks slightly scarred from pimples. She looks like a deer. It makes sense. Her parents Don and June owned a place on Lake Winnipesaukee. I went up there once with Toots when I was sixteen. She said we could water ski and drink all the beer we

wanted. They'd never know. Her parents were perfect nou-
veau riche. Her father was a Lincoln dealer. Don La Bert.
They lived like kids. Up at the lake they drank and ate and
laughed. Paid no attention to us at all. Everyone was kind of
overweight. It was hard to see Tootsie's fine features in her
parents. Getting June into her jeans after the laundry was
a joke. Supposedly Tootsie and her sister Linda had to do it
together.

All day long our project at the lake was gathering beers
two or three at a time and carrying them into the woods near
the driveway. They'd be warm by the time we went out but
they'd be easier to chug a lug said Toots. I hated warm beer
but I could get it down. In the afternoon we water skied on
their boat, the Gallant Fox, which was black. I wonder where
they got such a name. Tootsie thought probably her Uncle
Fluffy. He's the only one with any kind of brain. They were
eating pepper steaks when we left. Sure you girls don't want
some said June, playing Mom as we left. Her mouth was full
of food as she spoke and her friend mocked her. Shut up Rose
she yelled still considering us. We'll eat at Weirs said Toots.
Here she said going for her purse, clutching the pepper steak
in her hand. Let me at least give you girls a few bucks. She
pushed a ten in Tootsie's hand. Bye Dad. Bye Rose yelled
Toots. Hee-hee-hee she shrieked as our Keds hit the driveway. She had the most unbelievable giggle, almost a squeak.
It filled out the portrait of her as a cartoon character. My
friend Tootsie from Somerville. Tough girl voice, but kind
of scratchy, cute. The highs and lows got more extreme when
she got drunk. She had a kind of disturbing way of wrapping

her lips around the beer bottle she was drinking from. She looked like a baby nursing. She closed her eyes. Another one down. She threw it on the floor. She stepped on it. The car we had that night was great. Drive safely Toots her father said. Mr. La Bert was kind of handsome for a fat bald man. I guess I liked fathers.

We always drove cars with dealer plates. This one had power everything, huge car. Tootsie was a good driver. Same kind of ease she did everything with as if she were just one quarter of an inch off the ground at all times, so it freed her from care. So let's get subs at Jillie's. Then let's find some strokes. She laughed. Tootsie was always heading towards food like skinny people do. She'd bite a bit, swing her sub around in her hand as she spoke, then it would wind up on the floor. Strokes was one of the Hawkeses' words for men. We'd inherited it like everything else. The Hawkeses went to Marycliffe. They liked the uniform better an intermediary friend with an in told us. Oh Jeanie, Mary Ann was quoted as saying, I couldn't wear one of those beanies and she did one of those painful laughs that looked like crying. Marycliffe's blazer was navy blue and they could do whatever they wanted with their legs. Knee socks loafers, whatever looked cool. The Hawkeses loved Tootsie. In a way, she was just like them. Even more so. She didn't even bother living in Arlington, going to Marycliffe Academy. She couldn't see spending money in expensive stores, when you could steal clothes or work someplace like Filene's Basement. How's it going, Toots, said Barbara, changing her tone, indicating she was talking to a character. At these moments you could see she was a bartender's daughter. She practically asked what'll you have when she said hello. She is a hot ticket, said Barbara. Unbelievable said Mary Ann more softly.

We passed someplace that faced a green open field and a lot of trees. It wasn't even dark yet. So you reading any books, Eileen, asked Tootsie. Yeah, I guess so. My Uncle Fluffy reads a lot. You should talk to him. Fluffy was her mother's brother, the peace-maker when Tootsie got in trouble. The crowd at Weirs looked particularly creepy tonight. We went into a dance and the Blue Knights were playing. They were old men, in shiny blue jackets who played lousy rock and roll. It was depressing to see their big white faces and slicked back hair. We had to get out and we were laughing. We walked around town. Hi said a couple of big guys. Hellooo said Toots passing them. We had our beers in big paper cups and she was pretty well along. Her walk got stiffer and bouncier when she got drunk. She began to float. Hi she yelled at another pair. Weirs Beach was crawling with hunks she claimed. Camp counselors. College boys from all over who came to staff the myriad summer camps around Winnepesaukee.

Mine was named Tony. I can't remember if he went to Duke or Duquesne. He was big. He had wavy black hair—I think he had a Southern accent. His navy blue sweatshirt declared the name of his school in white letters. We were shopping for men who were products. Anyhow these two were right—we found them on the street at Weirs and the four of us piled into Tootsie's car. Want a beer, Tony, said Toots offering it back with her hand that wasn't driving. Her guy, fairer than mine, was sitting right up next to her. His name was Pat. It was such an intense scene. I think we had told them we were in Junior College. Tony had responded enthusiastically to the beer—but "Westpointlike" or something. Polite—"Sure do." I was glad Tootsie was still driving. She hadn't surrendered that.

At each stage of your life I'm aghast at how much it's just like the animal world. When we were kids, little, under ten, we would go into nature, change our names, say we were horses and then forget everything among the trees. We would run jump on rocks pick up sticks and become part of it all. It was a dream, the memory of childhood.

Now when we climbed into cars with boys the communication was instantaneous and similar. Tony never learned that I was more than Elaine and that relieved me. He was less than Gus and almost as soon as he had opened his beer and I had told a few lies we were making out and his hands were inside my clothes and I was thrilled by the realization, the safety of anonymity. In the front seat as she drove Tootsie was beating what's his name off and he had his hand inside her shorts and his finger was inside of her.

Tony pulled his zipper down and put his other hand on the back of my neck, moved his hand through my hair, pushing my head down towards his crotch. I was not in Arlington. I was in the backseat of Tootsie's car winding through woodsy dark dark roads. We were no one. I put my mouth on his cock. He sighed.

Tootsie shrieked. She slammed on the brakes. Oh no, oh no oh no she howled. Take it easy, Toots. Pat jumped out and took a look at the damage. Eileen did you see that Tootsie demanded. Yeah, what, ummmm, what happened? Tony was tucking in his dick. Tootsie took a glance. A deer, a deer she screamed jumping out of the car and then we all did. The honeymoon was over.

Tootsie shrieked again when she put her fingers toward the grill which was covered with fur. Off to the left of the car lying on the grassy shoulder was a very big deer. It did not have horns. What did that mean. It was dead, it was completely dead. We had killed it. Get the beer out of the car Pat demanded. I've got to call my father, I've got to call my father. Maybe you better call the police, suggested Tony. Pat and Tootsie headed over to a motel that was white in the single light of the dark road. Tony pulled out a cigarette and I smoked one too. We didn't say a word.

The game warden's coming Toots announced. Well that sounds better than the cops. Tony and Pat walked to the front of the car for a silent conference. We think we better get going said Tony. These guys were maybe 19 or 20. Pat was hugging Tootsie which looked nice. I just waved at Tony and he said see yah. I was disappointed. I wanted to see what happened when you gave a blow job.

The game warden showed up in his dark green car. He had a deep tan and a dark green shirt and a hat with a brim. It felt like he was in the army, but a good one. He carried no gun. With his partner he pushed Don's Lincoln to the side of the road. He looked at the deer. We'll pick her up later, girls. You better hop in, he said opening the car door. I already called your Dad he said to Tootsie. You did she piped. Sounds like he's just glad you're okay.

Oh sure Tootsie mumbled to me in the back seat of the car. The ride was lickety split, I didn't notice the feel of the road at all, just the deep reassuring voice of the game warden telling us how many deers die this way each year—it's a fact, girls. Early on he asked us what sex the deer was, the only weird moment with him. We were from Arlington, Somerville. How would we know about deers.

The fire was roaring at Tootsie's house. There was stone all around the fireplace. It was a nice house. I had never noticed it before. The game warden explained to Don La Bert the deer statistics again. There's just too many of them. It's a little sad to say, but this is one of the ways we keep the deer population down. These accidents. Mr. La Bert I would like to suggest to you that we be grateful these girls are okay. That deer gave quite a sock to the front of your car. Don took a fierce drag on his cigarette at that. Would you like a drink, Don asked. No thanks said the warden looking at his partner. This is a very common occurrence he repeated again, eerily, as the two men backed out the door. I felt like he was preparing everyone for something that remained to be seen.

I was certainly fooled. The twinkling lights of the fireplace. The maternal cast to June's face. The friends all gone to bed. Don stood in silence for a moment after the warden had shut the door. Did you have your license on you, Toots? Sure Dad. The silence grew. Don, said June, sidling over, touching the upper part of his back. Let me see it Toots. She pulled it out of her little black billfold. Tootsie had all these little masculine things. He walked slowly over to the fireplace, read it and dipped it into the flames for a moment till it lit up. He held it, looked at Toots. It flared and he dropped it on the flagstone and ground it with the toe of his black shoe. Then he grabbed Tootsie by the back of her jacket, shook her for a moment. She looked incredibly frail. He shoved her with all his might across the room. Piss for brains, he bellowed. It was so cruel.

There was a trip to Bermuda the Hawkeses organized. We wouldn't even need a car, Toots exclaimed. Bermuda was the perfect place for the Hawkeses, it being kind of British yet exotic. For years we'd hear about that cute cop. Apparently the cops' uniforms were unusual and handsome and as you might have noticed, we were a uniform-oriented culture. I didn't have the money, it was just out of the question. Tootsie went, Eileen Tracey went and of course the Hawkeses went and their extended community of Marycliffe friends and boys from Arlington. It was the beginning of the end of my communication with Tootsie. She was horrible, Eileen reported. Apparently she got really drunk and was driving everyone crazy. You know how she gets, said Ollie. She was disgusting Eileen Tracey said in her most severe tone. She had a voice that invoked the authority of her older sisters who she was in awe of. I think Tootsie didn't take baths or wore the same clothes all week too, that was part of the story. Then she was lying by the swimming pool passed out and everyone jerked off on her face. She was just lying there passed out. You should never let yourself get that drunk that people could treat you like a thing. I never heard what the Hawkeses thought, but to put it simply, she was 86'd.

A year or two after college I was driving a cab. I had my hair in braids. I was wearing a navy blue pea jacket. This was supposed to be a hip thing to be doing, but it didn't feel like that. I had a hangover. Actually, it was my birthday. I was 23. I remember writing in my notebook about that. I had just returned from an airport fare after which I stopped in Everett for a veal parmesan sub. I was so depressed. I was driving down Cambridge St. A woman was hitchhiking. I slowed down. It was Tootsie. She climbed in, her face more alarmed than excited when she saw me in the driver's seat. Hi, I beamed. It was the single instance ever when I felt I had the upper hand. It passed quickly. Eileen, you went to college. I instantly wished she was driving. I was terrified when people said airport and I had to go through that tunnel. My hands turned lily white with fear. I began to hallucinate. They turned into doves. I wasn't doing well. Naturally we talked about other people. We laughed at Eileen Tracey who we had always laughed at. We hated her sisters. We sat on the pink stools in the window of Dunkin Donuts and I swear I could see us from outside. Her in all black and me in my awful pea jacket as if I were sitting out in the parking lot watching. I guess I better go. Okay. She was in this drug program, methadone I think at Cambridge City. There was a moment when we talked about heroin. She said it was great and I believed her. Tootsie got everyplace first.

Gary came to New York several years later, maybe eight. He had looked me up. He was some kind of travelling salesman for cable teevee. It was good. They gave him a car. I think I heard that Tootsie died he said. We were sitting on a stoop on 4th St. Well she was hanging out with high school kids at Powder House. What a waste, he laughed. He wasn't commenting on the tragedy of her death. "Waste" was what we called someone. Well she OD'd. He squinted. Gary always squinted. Even in grade school. Yeah I'm pretty sure I heard that, he said. He looked at me. So you're queer now or are you bisexual. I'm gay I said, puffing on my cigarette.

1969

You can't force a story that doesn't want to be told. It was that kind of year. I was walking down the hill to Falmouth Heights in the blazing sunshine that amplified Good Morning Starshine on everyone's radios passing by on the street that wrapped around the ocean and down there on the beach millions of pebbles were gleaming and darts of light animated the Atlantic Ocean. I couldn't have handled anything less. I was going down to get some coffee and the *Boston Globe* to make me be something. Everything I did was something to fix me. With all my heart I was trying to be dead. I'd get my coffee in a big white wooden building that hung over the beach and had a porch out front where you could drink outside on weekends. We'd drink these large pink Planter's Punch in the scorching heat and get hornier and hornier and go into blackouts. I shouldn't get ahead of myself, though. This is only the morning. I was trying so hard to get placed in the world that I even had high expectations of the *Boston Globe*. I read each editorial and a couple of the more literary columnists and then I dutifully read the comics, a tragedy. I had been wildly addicted to comic books and comic strips in childhood but now I failed to see the humor but was carrying on some tradition about myself. I was 19. I wore a blue workshirt and a Villager bikini and a pair of Doctor Scholl sandals that made a dragging clucking sound when I walked and turned me into a toy. Getting extremely drunk was a regular part of my life and the stories told in the aftermath always included: "And then we heard Leena's Doctor Scholl's coming down the stairs . . ." Part of the comedy was that I was so beautiful that year. Everything clicked for a moment that summer and I came out looking like some kind of unwitting hippy wasp model who had absolutely no defenses against the boys and the men who were looking at her on the beach or were offering to buy her drinks in bars.

The attention of women was softer and more pleasing, but I didn't know there was anything you could do with those feelings. The best solution I ever arrived at was to try and control myself and be dead. I carried a tattered copy of *Crime and Punishment* around everywhere. I'd often be found passed out on the couch of the house I stayed in that summer with *Crime and Punishment* on the floor next to my toes. If I could finish that book that summer then my life wouldn't be a complete waste. I had a boyfriend. His name was Mike and he was also a blackout drinker. He was 21 and had just graduated from college. I thought we looked alike. He would always get drunk and say to me, "Leena, I ain't gonna march." I always felt like I was in a movie when he said that. Who does he think he is, I wondered. He wasn't going to Canada. The war would end. Something would happen. He just wasn't the type. When these foreign things would erupt from his soul it would just be so strange. It was like he was turning into a thing. I'd grab his dick and the crisis would be over. He was the first person I really had sex with. I don't mean in terms of quality. Earl Cook of the Checkmates in the darkened bedroom of a Kenmore Square apartment going "I want to eat you—" "What do you mean, Oh!" That was sex. Sex with Mike was the first sex I was willing to own. Boys in high school were always trying to get you involved with their dicks. And then announce it. It seemed like some struggle for mastery. I would let them finger me. Since it was inevitable that I would be talked about I wanted to be the one getting it. The thing with Mike, though, was that even though it was mutual, it really wasn't either. It was like my tits, my cunt, his dick, fini. My body was a hallway to his. But I loved the power. In any situation if I could get my hands on his crotch he would instantly be reduced to a child. That control made the mysterious things that poured out of his mouth bearable. The one that's most opaque to me now was the future he happily projected for me. "Leena," he'd go, "I can see you in a big house with all these kids. You'd make a really cool Mom." I had never ever said anything which indicated in any way that I wanted to have a lot of kids and be "a cool Mom." I could see that house and I could see that he wasn't in it. That was the point of the story. But if he wasn't going to march why should I? Getting drunk by the ocean made me feel like a part of nature. We were standing in a big field when we had this conversation and we were across from a bar called Navigator which was across from the street from the ocean. When "One small step for mankind" took place I was riding in a car in Falmouth Heights on my way to the

Navigator to watch us land on the moon. The radio was actually better.

Across the way from the house I was staying in that summer was another dwelling called "the chapel." Both houses were listening to the same albums—The Beatles' "White Album," WAR, Otis Redding, Richie Havens' Mixed Bag and Credence. But they were all taking acid, whereas we had men with SPECIAL FORCES stickers on their cars crashing in on us. Also the chapel played Their Satanic Majesty's Request, which I thought was out of the question. I went over there once with my beer and sat down on one of their couches in their darkened rooms and listened to the music. "Joint," they'd go, passing it. No thanks, I'd say. "Why do you have Green Berets staying at your house?" "We do?" "That's what SPECIAL FORCES means." "I don't know . . . I didn't know that."

I hated the war, but even more I hated knowing people who had brothers or boyfriends in Da Nang, or in Hong Kong on R & R. And of course these guys were just as bad as everyone else, maybe worse, when they got back. They would criticize you for drinking, pushing joints in your face, then trying to fuck you. And always wanting to talk about it, "Nam," when they got drunk. Just knowing people like that was so lower class. It seemed like if you were "right" then you went away to school and you didn't meet people who went to "Nam," maybe you had never known anyone who went. I had gone parking and drank with them in high school. These guys came back with great stereos and married girls who would marry anything and together they would be some kind of nervous hippies.

Of course I never knew that Duke was a Green Beret. He was this giant guy with a small head and a close hair cut. He wore grey athletic teeshirts and he brought cases and cases of beer with him whenever he arrived. And it was cold beer unlike others I'd met who bragged, "We always drank it warm in Nam!" We loved Duke. He wore wire-rimmed Raybans. He looked like a newscaster. He'd always been nice to me. "Well, I gotta go," I said to the guys in the chapel. They called it the chapel because it was a run-down version of those gingerbready looking houses that were all over Cape Cod. Only they had put that crummy-looking stick-on stained glass on all the windows. I had always wondered what it was like inside. It was dark. "Bye," my shoes clacked out, "Thanks for the . . ." I realized I drank my warm Schlitz and they had their pot and their . . . "music." Satanic Majesty's Request. Weird.

My house was definitely different. It was like this: there were ten of us, all women aged 19–25, and we each had a share, but once you divided a small house by ten it was hard to see what anyone got. A couple of girls, Debbie and "Mo" had staked out one of the upstairs bedrooms as their own and that was a safe place. All these women with the exception of me and one other, Joan, were sort of office-secretary types. They worked for Goldman Sachs, Merrill Lynch. They did things like have affairs with married men and got abortions in London and Puerto Rico. I had hung out in high school with Madeleine. We were both Sagittariuses and had enjoyed standing outside the library at night, smoking cigarettes and talking about sex. We laughed a lot. Well, one of the other women, Sandy, was Madeleine's sister and all the rest were

Sandy's friends. Sandy had been some kind of high school star-let just four years ago. Her boyfriend, Fred, was the captain of the hockey team and then went to Yale on a scholarship. There he had gone bad. Started smoking pot, had a ponytail and was thinking of quitting school and joining the migrant farm workers. Did he break up with Sandy or did she break up with him? I don't know. Then she dated Jack who went to Notre Dame and was now distancing himself from her as he began to wonder about his life. Sandy was drinking a lot of Jack Daniels and getting fat and the boys she used to date were beginning to see she was clearly on the far side of the great cultural divide. She was very funny. By mid-summer she spent the weekends in a pink nightgown fucking everybody. She even picked up a little hippy from next door. I thought she was sort of a Liz Taylor figure. I was the resident college girl, or intellectual or hippy—whatever role I was needed to fill. I was broke and always wanting beer so I was not intimidating but kind of a mascot. I was also like bait. I would go out with Madeleine and I don't know who the third woman was, but we'd go down to the Navigator and our combined sensibility and effect would invariably find us three men to buy us drinks and take us in their sports cars out to dinner. The other girl who didn't belong in our house was Joan. When I look at her all I can think about was what a scavenger I was, everyone was. She was different from the other women in the house on the basis of hitchhiking and "ripping off." She was always coming home with cans of clam chowder in her Greek bag, and the men she picked up were definitely there to support her, buy her dinner, take her places. Her great coup was hitching a ride to Martha's Vineyard on a boat. She hung out with him for three days. You just get out there on the rocks with your thumb, she said. Everyone was suspicious of Joan.

Paul Markey sat out on the porch. I'm sure he was tripping. He was extremely skinny and wore a green shirt and corduroy pants and had long hair for our house and he sat out there laughing all weekend. It wasn't much of a porch. It was more of a runway. I must say right here that our house didn't even make it to Labor Day. We were condemned by the Board of Health and they nailed our doors shut. Paul seemed extremely drunk but he was definitely tripping too. Everything seemed to happen on the same weekend—the whole summer was like a broken movie. And Paul would be out there all summer. His friends: Spike, Marty, Danny, who else . . . they were all kind of well-off recent college graduates. They all seemed to be working for their fathers, had cars. Paul was their hippy. It seems redundant to mention that he looked like Mick Jagger. For twenty years we've been saying "She looked like Mick Jagger." "He looked like Mick." It means skinny, brown hair, big mouth. But that's the way he was. So, it was natural that when that whole group of guys and the girlfriends they had absorbed from the house, Debbie and "Mo" from the upstairs bedroom, decided to go to Woodstock I would be invited to go with Paul Markey.

Oh, we love Paul, everyone exclaimed, that is, the girls, when I wondered aloud if I should go with him. I had always thought of him as more an "it." Something out there laughing on the porch. It was a good position to take. Particularly in relation to some of the other animals who came to us that summer. Who was responsible for the Ice Man showing up? The Ice Man was Jimmy Burns, big, big guy who tended to pin girls (like me) against the wall in front of their boyfriends and say, "You know I think you're really cute," and cop a feel and give them a big wet smooch and no one dared lift a finger. It was really terrifying. To be pinned like that by one of the biggest guys you had ever seen who was drunk out of his mind in front of ten of your good friends who just stared in horror. Then he would just kind of turn to everyone and go: "She doesn't know I'm teasing. Do ya, Linda?" The Ice Man was reputed to have killed and maimed many kids in Watertown during his wonder years. He was like something that would eat you alive, in that sense that giants would when you were a kid. He would get drunk and go, "I am the Ice Man!" and smash his hand down on a piece of furniture or the stereo. He ripped our front screen door out and our bathroom door off too. Years ago he had bit somebody's ear off. That's always part of any true animal's story. The Ice Man did it in a football game. He went a little beyond the boundaries of sports. Nobody in Boston knew what was out there. He was a dangerous man.

I wouldn't have gone to Woodstock with Paul if it wasn't for how badly Mike was treating me. He had this way of fading in and out. His alcoholic Aquarian nature. My mother went on a vacation in Maine with my sister and Mike and I had some kind of honeymoon in my house. It was insanely narcissistic. The two of us were naked on the couch in the parlor opposite a big mirror so we could look at ourselves. Everything in the parlor's decorating scheme was cool and metallic—the dull rose wine rug, the shiny green couch. After my father died my mother had the parlor done in this chintzy gleam. There was a definite pall over the room. We placed a basket of grapes next to the couch. I have always been dedicated to beauty. So was Mike. Our own. If either of us reflected well on the other, then alright. We even involved the album cover to Romeo & Juliet in this particular still-love vignette. That was Mike's joke I remember. Only I knew we were grabbing and fingering each other on the same couch on which my father had died. I always had the last laugh. Generally mine was internal.

Later, we fucked upstairs under the eaves with light blue and silver milk duds trailing down over the yellowed wallpaper that had accompanied my journey through puberty and finally to sex. "Is that all," I asked as his dick "entered" me. That's all I've got, he said. The next night we had a big party and I don't remember how it ended, but I don't think he stayed over. I had an extreme hangover the next morning pedalling to work up Mass. Ave. to Cambridge past all the Porter Square bars where the boys I knew had already begun drinking. Once they started playing street hockey on Sundays and going to those bars there was only a house and a few kids between them and the wake at Grannan's Funeral Home and the notice in the *Globe* Obituary column. That afternoon after work Mike was sitting down in the shiny beige man's chair in the parlor and he may or may not have been drinking a beer and now that I watch it I think he would've liked me a lot better if I had my own apartment. He liked visiting his girlfriend in a home, her home, without her family. As it was, I didn't impress him. He lived with his family too. I dropped by his house one night on my way to the Cape. I can't imagine why. He came out of the big old porch house, a two-family surrounded by trees. I think he was barefoot, and he was holding the book he was reading, *Lord of the Rings*. The trees were so leafy and he seemed protected by his environment and it explained him in some way. I felt like he was my son. It was so sad. Listening to him explain where he was in the trilogy stirred up pleasant associations but depressed me that my boyfriend had only discovered reading in college. What was he doing before that? He was playing hockey. How could he ever catch up? I couldn't show any of these feelings. I had to act dumb. I had to keep losing so he wouldn't know I wasn't normal. It was like being in a bowling alley and listening to the pins drop incessantly as your score got lower and lower and men were beginning to smile at you. I'll never forget that night. Watching his back go up the stairs as he returned to his dream, his house.

Will I always be mean when I think about other people's feelings? Their aspirations, their vision of themselves. I didn't see Mike for several weeks. He was off on his man adventures, being lonely, visiting Rick on Nantucket and Benny up in Maine. He was playing the lonely man, visiting all his captured boyhood friends who'd been tamed by friendly women who Mike approved of, though he commented that Rick had grown fat, and Benny was sad. The point of his trips seemed to be him, as compared to them. Him ultimately winding up alone on the beach, drunk, or drinking in the local bars with men who had recovered from the young married illusion of being "with" their wives. I was down in Falmouth, getting drunk and weeping nightly, picking up more and more men in sports cars. My sadness only made me more intriguing. I could have gotten married about 10 times in 1969 if that's what I wanted to do. I didn't know what I wanted to do. I wanted to finish *Crime and Punishment.*

The rumors began to travel down to our house that Mike was dating someone, Ellen, a girl who was by anyone's standards normal, "right," and cool. I was not normal, this was my pain. I cried about it to Mike one night at a party in the basement of someone's house in Cape Cod. I remember what I had on—teal blue Villager shorts. In the middle of my tears someone came up and asked me to dance and I did. It became a joke with us. "Well, it was completely weird, Leena. You're crying your eyes out about not being normal and some guy comes up and you go off and boog-a-loo." He emphasized boog-a-loo like it was the essential definition of what assholes do. "I forgot you were there," I cried, after I danced. The dancing felt good. It was like that. Mike never danced.

That's how I went to Woodstock with Paul. I wasn't normal, I never would be, so why not go with this guy who sat outside on the porch all summer laughing. Nobody could stop me. Nobody could watch, I'd be all alone with Paul. Everyone knew we were a couple of weirdos. But not hippies. As soon as I got in the car and opened my first beer, a Piels big mouth, we had a case of the stuff—and cold—immediately me and Paul went into hippy talk. We were going to go and be with the people, and ball, we would ball a lot, and we would get together and meet the heads and it would be beautiful.

Rightaway I knew I could say anything to this person sitting next to me. It was fun. Paul Markey. He wore a clean white shirt and a pair of chinos. He was just kind of a preppy looking hippy, collegiate we called it then. It suggested you had money, I thought. He talked very slowly and carefully. I quickly discovered that Paul was really smart, some kind of genius. Though they were constantly kidding him, his group was sort of in awe of him. And they were all keeping an eye on him like he was their little brother. He liked to get high and it seemed safe in this context, Spike's station wagon with a good radio and all this beer. It was a long ride and for hours I studied Debbie's wrist with some pieces of gold jewelry on it lightly nestled on Spike, the driver's neck. Normal, my reflexes scored. It reminded me of my parents on a trip. Danny, a beet-faced guy with oriental eyes and a receding hairline also sat in front. I liked Danny because he was quick, but he did get a little mean, slightly scarey when he got drunk. He played with Paul the most, they had some kind of secret joke language that you slowly got let in on when you were around them. I liked the world of men, but I always wanted to be accepted by them as a peer. It was possible too, relative to the extent to which you were obsessed with one of the men in the group. If that was the case it was impossible. Here it was nice. By the time we got to Woodstock I was deeply in a blackout. The ride had been fun, but hopeless. We stopped at a lush rest station in upstate New York. There was so much green and there was a gas station made out of stone, individual stones, it was beautiful. Some people were holding this months-old baby in their arms. I guess they were taking turns holding it while they peed. I was really smashed by then and I got excited about that baby. It was beautiful, it was so beautiful, it was the most beautiful baby I had ever seen in my life. I was full of that kind of excitement you have just before you lose consciousness. The baby had blue eyes, intensely blue eyes, and very black hair—it seemed like a magic child, a special baby. The light was that dull grey blue, just before twilight and so everything seemed more itself, stronger than it would be in the constant light of the rest of the day. A baby! Such vulnerability, here of all places, held in its parents' arms in a soft white blanket outside the stone comfort station on the green median strip in the middle of the highway in upstate New York, a place I had never been before in my life. Look Look Look I kept telling everyone—Look at its eyes—isn't it the most beautiful baby you have ever seen before in your life? C'mon Leena, we gotta get going. Are you going to Woodstock too, I asked its parents. They weren't hippies but mellow kind of people from Cambridge. I think I was scaring them. All their replies were very guarded. No one could see it my way, with the falling light and the lush green and the beautiful stone house. The safety of it all, the baby being held by the parents in the middle of the highway. Going home. Not even going to Woodstock.

Liked that baby, huh Leena? "Mo" asked me that from the front seat. I was that kind of Leena by now, and that was the end of the first night. Joanie Mitchell didn't show. Do you blame her? I finally saw the movie in 1987. It would have been painful before then though I didn't know why.

I slept in the backseat of the car, they said it was impossible to move me. I woke up walking over a crowded hill in the blazing sun with a roaring hangover and Canned Heat doing their incessant falsetto. Paul and I had split off from the rest and the plan was we would meet back at the car at six. I didn't have shoes on and Paul had all the pot and a gallon of warm red wine to which I kept going, ugh, okay, and taking a swig. Crosby Stills and Nash were really sweet. Something different was going on while they played. Joe Cocker was an avatar of the 70s, his unchecked awfulness. The crowd cheered. We walked down the road and met a blond kid named Evan who had a vest over his fifteen year old chest. He was kind of honey colored. He talked in super-duper hippy language, and he seemed to have all the information about where you could get food and how this whole festival was perceived from outside and about traffic conditions and road blocks. "Sure, my parents know I'm here. They're cool. They're very-special—" he took a haul of the joint, the little hairs on his upper lip shone with sweat, his eyes glistening out of focus—"*people.*" He laughed at his own joke, one on his parents, I guessed. We hung around with him a lot, maybe forty-five minutes.

Paul was great, Paul liked people. He was constantly interviewing them and engaging them. This was what was interesting about being here. I never thought about that before, mostly thinking I knew everything about a person by the way they dressed. We would walk away and he would say he was alright, Evan was alright. Then he would do this great kind of animal laugh, silent. His eyes would get kind of crazy, blazing. He would almost convince me, even though I thought there was something slimy about the kid. He smoked some very strong cigarettes, possibly European. Or did he roll his own. That would go with the vest. Paul smoked Pall Malls like a prisoner. He made them look really good, pathetic, his fingers all brown and smoking them down to nearly burning himself. He would kind of put his arm around me as we walked down the dirt road that led around the place. He was so skinny and his shirt was damp but there was really something sexy about his scrawniness. All weekend I'd succumbed to the sensation of being Paul's girl. I'd never felt it before or since. Just walking down that road with him and his skinny little arm around me. It felt like Twilight Zone.

Lying on the ground in the mud, in the rain, I felt like the whole place had been turned into a giant mouth. It was terrifying. The sounds of feet traipsing all night long up and down the muddy hills turned into a gigantic rhythm like a mouth smacking its lips continually. I had been smoking and drinking all day so this hallucination was what my night had become. I whispered to Paul who was lying next to me on the wet rag of a blanket we were spending the night on. "It sounds like a mouth." He cringed and put his arms around me. A speed freak with spidery repetitious gestures danced in front of us all night long. Kind of a conductor. Way down at the bottom of the hill the musicians were like dark trees lined in light wavering in front of our eyes. One more, just one more uttered some distant part of my will or mental faculty forcing my attention to stagger along with the entertainment. This is history. It was really horrible but my alternative was to try and sleep on the muddy rag. Impossible. In the early morning a tall blond stranger stood at our feet holding a thick, fresh khaki blanket. He was really saintly looking, pink and healthy in a light blue shirt and a blond mustache. He bent down and put the blanket around us and tucked us in like we were kids.

Peace, he said, making that sign and he backed off into the crowds. I was still in college and I knew he was a Christ figure. Who was that strange blond man we laughed and laughed and asked each other. It was part of the story we would take to the bar.

All signs of the times were the most moving parts of the event. I love cliches. I love the obvious. Woodstock was the biggest cliche of them all—and the end of the 60s. A jet made a giant peace symbol in smoke overhead and helicopters dropped roses and Drakes cakes and oranges. Even the most hardened cynic had to be sentimental about their own appetite being gratified by the sky, and I have always been in awe of skywriting.

But Jimi Hendrix was the best. It spelled destruction, it was so sour and noble. His Star Spangled Banner was the end of America for me. We were through with it. It was the most ironic end of an empire song any culture ever played for itself. I was so glad to be there to hear it. To know it was over. It was the thing we were all waiting for and had come to hear. After that hundreds of cars slowly drove out and they welcomed the carless to come aboard. Paul and I climbed in, never having found our friends.

Our ride dropped us off in Brookline. Paul made a phone-call and we took public transportation home. I didn't make a phone-call. We went to Harvard Square. We went to Charley's Kitchen. Paul and Mike shook hands in that man way that always sickened me. Do you guys know each other? Paul, this is Mike. Big grins all around. We were completely covered in mud. We were heroes. We got to watch it in the news on the big teevee over the bar. "In an amazingly tension-free three days, almost one million young Americans shared 'peace and love' in x acres of land in upstate New York." Then some politicians came on to say how really great it was. Paul kind of vanished. I slipped into a booth next to Mike. He seemed to have some money. He bought me Schlitz upon Schlitz. You know, you don't have to ditch the guy, Leena, just because I'm here. I know, I said vehemently. I didn't know it at all. Mike was like my job, my family. He was the real world, where I belonged. He didn't even like me, and he probably was sincere about Paul. I probably could've gone on hanging out with him for at least that night. Paul. This guy I went to Woodstock with.

I could stall around a little and tell you what else happened in 1969. Paul worked at a bar called the Tam on Commonwealth Ave. It was a BC bar. That's Boston College. A school where nice middle class Catholic boys go. Paul went there. He waited tables, bartended. He wore a clean white shirt and looked cute. The one night I went with my girlfriends I was so happy to see him, and wondered if I shouldn't keep seeing him anyhow. But I didn't know how to have two boyfriends, one who liked me, one who didn't. I had to choose the one who didn't like me. I think we dropped Paul off somewhere when the place closed. He had let us sit and wait for him while they closed up. They served Bud there, and they tasted really sweet and I could've drank that stuff forever. I liked Paul more and more. He kissed me when he hopped out of the car. Okay, he even asked me to go to the BC/Army game with him. Call me, he said. How could I ever call him. It just wouldn't happen.

The next time I saw Paul he was lying down. He had brown rosaries in his hand and a grey double breasted pin striped suit on, and a tie and his face had a fine covering of makeup on that infuriated me and made him look queer. Paul was dead. He was surrounded by flowers and that dense thick smell pervaded the air. Spike was there, in a suit, very subdued, and Danny looked insane, his eyes completely red, he couldn't stop crying. Maureen went "Leena," and gave me meaningful looks. I felt furious. It's all I felt. Oh, I had a lot of dreams. I thought about how if I had just stayed his girlfriend, God, just for a month or two I could be incredibly sad now. If I knew he was going to die I would have cared. This was not Paul. I don't think it's Paul. Did you see the makeup. Did you see those rosary beads. That was so un-him. He hated liturgy. How did I know that about him. There was his father. To think of Paul having a family. I keep thinking Paul's going to show up, said Danny. He was so crazy . . . crazy, crazy . . . you jerk Danny yelled at the coffin. Paul was lying there with his brown beads in his fingers. What am I going to do without him. Who am I going to laugh with. Danny was laughing and crying. Paul's graduation picture was prominently displayed nearby. Very clean cut, serious, though. He was not smiling. As if he knew he'd be dead this year.

Apparently he left the Tam one night and everyone said he wasn't drinking. He had a car. Everyone was impressed by that. Nobody knew what Paul was going to do once he got out of school and he was in that kind of high expectation crowd. They thought it was good that at least he was working. Supposedly he was saving money to take a trip. But he had bought this car, a used one. Two-tone I heard. And he left work and he plowed right into a stone wall around 2 A.M. It just looked like the car went off the road. He wasn't drunk his friends insisted. They saw him that night. Though he was a little quiet. It was funny that he wasn't drinking, but Paul was like that—he had a mind of his own. Nobody would even say out loud that he did it to himself. I felt that. He probably already had his life. There was no place for Paul to go. He had that great laugh.

FEBRUARY 13, 1982

Time passes. That's for sure. It's the nightmare of having what you want that I'm interested in today. I had a book party five years ago. It took place in New York where I live and it was the beginning of the end for me.

I'm a very different person today. Bill's coming over to build shelves in the kitchen. Things have a slow progression, kind of a pleasant listiness. A big part of my list is the past. I went over to Rose's to plan the book party. Power Mad Press, which was Barbara, was publishing my book. Barbara lived with Rose in a loft and that's where we were going to have the party. Rose is an astrologer. She pointed to February 13th on her calendar. It's got to be this date, she said. Absolutely. But why, I asked. A lot of things will converge for you on this date. Your Mars, a lot of your aspects . . . I don't know how to explain it, but this is YOU. Maybe you don't want your party to be such an intense experience. It could be a lot quieter. It depends on what you want. Rose was like a lawyer, or a salesman. You never knew if she was making this stuff up—if she really had her finger on the pulsation of the orbs and if she did, I mean, if she really had the power, was she on my side.

I watched the way she played with her cats. What if she was just very powerful and intuitive, but to her we were all just cats. It was an interesting place to be and I decided to go with her suggestion.

I made a very nice white on black invitation. I sent it to significant people. Mostly the party was publicized by word of mouth. I bought some cocaine. I was a very down and out person. Glamorous, but down and out. Sort of a beer drinker, really. The kind of person who always had diet pills in her faded jean pockets. My main concern really was that I didn't get so drunk that I fell down or turned it into an embarrassing night in some way. It was an early evening event. I had slept with this girl who was a musician and who I was currently in love with. She left around noon, left me to my cigarettes, and a nice foggy musing upon my pink floral sheets and the birds outside the window and the slender branches of the trees. I have an old cemetery outside my window and I felt like Keats in the 80s or something. I could feel the nervousness rising in me like some kind of strange spring, inside and out. The winter had a way to go, but there's always days in February when you forget that. For me to put down one hundred dollars for cocaine was something, but all in service of this wonderful amazing day—the long-awaited book and of course my new life.

I suppose I had the typical horror of what if nobody shows up. I went over to the loft relatively early and I know I was full of the deep calm of one who is in a total panic. I smoked significant cigarettes. The whole thing wasn't very professional. We didn't even know we could sell books. We had maybe twenty available copies. The rest of the books were there in the loft but a couple of things were missing from them. One was the name of the photographer who did the photos front and back. Irene Young would be pissed if she didn't get credit so we had a stamp made and dutifully stamped her name in red ink on the credit page.

The other thing missing from the book was a whole stanza, the last stanza of a poem called "New York." Here's the stanza:

> Then entering the subway, pushing through
> the crowds at 34th, I saw a
> baby sucking desperately on its bottle
> tears streaming down its tat dark face.
> As it sat in its carriage. It stopped me,
> I turned, examined some flowers
> for sale, cloth on silky green leaves
> mounted on a comb. I plucked
> up a black one, a black rose, paid the
> guy a dollar. I love it.
>
> I'm softly fingering its petals on the
> subway home, it is so artificial
> so dark and so beautiful.

I thought "it is so artificial / so dark and so beautiful" referred to New York. Now it strikes me that I was talking about my life. Line four should read "fat dark face," not "tat."

So what happened once the party got going was that as

people wanted copies of the book I had to go into the back room and stamp "Irene Young" and the final stanza of "New York" into each copy. My book was called *A Fresh Young Voice from the Plains*. I had always figured if I had a book I would want my face all over it. The experience was like television. Every book hanging off the end of someone else's hand was like another tiny monitor. As more and more people began to flow in it meant that that many more pictures of me were bobbing around the room. What a horror. Particularly in relation to the people I didn't know. They would look down at their book and then up at me. Oh, it's you. Here it was a big moment in my life and to them it was just another party. I began to join that group. Some beer, some coke. Some people you know. I would go in the back and people would offer me some coke and then I would offer mine to other people. People seemed surprised that I had my own coke. Of course. It's my party. It's a self-serving event.

Allen Ginsberg asked me to sign his book. I must've stood there for five minutes drawing a complete blank. Hi Allen, from one howl to another. Dear Allen I'm glad you think I'm a poet. Love, Eileen. I'm the only woman you like, right Allen? Only the craziest thoughts passed through my mind. Finally he started getting embarrassed. Just sign it. Come by and write something better when you think of it. I scrawled something. I forget what it was.

I was "The Fresh Young Voice from the Plains." I felt so foolish signing books. "Mark, you're going to kill yourself if you keep drinking the way you do. Me too. Eileen." The wrong lines kept flashing through my mind. In David's I wrote: David, I just wrote something really horrible in someone's book. People I didn't know wanted copies and I would put them off and they'd offer money, go "C'mon, I'll pay for it." At the end my pants were full of these wrinkled dollar bills. It made me feel kind of sleazy, though Barbara was the most laissez-faire publisher ever and I'm sure she didn't give a shit.

Rene was skipping around. That made it a real party. He was talking to Ted who was there in his dark blue short sleeve shirt. Ted found my discomfort so amusing. How're you doing, *Eileen*? He put this faggy little turn on "Eileen," like it was a made-up name, something I'm pretending to be. It sounded right. It sure amused Rene who kept telling me how fabulous my book party was in a way which made me wonder if this wasn't the worst party of all time.

The girl musician was blowing her saxophone in the middle room with all her musician friends who were taking this party as an opportunity to play or impress each other or whatever musicians do. She seemed to think they wouldn't let her in on all their men things if they knew she was a "lezzy" so I could barely get a hello out of her.

My couple didn't come. I sort of moved in on this couple of poets that winter. I liked him, but I adored her and that was all falling apart around this time, but at least they could come to my book party. I used to wear a Timex watch and she was always asking me what time it was. I planned to give her a watch of her own at the party but she didn't come. Suddenly I had this extra watch. I had also guiltily bought him a purple striped tie. What was I going to do with that tie. I asked my sister to hold the stuff in her bag. She wound up going back to Boston with the watch and the tie and eventually they came back in the mail. Then I gave Mark Breeding the watch. The tie just hung out with my other ties for a few years until I realized I didn't wear ties.

Yeah, my sister from Boston came to the party. A representative of the Myleses from Boston. Unfortunately, she had just broken up with her boyfriend the night before. She thought the trip would be good for her, a distraction. People always think that until they get a few drinks in them.

I wore a striped boat-neck shirt. There was a poem in my book about a dog named Skuppy who sailed the seven seas and lived in his own private boat. I secretly knew that I was a dog who lived in a boat. The floors in my apartment had a definite slant and the trees outside would get going in the wind and I was always kind of staggering around so it was a pretty natural image to grab onto. Vickie picked up on it and greeted me: Hey Skuppy! I barked. She had the same shirt on. Mark told me he had also considered buying that shirt and would have worn it as well. I guess it was 1982 and it was an obvious shirt to have that year.

Chassler, who also lived in the loft, had two kids from his last marriage. They were great, they were sort of the pets of the loft. These kids always had some toy that we were all playing with. Nora had a parrot on a stick. You could make the parrot bite by moving the stick. Once my sister got a little loaded she started nipping at me with the parrot. She started aiming for the crotch a lot, and I started to get the picture that my sister was going out of control. She wasn't mixing very good and she kept turning to me for love and affection . . . and then these kind of odd sexual gestures.

It wasn't my day. Or was it? Chris showed up. She was living in Maine with Judy. She didn't look so happy and she looked like she had put on some weight. Somehow I think the experience of being in New York all of a sudden with its great frank energy was completely terrifying to her. People walk up and say things like: I don't mean to offend you . . . but you look really big. I mean, it's good. Do you do anything there? What do you do? Christine looked immediately like she wanted to cry and eventually she did. Judy seemed like one of those nurse-type girlfriends. She had her arm around Chris who wouldn't look up. We gotta go, Judy smiled. But thanks a lot! Don't forget brunch tomorrow! People started asking me if I was having a good time. Are you okay?

The thing I couldn't look at was that book. On the front I stand with these crooked bangs and big bags under my eyes against the white wall of my apartment. You can see the buzzer about maybe a foot and a half from my right shoulder. My face looks puffy and shapeless, fortunately I have kind of a big mouth so it sort of works. My arms look weird, though. I had been doing a lot of speed in that period of time, so I'm thin but it looks like bones with all this loose flesh tied on. The arms always look scarey to me. Old. Folded across my ribs. There's other things that bother me about the front of the book, but look at the back.

Here I am lighting a cigarette, here is my can of beer on my desk. There's the typewriter. Poems all over the desk. I used to know what that big one was, but I can't remember now. And here the skin that my arms were made up of now makes up my face. I look like an old lady. It is really scarey.

I had been to a million book parties since I lived in New York but mine seemed made up. I wanted to go home. There were three places to be in that loft: in the back room doing coke—it was actually most comfortable back there. It was smaller, and it had that kind of enforced closeness that feels safe in a screwed up way. But the coke made me feel more and more like one of those cubes of glass they use to create partitions with. Can I put on sunglasses? I wasn't sure.

I'd go out into the fray passing the musicians' area each time. They weren't playing music like you could dance to, it was an inner experience they seemed to be involved in. I think they were all junkies. I still could hardly get a wave out of you know who. I leaned over and said, We're all going someplace in a while—you wanna come? She nodded.

The front room was still loosely packed with drinking smoking people—oh, yeah and there were all kinds of joints circulating and for one lucky day in my life I managed to say no to them. Since I was already completely paranoid I couldn't imagine where I'd go if I smoked pot. People were beginning to leave, they were saying you want to eat with us, or we've got another party, or I've got a rehearsal or you know me—when you get to be my age (turns up his collar) we go home when the getting's good. He raised his eyebrows. Hey Allen, wanna share a cab? The Dads are leaving I thought. This means something.

Rose's girlfriend from Chicago was in town and I was part of a troop going to Cafe Society, one of those part-time lesbian bars. I was bringing my sister, I was bringing the musician and I was completely depressed, but my face was frozen into a grim smile. Eileen, Rose screamed as we piled into a cab, did you have fun?

She was using the same tone she used on her cats. Yeah, it was great, Rose. Thanks a lot. Where are you going, squinted the musician. I felt like tying a rope to her leg. I was so convinced she wasn't going to stick around at all. I was right. As soon as we got inside the kind of glitter ball, tall hyacinths-in-a-vase Italian lesbian disco environment I could see her squirming free. I sighed. I hate disco, she said. You can't tell me you like this. Like? I didn't even know what that meant. Well, no, but . . . Listen, I gotta go, she said. It was that fast.

My sister seemed ready to go off. She kept putting her arm around me like . . . you know. I guess she was really upset about her boyfriend. I couldn't handle it. She kept saying sentimental things to me. She was really bombed, and I wanted to be nice and I knew she was a mess, but I really didn't want her touching me. Especially now that the musician had left. By the time we were all at the front of the bar the situation had reached its crisis. My sister had her arms around me and her head on my shoulder and I absolutely couldn't handle it. We had shared a room for seventeen years. If she wanted love and affection why couldn't she have asked then.

Everything was all confused. At the party people kept saying the musician looked like a younger version of me. I thought she looked like my sister. Lookit, I said, why don't you sit over there. Unhinging her arm from me. She held her head down and shook it grievously. The attack. You don't care about anyone but yourself. She was bombed. I could tell by the way she was shaping her words. That's it. That's the whole story. She waved her arms with a referee's gesture of closure. You don't care about anyone but yourself. All you think about is yourself, you don't even know other people are alive, you're so selfish. It's true. She doesn't care about any of you. Think she does? She doesn't. I know her, she's a phoney. A fucking phoney. Well, I hate you and I'm leaving. I'm going back tonight. She still held the parrot on a stick. She grabbed her suede jacket off the stool and her bag was on her shoulder. I hate you and I never want to see you again. You are so, and she broke into sobs, selfish! She ran out the door. I looked up at the faces that surrounded me. She's your sister, Eileen. Eileen, this is a very important night for you, said Rose. It counts. Should I go—I don't want to go. I was thinking: It's my night. It's my party. This isn't fair.

I caught up with Bridget on 5th Ave. and we jumped into a cab. I tried to sort of pet her. Don't touch me, she shrieked. You can't make it better now. I never want to see you again. In my apartment I watched her call the trains and discover she had just missed the last to Boston. I'll get a hotel. I will not stay here tonight. She didn't have far to go. She threw herself down on my bed and I took her boots off. In a few minutes she was out like a light.

I wanted to be anyplace but home. It was 12:30. I was sitting on my couch. On the coffee table I had my cigarettes, my little vial of coke and the red phone. And a mirror, of course. A big piece of thick broken mirror I had found in the trash. This is the picture that should have been on the book. I could see my sister's legs and skirt. I had to keep telling myself that woman is my sister. It just seemed so odd to have a passed out woman on my bed. Who I know the way I know my sister. Family, great. Look at me. No one to call. My book sat on the coffee table. I felt great. I felt frozen, completely frozen in my life. It would never stop being exactly like this. I was a great poet and I would always be alone. This was my curse. I took a couple of valiums and fell asleep on the big brown velvet couch that always felt like a casket. I always heard a little voice yell my name just before I lost consciousness. I thought my death would be this way. I loved it.

VIOLENCE TOWARDS WOMEN

Jane Maxwell? Then how come she looked so familiar. It was an anonymous face, thin, the eyes dark brown and so filled with themselves you couldn't see in. Like an animal's eyes. Made of something else. Another shift in the office had just occurred and Jane who had been someplace else was now here, and we had a club. I was always losing the thread of how people dressed these days and Jane nonchalantly pulled me back in. We rolled up the cuffs of our jeans. Shirts were loud. Rock 'n roll in the tropics it seemed. 1973. Anything to kill "hippy" which had left everything and everybody looking depressed. I wished I could grow a moustache like our boss John. He had sad eyes, was 30, smoked a lot of pot. John was gay and a topic of our office, mostly instigated by John was how nice his ass was. He wore tight pants, and there it was, the target of shoptalk, John's high, tight, well-rounded fanny. I wonder if John is alive. We all worked at Little Brown, underpaid but prestigious. We were the Boston office of *The Lancet*, a British medical magazine. The *Enquirer* would occasionally call: Is it true as you said in your Dec. 1972 issue that plants in fact do kill patients in sick rooms? At Christmas the white flakey snow would fall down on the low pipe-cluttered roofs of Beacon Hill and we all would joke about being Bob Cratchit. There was no Uncle Scrooge. Unless it was the conceited place itself. Jane, of course, was in love with John. Someone who had once drank and taken drugs a lot, her impossible taste in men was now what she used to escape. Currently she lived with Walter, a Cadillac salesman who drank too much, like you Eileen, she sneered.

I was an alcoholic at 23 and she was the first person to tell me that. I was in love with Jane, but didn't know. So why do you live with him. He likes Jenny. She was her little girl. Her ex-husband the Maxwell was an A & R person at a record company. He screwed around so much she had to leave him. She and Jenny were sleeping in the extra room of a friend's apartment in Cambridge. She cried and cried. One night she overheard them talking about her. If she doesn't stop fucking crying I'm going to smash her. I can see the dim light from the kitchen creaking into the small bedroom with the weeping young woman and her four year old child on a mattress on the floor. *Me?* Isn't there a moment when you hear something cruel and you can't believe they're talking about you. Doesn't it make you think you're going insane.

For Jane it was a moment of truth. She shut up, got over Brian, that prick. He gave her child support. Though she had to nag. Actually she seemed to like it. A look of glee swept over her sharp-featured face. Jenny needs shoes Brian. He's very guilty. His mother loved me. We're still friends. She told me giggling about the time she had taken Jenny to the in-laws for Christmas. Brian came with one of his bimbos. She asked his mother in front of everyone if Brian had been a grouchy little boy. Oh Lorna shut up he exclaimed. See what I mean, said Mrs. Maxwell. Ever since—she clammed up. Poor Jane was there, though poor Jane was who she'd rather be speaking to, not this dumbo, Lorna. Jane seemed happier than I had ever seen her when she described how kind everyone was to them and she and Jenny were very humble and quiet and left with little bags of food. If he's ever late with a payment he knows I can call his mother.

John hired me because I was gay. It's odd to be hired for a trait you don't know you have. Gay people liked me. I knew that. Nobody would ever come right out and ask. San Francisco, John queried. Yeah, I just came back from there. John had lived in San Francisco. John had lived in New York. One of his best stories was about sitting on the New York subway coming back from a Halloween party in some kind of green elf costume. It was an adorable story, and John regaled us with his tattered narcissism in a way that enabled us to laugh at him *and* feel what he felt in one fell swoop. Though he occasionally got in trouble, John mainly had charmed the stodgy old queens upstairs into letting him run our department according to his whim. Which was to occasionally poke his head into our reality, be managerial, asking for less talk and more work, otherwise only coming in to entertain, gain attention and praise from those he had hired for that purpose as well as to satisfy his occasional interest in us. We loved him.

Jane was Janey Coyne. She grew up in Milton. I knew her. I saw her white-faced with heavy makeup leaning out of a bathroom stall of a high school dance called Town & Country. She had been gang-raped one night and never seen again. No one in her school would talk to her when she came back. The boys would cough and say her name, Coyne, under their breath. She never got drunk again. Her sister had to walk her home from school in junior year. In senior year she went right home from school and cried. Nothing should take that long she said. Mostly she hated her name. And that's how she got married. She never wanted to go to school. She got a job at Capitol Records. That was cool. A friend of her mother's knew someone. "I know you've always liked rock 'n roll," her mother began. She was sitting in her room. Capitol was where she met Brian. He was so sleazy she said, but he was really cute. We just got married cause I got pregnant. I wanted his name. No more Janey Coyne.

I fell in love with Jane Maxwell. It was so strong I could barely look at her. My heart was pounding as I walked to my desk at an angle from hers. I had the windows, she had the corner. I smoked my Marlboros for her. You're an alcoholic, Eileen. No, I'm not. Did you get drunk last night. Yes. Do you get drunk every night. No. Big deal she laughed. I thought being an alcoholic made me dirty to her. I loved her because she had been raped and because she was tough and because she had a little girl and because she looked me right in the eyes and laughed at me, teased me as if I were a man. That's how I felt. I have never been so embarrassed in my life. Without doing a thing I was showing my cards. I was feeling all this and she knew it. Take a shower if you want she said when I went to her place for dinner. It would feel good but I was too scared. Once after work we stopped by her friends' place to pick something up. This is my new boyfriend Eileen she said. I was wearing light blue corduroy pants. They're all I can see. I felt huge. Why did she say that. They used to be good friends when I was with Brian she said. They were bitches I think is what she meant. So she turned into one, mean, when she walked into their place. I got sacrificed, my comfort for hers. It's happened before.

I was completely drunk in front of Jane at a party once. I was so excited to see her. I remember that. Anything could have happened in those days. It was a Friday night. I would have forgot for the rest of my life. Jane was in love with John. She couldn't help herself. Poor Jane. They used to go home to his place in Beacon Hill, and smoke pot. They came back so giggly. Her and I were so close. Don't you eat she asked me. I thought I was dieting. Alcoholics don't eat, Eileen. Oh.

I was leaving and the three of us had lunch. John who never drank got drunk. I'm an alcoholic he said. He had told us stories about throwing up on a camel's hair topcoat in college he was supposed to return. It was nice to know that John had been straight. Now he lived with Richard, a handsome dark-haired man. They talked on the phone a lot. Boring he would say when he described his life at home. He made it clear, they didn't have much sex. John, Jane and I went and had that last lunch. The whole office went, but we three stayed. You two have a crush on each other don't you. Don't you have the hots for each other. We looked so fast, her face was pink, then we looked away. If anything ever happened it would've been then, my last day at work. The corner of the street from where she's long gone reminds me of her. I know she's alive. I loved her because she was gang-raped. I'll always know that. Changed her name and moved on. They're all men's names, what's the difference. Her name is Jane. Janey.

TOYS R US

Myles's social observations are scattershot, and when she turns her eye exclusively on herself, as too often she does, she sinks to sharing sappy diary entries. "I'm not just one person. I am every other one person in my culture."

—Laurie Stone, *The Village Voice*

That's when I knew my play was over. Sara asked me to go to Roz her sister's party for her six-year-old son Nathan. The party was in Great Neck. She was currently battling with her seventy-year-old father who treated her like a taxi or simply one of a chain of female ears and hands and arms that served his needs. A typical conversation with her father went like this: they conducted the business of the conversation—the ride he wanted or the family party he would like her to attend as well as picking him up. Then when Sara asked him how he was he would go, "talk to Riva," handing the phone over to the 65-year-old woman he was sharing his life with. Which raised the horns of the rest of the family. Sara's mother had died 10 years ago and since then he had married again, buried his second wife and now was on his second girlfriend after her.

Today, as well as wanting a ride to the party he wanted to go to Toys R Us to buy a gift. Sara's father had been in a concentration camp, Auschwitz, so had her mother, so had Riva. Riva even had a large crudely printed number on her forearm. In me it encouraged a childish urge to alternately stare and look away. When I was in college I worked in Filene's Basement and several of the women there had numbers on their arms. The meanness of one in particular was always explained away as a result of her time in the camps.

Riva had large innocent eyes and Yanik, Sara's father, was a dapper little guy, and typically macho in that way of being extremely charming when he was asking you for something and then dismissing you after you had been of use. He turned his back to all of us in the kitchen when he made phone calls. It was clear to Yanik that Sara was a lesbian, though the only way he acknowledged her difference was his financial unwillingness to buy her a house. After the four of us had a little whitefish around the table, Sara and her father went into a bedroom to fight. I explained Sara's case to Riva who understood of course but Eileen, Yanik loves Sara. And what is so good about this house that she wants. And then, Eileen may I ask you. Have you ever been married. No I replied. You don't want to she continued shaking her head no for me. No I have no need of a man. You like girls? Yeah. A scene I have never had with my own mother I am having with Riva who is actually the mother of Francine who I met last winter in Miami and is not gay. Sara too? Yeah. The only thing she didn't ask was if we were lovers. I suppose we don't want to hear the total truth.

Lacking the privileges of men and the protection accrued from hanging round with them, lesbians have kept their closet especially shadowy. How many out lesbians can you name in public life? Compare that figure to the number of out gay men who, by being themselves, chip away at fantasies about them. But what could be more tantalizing to a performer/writer than showing the self to the world and demanding, daring the world to love you as you are—the whole you, including the sexual you, the part insecurity makes shakiest? . . .

Sara and her father came out of the bedroom. We all go get the scooter said Yanik. It wasn't what they went into the bedroom to discuss but it seemed like something was resolved. And we were all glad to have something to do. Just an exit or two away. Sara drove. It took a few minutes to find the scooters in the midst of the biggest toy store in the world. All of the toys were in boxes with plastic windows in the front as if kids wouldn't recognize their wishes unless they were displayed like on teevee. I looked for "bikes" and found "scooter." It's over here I called to the group. If I was a little bit useful I might be okay. The scooters had hand-brakes, there was a boy scooter and a girl scooter, finally we settled on a blue one that seemed right for this boy. Sara and I began to get excited about the bikes one aisle over, rolling them out and trying them on. They were a really good deal, brand new and cheap. You could sort of see the advantage of these huge stores.

We walked down a long hall with our numbers. It was then that I thought about a century that could exterminate millions of people and then create such huge dehumanizing toy stores that would both serve and frustrate the survivors of those same camps. It seemed like a single impulse to me. I almost laughed as we walked down a brightly painted concrete hall, earnestly holding our number hoping our scooter would come up.

Outside we stood on a flight of stairs with a metal railing along with a lot of other angry toy purchasers, some with kids in tow which made us feel fortunate, and it delighted me even more to think I would never have them and need to take them here. Sara and I moved away to look at some water at the end of the parking lot and an industrial landscape. Don't you feel like dying she said. I am so depressed. Isn't it weird, it's like the air inside and even just being in the car with my father and Riva. I know. I feel like I'm with *my* family. I thought about my family, I suppose I should bring Sara to meet them. It's just my mother. It was beginning to feel too late.

It's red mourned Yanik. He doesn't want red. He wants blue. Red is not good, Sara, Riva pointed at the offending scooter. Red is good, red's fine, he'll like it. I don't know, Sara, said Riva. Yanik let's take it. Maybe Sara's right. Red is okay asks Yanik. Sara, get car.

Roz's house was very nice. We walked into the green back-yard and a dark-haired youngish magician was in the throes of some really pre-fabricated tricks. All the kids were seated in front of him on a blanket just like in school which made sense since Roz was a school teacher. I immediately calculated the combined income of her 14-year-old public school teaching job and her dopey lawyer husband's salary. I'm amazed what it costs to maintain one of these one-child suburban marriages. Roz looked like Sara. I was pleased. That's what I came for.

I wanted to see a woman that looked that much like my girl-friend plus wasn't her. She even laughed like her, or a varia-tion of the same laugh. It was more like a mouse than Sara's. I thought about the generations of kids that would go wild when they heard their teacher laugh like a mouse. Roz was cute. I had seen baby pictures of her too, hovering over the innocent baby Sara with a malevolent five-year-old smile that spelled sisterly hatred. We called the girl in that picture Devil Child.

These kids were well trained, sort of, and buoyed up by the magician's ego were truly wowed by some of his tricks. He was such a kit magician—wands with banners that said boom on one side and had a picture of a rabbit on the other. I was fascinated by the relative sincerity of his delivery. I started to think of this suburban backyard magician as someone less smart but sightly more successful than most poets I know. It's not like we can farm ourselves out to bar mitzvahs and wed-dings like saxophone players can, or this guy. Even a clown can work the kid circuit. How have poets managed so utterly to get no piece of the pie. It is some kind of trick, a vanishing act that we have performed on ourselves.

There was a row of white chairs against the wall of the house for the adults. There was one elegant-looking long haired woman there, a parent, who I later learned was Iranian. I just quickly decided she hated me for not having a child, but actually she could hardly speak English. I think I tried to joke with her over the black cherry seltzer. Some kids tried to get up from the blanket, some wild ones actually advanced into the unclipped brush between Roz's property and her immediate neighbors. The magician became sullen and punishing towards these transgressors. No Wyatt! All these kids had frontier, biblical kinds of names. No Bobs or Sues in this yard. That's not what we do here. Kids can we tell Wyatt to come back. All together, Come back, Wyatt. Wyatt felt foolish, embarrassed by the crew, just as he would be embarrassed years from now in business school when he committed a boner in front of the group. But it was clear that this scene was breaking down and the magician performed one more silly miracle and it was time for food.

Everyone could have pizza now, but first they must sit at their spot on the eating blanket. Kids were moved from module to module by the discipline of brightly colored shapes placed on the sensible lawn. I was starving. I wished the kids would settle down so we could get some food. But the adults were fed as an afterthought, it turned out, the implication being that kids' parties were a spectator sport, and that any real adult would have known to eat before they came.

Finally when everyone was fed the magician played his final card. Okay kids I'm going to make animals, or anything you want out of balloons. Just tell me what you want and I'll fix it right up for you. "Everything" wound up being either love birds kissing or swords. Whatever the kids asked for he would somehow twist it that way. Eventually, one brave girl asked for a sword since all the boys were having fun fighting with them and nobody could figure out what to do with kissing birds except put them on their heads. The girl got a pink sword as did any other girl who asked for one. Boys' swords came in all colors of course, so did the kissing birds. I spent the next half hour wanting to ask the magician if he could see how he was trivializing the girls. I overheard Roz asking the magician about himself and he revealed that he was a young married now too. He still did as many parties as he could though. His wife was always trying to get him to stay home he chuckled. Roz smiled.

Then the parents showed up. People my age, people younger. It was Sunday so they were in their running and backyard sporty clothes. Everyone was straight. Why should that be a surprise. Yet it was an exotic environment to me. I don't travel in young married sets. Parents of Seth and Tamarindo and Hester. Roz's horny husband Jay (Sara had told me some tales about him) never once took his eye out of his video camera. It supplied him with an opportunity to stare and not relate, except to shove a few slices of pizza into his fat gut. I had worn a black mini skirt thinking I would seem straight but instead I looked like some kind of cheap slut. Jay's camera loved me.

[She] wants to make us see her as beautiful if we thought lesbians were ugly, as ugly if we thought lesbians beautiful, powerful if we thought them weak, vulnerable if we took them for Amazons.

When Nathan, Sara's nephew, was finally alone with his toys he could open them. This was understandable to everyone but Sara and I. The logic had to do with the communication between parents which is what this party was all about. If Nathan madly opened presents the cards would get lost and how could Roz write thank you notes which Nathan would sign. So Nathan opened his presents in the controlling presence of his grandmother, Mom, and aunts and uncles and the video camera and if he went too fast or mislaid a card he was told that he might have to stop opening them unless he calmed down. Just as bad was if Nathan got involved or excited by a new toy and stopped the brisk pace of gift unravelment.

He loved the scooter. Which immediately employed the services of one of his uncles who was an engineer. His name was Jay too and as soon as he finished assembling the scooter he put up the basketball hoop. And then he went home. Jay loved to work. Roz snubbed Riva because she wasn't wild about the idea of her 80-year-old father "just living" with a woman. Has he changed the will she whispered to Sara when they were out of earshot. Riva had relatives in Great Neck and she sweetly went off for an hour so the true family (except for me) could really get down. Nathan got yelled at for losing the caps for the tires on his scooter. I logicked that he put them down when he was opening another present. I handed them to Jay, the engineer, and announced my fruitful deduction to Roz who smiled significantly at me for the first time all day.

There's heat in the opening sections of Eileen Myles' FEEL-ING BLUE. The author stands on the stage—hands threading hair, cowboy boots shuffling. "You know how exciting it is to be with someone who has a gun, especially a girl who has a gun." The audience laughs.

By the time we got back to Manhattan we both felt sick. Sara wanted to get some heroin, I wanted a big glass of whiskey. We parked her car in her usual spot, the lot on 7th between C & D and just shook our heads and shuddered all the way west to First Avenue, and her street, 9th, where we spent the night.

NEUROMANCER

I wish *I* was tripping now, said Chris, her face lit by the glow-ing candles on the table at the Orchidia. I loved the color it made her, honey light and I wasn't even tripping yet. Yeah. I wish you were too. I had just taken a tab right in front of her, though I had offered her half and the opportunity to break her date. She was going out with Tina and they seemed pretty bored. After all their little relationship had cost them it seemed they had to stick together for a while. Poor them. I had plans.

I was supposed to meet Rose and Andy at some opening at Parsons. They said you have to come, all these great women will be there. I hadn't been to a hot lesbian event for a really long time, years in fact. About three or four years ago there used to be these great parties at this place called Medusa's Revenge. They were the best parties I had ever been to. I was lifting a woman up behind black velvet curtains. It was rain-ing out and I anticipated the acid coming on as I walked over to 5th Ave. I loved these moments of intense privacy that drugs gave you like you were between two warm buildings while you were waiting to get off. No longer hungry, broke, the rain was something to walk through and I was feeling terrifically strong. Acid always made me feel like a fantasy character. The color of whatever I had on would really come splashing up. I had on a striped shirt, purple red blue peach and something else that was pretty in a way things looked when you were a child, disordered and bright. The more the merrier. Child values played very well when one was tripping. I was pretty wet when I arrived.

It wasn't pouring, but a steady drizzle that made my hair wet and it added to my sense of myself as an adventurer. Kind of a man among all these girls. And what a sight it was as I came in. And of course I was just getting off. Huge female torsos coming in from sea. Just big bizarre female monuments that were supposed to be incredibly serious and wonderful or something, but I just wanted to break out into hysterical laughter at these huge tits. My sense of myself as a boy, a wet strong one from outside was expanding by the moment. I would look and turn away, feeling spasms of laughter ready to rock me. I kind of snorted and lurched away, gasping, and some women heard me and stared suspiciously and then I saw my friends. I was wading toward them, splashing my drink. These photos were huge—floor to ceiling, black & white the artist and probably her lover and several of their friends were in uniform, tuxedos, maybe with tails, I think. They looked like penguins I gasped and I was really going down for the third time. Look who's here says Andrea. It sounded like it came through a tinny loud speaker. Her small dark pretty face was an oasis of calm in this art amusement park. Good you've got yourself a drink I see. Why are you so lit up tonight, I shot her a huge grin that felt like it went both inside and out at the same time. It was mild acid, happy stuff that only enhanced, shook and ampli-fied without you know turning your friend's face into twitch-ing mandibles at the front of a column of marching ants. Rose is up there, and she was tugging me, going come on, come on. And *Elizabeth!* You know how happy I am when Elizabeth is around Oh look Rosie has her pinned. We walked upstairs to a balcony that surrounded the room and the strong effect of the torsos was withdrawn in fact I forgot them. It was like a yoyo, acid. A yellow Duncan yoyo. Mine was back, intact, all reeled in and safe. I couldn't take another gale, those gagging laughs that threatened to leave me writhing on the floor. There's some food, Andrea pointed at some crackers with white stuff. No I couldn't do that. Are you on some drug she asked suddenly getting the picture. Now I went mute. I nodded. Acid she asked gleefully? Yes I smiled. She took in the whole room and looked at me. And you look so cute! I don't know how—you look so *healthy*, she was doing that slight groaning way of com-plimenting, when her voice got a couple of octaves lower. But if I ever took Andrea's flattery seriously I was in trouble. I would sort of fling myself at her when I was bombed and she would flat out reject me. It felt the rules were to not reciprocate. We took a tour of the room, I was like Andrea's seeing eye dog. She wanted to know what appealed to me here in my state, but she didn't get much because the really great things had gone dead, and some I just didn't want to open up. Those women in the tuxedos were scarey and mean now. They all wore glasses and looked old. You could see their skin and it didn't look too nice, it seemed like a waste, this kind of extravagance on these toady women, but that's the way it often was, you could either have fun or get things. So the room was just a mine field of *no, no, nos* me leading Andrea around in circles until she got tired of it. I kept seeing my own image in flashes like some part of me was taking pictures of the rest flash flash the lights were fluorescent in here. Yellow sneakers. Flash. Tight green pants. Flash. Magic shirt, wet hair. Small. Help me. Andrea I've got to get out of here. Let me get Rose, we're going to go eat. No I've got to go someplace. Do you need some money she asked. Yes I admitted. She gave me a twenty which was incredible. I could have taken a cab but I preferred to walk and glow. The reading was by a dark-haired man from California and I made him some kind of knight, I romanticized him to heraldic proportions. His work seemed to beg for it. Later in the bar with my boyfriends surrounding me I glared at his wife. I don't know why it was just fun. I couldn't stop myself. I was a dot in bed that night. Just that tiny. It warbled and glowed. No Chris.

DOG DAMAGE

I read about how some other brilliant child tried to win her family over with messages on their pillows and notes posted to the lid of the toilet seat. I pasted, "The house of neither a dog, nor a cat is the house of a scoundrel" on my mother's pillow. I thought my parents were not impressed and yet when I came home from school one day my father said, "Eileen, go in the bathroom and wash your hands." I looked at my hands and didn't know what kind of joke he was trying to pull. "Eileen, go in the bathroom and wash your hands." Daddy, they're not dirty. Eileen, do what your father says. I opened the door and there stood a small tan puppy, looking scared. Mom, I turned with accusing pleasure. I didn't think it was real. What was the joke. Taffy stepped out, a noble and unhappy little puppy. There's a picture somewhere—I stand holding her in my arms. The back of the picture says My Dog Taffy— age 9. I can't describe the place that Taffy went in my heart when I realized this living breathing puppy was mine. The dog became my heart. I was afraid to touch her, break her. She slept in a little box with a towel wrapped around a clock that ticked and made her think her mother was there. She cried and cried all night. My mother said, Eileen I can't taken another night of that crying. She has to go back. It was like a conspiracy between my father and me to bring crying things into the house. I think my mother always needed a good cry, and here comes one more who's going to get all the attention and wreck all my sleep. Here's another one to clean up after. If I could have held my mother in my lap and patted her head, if she could have told me that's what she wanted it would've been alright. Nobody knew that, and I am probably wrong, but I had to bring the poor little doggy back to the Animal Rescue League the next day and the woman who received Taffy said what was the problem. She probably has worms, my mother shrugged lightly, she never stopped crying once all night. Mama, I wanted to scream. "They all cry the first night," the woman looked my mother straight in the eye and pushed a paper towards her to sign. In the photograph holding the dog I look just like a boy. I really do.

MY COUPLE

I went to them because I was hungry. It was something like
that. I was finally through with all the business with Chris (or
thought I was) and came back to New York elated to be utterly
free and decided I would not get involved with anyone but
was simply into sex and immediately called Ybette who I still
wanted to have sex with and she practically hung up on me. She
said I'll call you back but that's the absolute easiest way to get
someone off the phone. I was sitting at a little black cafe table
on the sidewalk on the upper west side and I was sipping the
tastiest vodka and grapefruit juice I have ever had in my life. It
was the taste of freedom. Maybe I had two Marlboro lights left.
They rattled in the box and I was so fucking high. I was starving. I headed over to Ted and Alice's. They were usually good
for a couple of bucks and I could always get a fix on what was
going on in my life. Ted would tell me and then Alice would
say something even smarter. They were the ones who advised
me to go over to Grace and Keith's. They always have nice dinners Ted said. Do they have meat, I asked? I was looking at the
translucent leaves shaking in a window pot. I was practically
hallucinating from hunger. It was the hardest need to satisfy.

I had a million ways to satisfy my hunger on my own, usually getting credit at any one of the local supermarkets on First Ave. But I owed them all money right now. People would offer me drinks, drugs even buy me cigarettes, but no one would feed me. And I didn't want to ask. I was 31 years old and it was too humiliating to admit I wanted food. I wanted a steak. Well they have money, I think they get supported by Keith's parents and Grace gets her salary from the church. You could probably go and get whatever you wanted over there. Think you could walk in on dinner just about now. He looked at his watch. Have a pill. He bent his head towards the clear golden pharmaceutical container that had slipped under his belly. He picked it out like a little boy—it was one of those half green half speckled capsules from Dr. Sugar. I went down and called Keith. He yelled Grace and went away for a moment and said can you bring a six pack. I said no but I can go out when I get there if you have money. It wasn't such a good introduction but it seemed just fine with them. Dinner wasn't so great. It was pasta with vegetables, pretty boring, but since no one else was interested I kept shovelling it down and drinking beer. I felt like I was something very interesting just by sitting there which made me feel very comfortable and safe in the knowledge that this relationship would continue. I looked down at the poem I had written in my notebook when I was starved:

LARAMIE

Here we are in Wyoming
Stopping for a can of soup

Here we are a string of leaves
running down the window pane
green, limey, running by a bluish sky.
Laney, come by and feel the breeze outside.
This window, Laney—
won't you please come by & put down
your spoon.

    I was obviously losing my mind. And now I was full. I was smoking Keith's cigarettes. They were telling me all about their marriage. They had kind of fascinated me in the past. I was part of this extended family of poets and as one of the younger ones I had watched this "generation" of people just older than us trotting out their friends when they came back to New York from their various desperate attempts to have lives outside of the East Village. They all seemed kind of pathetic to me. Keith and Grace had been lovers at different times with Marie, who was central to their scene. She was its ruler and everyone seemed to tag along with her to her next kingdom which was really a buddhist retreat in the Rockies and they would have bad paying teaching jobs there and get involved with students. Some others had stuck around New York and become art writers like my former friend Pat. I guess I'm fascinated by anyone's history. And it's the best part of being drunk to sit down and share it, to pour your guts out to one another. Which is what they were doing. It sounded like they had gotten together to say fuck you to Marie. Maybe not. I had had a run-in with her a few years previous. Just before she got married. Everyone's a lesbian, I think. Except for fags and a few of them are too. Marie wanted to have kind of a fake affair with me. I just wanted to fuck her, but felt I was some kind of repulsive drunk to her. I had a girlfriend like that once, who just wanted to have a big romance with me in public and would ice me privately. It's a very confusing turn on. Anyhow there was obviously a big gaping hole (Marie-shaped) between these two people. They had lived in the Berkshires for several years and would reappear in New York as hippies from time to time and give readings that you knew were just the sort of readings they had been giving in the sixties. There was a kind of group posture, hands on hips, that the others would occasionally slip into too when they weren't on guard. It kind of made you feel grateful that time had stood still for someone so you could really see it. Even by the seventies people had started to want to look rich and these guys didn't even know about it.

A lot of my way of surviving, it seemed, was to get involved with these families. None of them talked to each other anymore or maybe they had professional relationships but they all secretly seemed to think they were doing "it" wrong, or were doing it the best or were the only ones still doing it. It was hard to know what "it" was. It's hard for everyone to grow up and I think for heterosexuals "it" starts when they have kids and there's an outside to their romance now which is not their friends and seems to be a reason not to stop. To go on seems to be about addressing something outside of yourself all the time. I loved sitting there, hearing about their "it." These people were so disoriented. New York had changed a lot in fourteen years or however long they were gone. She got a job, that's why they came back and they had a huge apartment that they complained about all the time, how expensive it was, etc. I think they were the first people who I ever heard use the word "gentrification." They were against it. My position was who cared, if you had no money all the time. I asked Marie about this once and she said it just meant there were more pastry shops and she liked pastries. Marie drove them nuts.

When I was leaving that night we were all pretty blasted. Grace had always seemed pretty shy to me. She was kind of pinky-faced which was sweet in a woman pushing thirty-five and she drank a lot so every now and then I had seen her looped and she would say things like "The Language poets hate me now" or something indicative of her fears. But I had heard in her former incarnation as a female poet in New York she was a real slut and had this one boyfriend for years and fucked everyone in her workshops and horrified Marie and everyone else and liked having a little cult around herself. Now I would never willingly participate in something like that around another woman. I worshipped Alice, that was different, I was hot for Marie, but the Grace thing seemed to be about some male kind of intellectual power. I didn't get her work. It just went on and on because she was an orphan. I liked his work better. He was an easy man, so it seemed, but he got stuck with the kids when they came back to town so he was probably needier and you were nice to him for that. Often I would see him on First Ave. and it got to be a fun fantasy to think about going home and fucking him, not because I was attracted to him but because it would kind of make me male and I thought he would like that too. I've read about wolves and their kind of submission, all kind of grinning and stooped, but the problem is wolves never really submit so it's just this meaningless performance. It's a big fake grin and I wondered what was behind Keith's. I remember encountering him one particular day in a flurry of snowflakes and later such a day turned up in one of his poems so I am convinced that many of us do live in each other's worlds. I guess it's a belief that makes me feel less alone, but also pretty paranoid.

I have a crush on both of you, I said in lieu of goodnight. I feel like Keith said "Grace" again like earlier on the phone, but anyhow I was in their bed right away. It was great. They were both getting to be unfaithful at the same time and I was getting to be fucked in a new bed in a house with kids which seemed sleazy and sweet at the same time. It wasn't like I was "ruining" their marriage. I was expanding it. Instantly I was in love with Grace. She seemed to be such a lesbian. She would go look Keith look as if I was the first woman who ever had a cunt. If you have any doubts about your femaleness, existentially, I mean, then this is the greatest thrill. Not red hot, but something else. Being in bed with a married couple isn't like menage. It's more like being a child. They had two kids. No they had three. Two girls and baby boy. Instantly I was a fixture and would get up and make the kids toast and watch cartoons with them. Keith and Grace loved sleeping in and I adored having children to hang out with. I really wanted to look at their drawings. I liked their clothes. Their toys and things were strewn everywhere, the place was a mess. Our mornings were purple and tan. That was the feeling, kind of wooden and royal. The kids were the reason Keith and Grace had dinner so obviously they were the power in the family, the real power so I felt a deep connection to the situation when I attended to them.

Garth, the baby, was so new that Grace was still nursing. This was amazing. It's one thing to suck a woman's breasts, when you are female. I mean, it's the absolute best thing from either end of the equation but I beg you to consider sucking the breasts of a woman who has milk in them. It was almost too scarey to do. And naturally, soon after, I was sitting in a cafe with a group of people I didn't know too well and one of them, this guy, was arguing for the joys of, what, being a man, I think. Straight guys always think that's what lesbians are vying for. Have you ever, he sort of leered towards me, sucked a woman's breasts when she was nursing. The women with him shrieked, Oh Larry. He looked me in the eye. It's really great.

I would be doing myself and you an injustice if I didn't admit I fell madly in love with her. Maybe the worst ever. Most of my lovers have been younger than me and this woman was maybe five years older but she was in several important anthologies and she had three kids and a job that was important in my world. We all kept it secret, our affair, for quite a while and that was the most fun part, I think. Writers together are ludicrous and dangerous. We sought literary precedents for what we were doing. I think Bloomsbury is what we came up with. Keith did most of our research, being home all day. Grace would go off to work and we would drink more coffee and he would scramble a couple of eggs, we'd begin to smoke and then I felt I had to go. It was like having a boyfriend, it was scarey, though I liked him very much. He would cajole me to stay. It never felt exactly sexual but how could it not wind up there. None of us ever had sex alone. I tried desperately to get her but it seemed like leaving her marriage was what our sex would mean. He would try and convince me I was not a lesbian. Then why was I fucking him. Well for one thing he had a vasectomy. It would be impossible to say, I love your wife so I was silent in my own defense. Or merely replied I am. She would go into the kitchen, I'd come behind to hug her while she prepared food. A woman in the kitchen is completely hot. Especially if she's not me. We'd send him out to get more beer and make out furiously in the kitchen. He'd stroll in and we'd include him, of course to make things okay. Any separate arrangements would be unfaithfulness to someone. We all leaked it slowly, but once everybody knew it was different. I missed the good old days when we couldn't get over ourselves. I guess I felt it was less about me once the world knew. Guys would get kind of lecherous with me and I'd go and fuck them too.

Mostly when I think of her kitchen I think of bread. A big bag of it with rolls strewn, tumbling out getting stale in the air. It seemed so outrageous to me, this tiny advertisement of plenty. That's what her sexiness was like. Once in a while I'd walk with her up First Avenue in her old world way stopping at different stores. No matter how many tumbled rolls I'd spotted this morning she'd buy another bunch and throw that bag on the counter too when she got home. Because she drank beer from morning to night there was always a refrigerator full of Rolling Rock. The kids were always drinking juice, everyone was smoking and occasionally Keith would indulge

CHELSEA GIRLS

with me in a couple of pills. For him it was dangerous and she would beg me to stop supplying him with them because then he and I would be even more adamant that we stay up till four or five and she had to get up in the morning to work and someone had to walk the kids to school. Also I think he got kind of nasty when he was speeding and they were alone. He didn't need to drink with his pills like I did. Pills alone can make you mean. I felt like I was right between them doing both. One night early on we took some photographs. Of us all nude of course lying around in bed. They came out great, I was delighted because you couldn't tell what sex I was. I mean you could but I looked like a guy. They had them developed as slides and the baby sitter, a nice girl named Carmen found them. You have a very interesting life she told Grace one night before she went home. Some poets who babysat saw them too. It seemed like simple revelation wasn't enough. We needed to give proof. You had to see us as lovers.

She would often look like she was weeping when she had to get up. I found that very moving. I'd go and see her at work during the day and we'd go out into the hallway with a big window and she'd look out that window into the wintery mid-afternoon sun and smoke and look exhausted. I'd get her to go for drinks with me sometimes at night and I would be really loaded saying please please please but I don't remember what I was begging her for. To leave him and come away with me. What a deal. They bought my cigarettes. They were completely nice and generous. When I first met them I was doing phone interviews someplace in the thirties at night. I was asking people if they knew what a VCR was. Nobody did. There was a lot of drinking going on at work. People would be fired for drinking martinis out of frappe cups. I quit that job and got a job at Paragon selling sneakers. She loved me working there because I would answer the phone saying Paragon and she wrote a poem for me with that title. I wrote a poem called "Wooden Floor" and a lot of good poems that wound up in books and a sweet little one called "Elk": "the hips / the long avenues / if you're going two ways / all you need / is one light / to move." What does that mean he said angrily. It's true, I said. You only need one light. He puffed. We showed each other everything we wrote. It was so twisted. Some I think I only showed her. Anyhow I think I quit Paragon because I was sitting in Union Square Park one afternoon at lunch time and I knew I had to quit something so I quit my job. Then I really lived off them which he encouraged me to do and she disapproved of. We took a vacation together out to Western Mass. We stayed at the Red Lion Inn. I think the idea was I was this weird-looking nanny. We brought some coke and things got really mean. Her and I had our first serious conversation about writing. It was almost more disturbing than to have never had it at all. She really believed she was the only one. Brilliant woman. Maybe her and I paid too much attention to each other and he got mad. Then she wept and blamed everything on drugs. We visited some old friends of theirs out there and that was fun. Poets I had never met and they seemed very interested in me and I liked that. Then they got it. The guy dug it, the woman disapproved. I remember her bringing us beers on a tray. She was a blonde.

I think we went from September to February. My phone

got turned off. It was nice in my apartment. So silent. I'd come home and write poems and go back for more. He would have had a separate affair with me. She wouldn't. We went to a Christmas party with her old friends. We got really blasted and danced in this crazy circle. That night was really fun. It was about how little shame you had. I ripped the seat of my pants and we kept dancing. I brought them once to hear a band uptown. Tin Pan Alley. This old friend of Barbara Barg's with the best Southern accent lifted her glass of whiskey to me down the row of the bar and said Ah really like your couple Ah-leen.

One night I decided to pay them back. I had gotten a grant I guess so I took them to the River Cafe, which at the time was incredibly chic. We got all dressed up. I had gotten him to cut his hair. Whenever he decided he hated me that haircut made him sad. But he looked pretty good. She was dressed too and I wore a suit. We put David Bowie's "Fashion" on the stereo before we left. That was a weird moment. A cab, or maybe even a car service swept us off to Brooklyn. Her and I spent way too long in the bathroom. We were already smashed. I gave him a handjob under the table when we got back and I think the waiter saw. We were really drunk. Somebody had rack of lamb. I think Keith. John Belushi was sitting at the table across from us. It was the week before he died, but he looked dead already. He was with two women, blondes, and they were all drinking champagne in tall thin glasses No food.

I think it ended because she was jealous. That was crazy. She thought I was taking her husband away from her. You're kidding. I don't want him. It didn't matter. She was jealous.

I came back one day, maybe a month later. I was broke so I called Keith. I had five blue pills and he said he would buy them. It was such a scene when I arrived. He doesn't need pills, she murmured through a crack in the door. And then she let me in. Their whole house had been rearranged. Keith had thrown his back out. Their big huge bed was in the middle of the room and he was in it. Raging. His hair had grown long. It was so Dostoyevsky. The kids were there. They stared at me like I was a ghost or a clown. I wasn't. I was their friend. I felt like he had invited me over to humiliate me. I gave him the pills. He gave me five bucks. It was a crude exchange. If the end of one's youth is a thin slice of cheese I ate mine standing in that room. I was there because I was hungry. That's all.

MARY DOLAN: A HISTORY

It was New Year's Eve, 1991. Vivien had requested that I show her my photographs. I lugged down a brown cardboard carton that was split on its sides and there they were, ranging from wallet-size and high school graduation folders to glossy 8 x 10s of me with famous poets, even photographs that suggested that I myself was a famous poet. Pictures of my sister, my brother, ripple-edged family snapshots, black 'n white from the fifties that dutifully bore their date: June, 1954. Something amazing like that. A Grandma on Sunday trip. We're having a picnic on the grounds of the mental hospital. Her face growling into the camera. And mine, oddly, under 10, more like five, mimicking hers. Here, my hand dashed into the piles of falling goodies: this is Mary Dolan. She was my best friend from fifth grade until I graduated from college. She was in love with me. It was like she was my wife. Vivien held the inch-by-inch school picture for a moment. Little round head in a navy blue uniform. A slightly wistful but determined expression on her 10-year-old face. It's hard to picture her as a sex object Vivien tactfully noted. I glanced over. It was true. Here was a picture of a little kid. Well, I didn't mean—Vivien laughed.

Mary's family moved into Swan Place in the fall of sixth grade. It's funny to picture someone's existence beginning at the top of a street right over a manhole. Mary Dolan is skipping around it. She wouldn't be in her school uniform, but I keep putting her in it. I know I'm not in my school uniform. I tore home from school as fast as my legs would carry me to put on pants and sneakers. To be real. My father wasn't dead. That's an important thing about that time. The energy was higher, in my world, in my life. Things were on the move because we were almost teenagers but there was no desperate chasm to leap over, no run for your life, in fact everyone seemed adamantly attached to games that smacked of childhood. Mary's new girl predecessor on Swan Place was Franny Fittante and she was a whole different ball game. At the top of the street was her house. It was in front of Franny's that we played. She was Italian, had naturally wavy bouffant hair which was perfect for those American Bandstand Annette Funicello beachparty days of 1962. Franny had been kept back. Nothing to sneeze at. Intelligence, diligence in school were things to be ashamed of. Franny didn't have those problems. She didn't like school, wasn't good at it. She liked childhood games, after all she was only 12. We played those handclapping games, my dolly's playmate, that required large amounts of girl coordination which Franny possessed abundantly. And being who she was bursting towards the future before the rest of us, or me, she managed to be sexy while she took part in childish games. It wasn't something you could aim for, it wasn't like being good, even really good at the game, it was just a question of who you were while you were playing it. Sexiness was amorphous, but already existed by 6th grade—sort of a spectre dousing all your simple pleasures with danger. Boys liked the three stooges around that time. They were always what you got at the movies if it wasn't little rascals before the feature movie, usually something with sandals and chariots or a horror flick like *House on Haunted Hill*. I thought they were stupid mostly, and violent which brought out the worst in boys. Yet occasionally they did something simply funny. There was this little dance, in the middle of their most aggressive kind of play. Mo would grab Larry by the arm and the two would rotate in a small foolish circle gleefully chanting: a woo ba dee poop ba doo, a woo ba dee poop ba doo . . . It drove everyone nuts in the three stooges when Larry and Mo did this. It was a stalling action—it broke up whatever was going on, declaring they were idiots, not adult and hardly masculine. I got my little sister to do it with me around the house but that wasn't enough. I found Mary. Before I met her I heard she was kind of a fink, was a year younger than us, was kind of a brain, read books. Oh you'll probably like her, Eileen, was the final insult. Actually I was intrigued that someone in the neighborhood could be less cool than me.

Within five minutes of meeting her I initiated her into the dance and we performed it to the horror of the other girls who were hanging out in their teased hair and capris, leaning against cars on Swan Place and we danced around the manhole again and again, laughing and laughing. I could feel the collective disgust of Franny and the others and that only drove my dance. I could act like a jerk unto delirium. It was a release from an interminable progress which I was being borne forward on kicking and screaming, by accidents like who moved in like Franny, and now another accident had come. Halfway down the street was Mary's house. Or half a house. Her family had rented a duplex from the Hills. The stink of it was apparent when you walked in. They were poor. Not poor like there wasn't any food or furniture. Somehow they had just come into their own half of the house, thrown down their furniture and got on with their lives. All at once there was a rushed, desperate, independent personal quality to Mary's family. She came from the child end of it and it went on for a while. She had a younger brother named Danny who I just don't think I'm going to discuss here at all. But look at her two older sisters and maybe her big, practically huge, mother, Peg. Who had a really large almost male presence like certain nuns I knew. Though I quickly surmised that her size, the amount of space she filled had to do with the size of the job she held in the world. Mr. Dolan was something sick. You knew that. Then he was something angry. He was red. Then he was gone. He was a scarey-looking man. He was an alcoholic. The bad kind. My father was an alcoholic too but he was more of a sad one, a lamb not a red frightening guy like Mr. Dolan. Whose first name I never learned. He was gone almost as soon as I saw him. The Dolans got separated. It was Catholic divorce. Things were that bad. And Mary said it was better. She was happy. But Mrs. Dolan. That's when she became so large she filled the house. I'm sending you a big bouquet of roses, she wailed. One for every time you broke my heart. The first time I heard this song I was fascinated. She always sings it Mary said. It's her song. We would howl and imitate her. We'd do horrible southern accents. I'm sand-ing you—sending the whole song up our noses which was funny. This game worked for everyone. Mrs. Dolan would wail and get to be sad. We'd feel it and dive in, making it be funny. Mrs. Dolan would yell back at us about how cruel we were. Laughing at her beautiful voice. We'd sing it again even worse. Every tahhhm you broke mah heart. Love was gross. One of the first things Mary and I had agreed on was that we would never get married. Wanted no children, thought they were useless. Interestingly enough, on the heels of this resolution the habits of our friendship began to grow. We would sit on the couch in their front room that faced Swan Place. Their couch was really soft, more like a bed. All their furniture was really crummy so it felt more like a kid's house, you didn't have to act reserved on it. You felt free to lie down. Mrs. Dolan had a full-time job. She worked at the phone company. It was sort of Mary's house in the afternoon. Mary had to do certain things for her mother like the laundry. Her mother would call from work and they'd have a chat. My mother says hello Mary would mouth from the phone. Hello Peg I would yell, never knowing if I was going too far. There would be refreshments: Hawaiian Punch, popcorn, with tons of butter. In terms of basic pleasures there were no rules in Mary's house. She could have things the way she wanted them. She could have furniture. The new Sears catalogue was on the floor next to the couch. The corners of almost all the pages were turned, it was rumpled, eventually it was no good at all. It looked like everybody in the family looked at the Sears catalogue. Maybe it was only Mary, looking at it over and over again. Let me show you something she said throwing it open on both of our laps. Look at this headboard. It only cost $59. It came in blonde and walnut, had sliding doors for books and two different kinds of knobs to choose from. I want one too, I exclaimed. Here make a list. Mary provided two pads of lined paper and pencils (her mother got paper free at work) and we would set to work, planning our dream bedrooms, then moving on to sportswear, athletic equipment eventually slipping into the kitchen, planning a whole house. It seemed like it was our future that we were doing divining out of the Sears catalogue, and how much the future would cost. I kept a real list and so did she—eliminating the kitchen, just sticking to the rooms and the lives we now lived in. How much that would cost to have. About 341 dollars. That was nothing, we cheered. I was more likely to achieve it first because I was older and was babysitting. Mary had an allowance and that was stable too, but not as much. Plus I planned to branch out and do more babysitting and there was my birthday money that was coming up—Mary's had passed. What was odd, of course—and kind of telling if you were looking for cold hard facts was that Mary bit by bit did get her stuff. First she got the headboard—I would've gotten blonde, I sniffed. And I simply stayed over at her place more because that made the headboard be both of ours.

The first time I went over to Mary's house she told me about her shoes. It's all so magnificent to remember, the tar path that led to the steps of her house, and those white pointed shoes. I think they probably came from Thom McAn's, though I could be wrong. Mary's feet were wide and these shoes tapered to a very thin point. They were made of some soft thin leather, had thin ties which laced through six or so holes up her foot. They were dancer shoes, Capezios or knock-offs of Capezios. Mary wore hers into the ground, cleaning them with the non-shiny white liquid polish that came in a small jar and you applied it with this stick with a blob of fiber at the end. Once you put this white to your shoes the texture was ruined forever. It was like with bucks—it was a choice between softness and whiteness and since it was the era that it was, it was whiteness and Mary maintained hers very well. And then she got a new pair. I could never see the specialness of these shoes though she nearly convinced me I wanted a pair. It was the ardent way she spoke of them. Made me look at her feet as we took the walkway into her house, white pointed shoes, slippers really, on black pavement.

In Mary's bed I would talk about the filthiest things. I don't know what would come over me. I would take scenarios that my brother had described in only the most cursory manner and expand them with my own passions and perversities. Boys and girls on bikes would meet in garages and there they would play sex games which mainly included girls peeing in boys' mouths. At the time it seemed that boys were really interested in what girls had. I don't think we even had a name for what we "had" at that point in our lives. But boys according to my brother were always getting girls to lift their skirts, open their shorts or slacks, pull down their underpants. Once my brother claimed he and his friends had put a rare stamp from one of their collections down one of my friend's underpants. All of my friends seemed to be doing amazing things when I wasn't there. One of them, a redhead, was naked up on the dining room table at another friend's house as all of the boys looked on. None of the girls ever shared their versions of these stories with me nor did I confront them and ask them if these things were true. I liked them being true—I thought they were exciting and would embellish them with details that I thought made them even better. If boys were always trying to get in girls' pants, what did they want? What could the girls give them? Pee it seemed to me was an appropriate gift. In a garage on Swan Street I described them for Mary in a line, boys with baseball caps, crouching under squatting powerful girls. Often the boys' caps would fall off in the excitement. Everyone's bikes were strewn in the driveway outside the closed doors of the guilty garage. Pee was streaming from between the girls' legs and landing in the boys' opening waiting mouths underneath. It was steaming, it was messy, it was the dirtiest thing I could think of. Eileen, are you sure this is true. Absolutely. My brother told me so. Terry was older than us. Very smart and he was not a liar. And these were the stories that I made up.

On Fridays Mary and I would stay up as late as possible, the night ending with a new episode of *Twilight Zone*. There was one about some people who had a hole in the wall of their house through which a dog fell, then a little girl, then a man went in and saved them both. The hole opened into another dimension, floatier than ours, mostly blackened it seemed and filled with amorphous glowing shapes, like gases and galaxies, going slow. In bed I knew that I was next to that wall suddenly I knew it and Mary had to hold my hand. Mary I'm going to go through. I can feel it. You've got to hold my hand. I'll hold your hand Eileen but you're not going to go through. I know you're right Mary but will you please hold my hand. I'm holding it Eileen. Mary don't let go. Eileen I'm falling asleep. Okay but just hold my hand while you're sleeping. Okay okay. And she did.

One day my father died. It wasn't a surprise. Watching the firetruck come up the street, the crowd assembling to see him be carried out. It was as if it had happened before, it was so familiar. Then Mary Dolan stepped up. Do you want to come over to my house. We can paint my new room she added and that was the clincher. On the third floor in Mary's house there was this large room with intense eaves. That's where we went when my father died. OK, Dear? Mrs. Dolan yelled out from the kitchen as we headed upstairs. Everyone's concern seemed strange—indirect or misplaced somehow. It was like I wasn't there, but was watching them. Mary's offer to paint made a lot of sense. I don't know where she got the paint, but there were several buckets of it. I kind of like the color, don't you? Mary asked. It was an ugly color and we both knew it. Sort of a grey-ish turquoise. Not even like the bottom of an old swimming pool—more like an institution that was trying to be a little bit different. More like a waiting room. It was thin, watery paint. The walls were impossible. It dripped down. No matter where you tried to cover, the past re-emerged, some old pinkish wallpaper we hadn't bothered to scrape—My mother always scrapes first I pointed out. My mother said we don't have to. Okay. The greenish paint stained the wallpaper, it did that, but little more. At one point I started to cry. It was just too impossible to put this paint on the wall. It was at a slant and even the straight part down at the bottom that had no wallpaper on it, even that was no good. It just looked terrible. Why are you crying, Eileen, Mary asked. This paint is making me sick I screamed, slapping the wall hard with the brush. A big patch of paint gobbed on somehow and really looked, kind of good. How did you do that, Mary asked. She yowled and slapped her brush hard against the wall. I laughed at her and did mine again. Ahhck I shrieked and smashed the wall. We started splashing each other with paint, it was getting on the floor—Are you girls okay Mrs. Dolan yelled from downstairs. We looked at each other, we opened our mouths wide in silent horror. Mary took her brush and painted the front of my shirt. I painted her legs. She had shorts on. Someplace in there we kissed each other and I don't think it ever happened again.

Now neither of us had fathers and that made us special. Someplace in there it seemed like we got married. Mary's house was halfway up the street. Mary was in love with me. She really was. Afternoons when I would go home from school she would tell me how I looked. She said it looked like I floated up the street. That my feet were several inches off the ground. I liked that. There were days when I was dreaming up the street, and there were days when I was dreaming for Mary. At the bottom of the street I'd be getting ready, being real relaxed and then the whole moment—the three-house width of the actual pass by the several windows of her gaze. She may have never watched me again, just that once but it got me home for years. I have always been afraid I would vanish, would cease to be, if I ever stopped trying to decide who I was, how I looked. Since childhood I had always been standing in the excessive glare of my father's eyes, even when he wasn't drunk. When he died I began watching myself all the time, for fear of being pitched into blackness.

I was Mary's boyfriend. I had always wanted to be a boy. To have women love me, to have extra rooms to go into, to be free. There on the soft couch in the Dolan's parlor as we lifted our tall metal cups of Hawaiian Punch to our lips, in the moment I was male and I was loved.

Our friendship hardly existed outside her house. By high school I actually snubbed her in the halls. It was her fault. She would usually say something very jerky and familiar like one of our private jokes in front of my friends. I'd look stunned and move along. My friends would ask, "Who's that?" Mary Dolan, I'd reply. She lives on my street. Once I even said, "She's sort of my sister's friend."

Mary had two sisters, Bess and Helene and they were as different as night and day though equally fascinating. Bess was brassy, always had a new boyfriend who was buying her things: a fish-tank for example. She drank, would gain weight easily and go on diets—Mary showed me many pictures of Bess at different weights. She had a great singing voice yet decided against a career in it. She had loud dramatic fights with Mrs. Dolan, would yell Hi girls having fun as she whizzed into the house to get dressed and go out. Mary and I decided that I was more like Bess and she was more like Helene, the quiet beautiful one. It wasn't really true, but it seemed like if I got to be like Bess, she had to get to be like someone so I just shut up. Bess owned a lot of comedy albums and dirty ones too: Rusty Warren's songs for sinners. Our favorite song was called Knockers up and Rusty Warren would inveigle the women in her audience, Ladies please will you get up and stand there, be proud, put those knockers up. Then she would sing a few stanzas of the marching tune and we would march one behind the other with our chests stuck out, our heads held high, our arms flailing. Often it seemed the phone rang when we were doing this. We're fine, Mom. We're just listening to music.

Bess paid Mary to feed her tropical fish. Around that time I had decided I would be a scientist when I grew up. The ultimate goal was to ride somewhere on a spaceship but it seemed you needed skills. I had a microscope, then Mary got one too and we set up a lab in the basement. Bess had worked as some kind of technician in the past so we used her old lab coats and started a science club. We would make observations of what we saw in our microscopes and record these observations in our book. Our main object of study was dead tropical fish. Often, especially if Mary had failed to feed Bess's fish for a stretch of time there'd be a couple of fish floating on their sides. Those we'd pluck off the surface and rush to the basement for experimentation and dissection. We had a code: Mary would call and say "Two on the side." I'd rush over. The dissection was a messy business. We didn't know what we were doing, of course. We weren't looking for anything in particular just stuff that would look good under our microscopes. That usually came down to eyes. A fish eye looking back at you. We recorded it in our book.

Helene was simply a movie we liked to watch. Mary assured me she wasn't nice at all and she never seemed friendly or faintly interested in me. But she was beautiful. She had brown hair and sort of brown skin, when she got a tan she really looked great. We loved her in white. She had the same boyfriend Mucca forever. He was really handsome and macho and he wore bermudas and had great legs. They played tennis. They went on trips. Helene hadn't gone to college. She just had a job and Mucca dropped out of college because he really wanted to be a state cop. We even liked that. They were the Barbie and Ken of our lives and we would quietly discuss how they looked after each occasion on which we saw them together. Helene was always watching her weight. Mary assured me that she had steak and salad every night, nothing else.

At pajama parties Mary was my partner. I didn't have to get involved in the competitive crush for Franny Fittante, I didn't have to take one of the Delays, I had Mary and we would dance slow assuring her that I was Mark Casey, her great love, and she was Stephen Gough who was cute that year. Her passion for Mark was broader and more long standing—they lived up on the best part of Pleasant St., his father was a doctor, he had nice sweaters, you knew he would go to a good school, maybe be a doctor himself. About 15 years later Mary did marry a doctor.

Once Mary offered me a pin and suggested we go steady. I told her it was disgusting. I thought it was queer. Once in bed she told me about her activities with Carla Ware and it really slowed up my staying over at her place. Carla was the poor girl on the block. Her mother was divorced and had boyfriends and often if you came in with Carla Mrs. Ware would be drinking and sitting on her boyfriend's lap. One day she brought a whole bunch of us in to see. Both of the Wares,

Bill and Carla had tons of pimples. Improving Carla was something that took place at pajama parties. Cutting Carla's hair. We should've popped her pimples someone said. That I couldn't have handled. Mary touched Carla's bush in bed. She also touched a breast and she let Carla touch hers. Carla was so ugly and gross. Stop Stop Mary I don't want to hear about this.

Both Mary and I smoked cigarettes by the time we got older. I think we might've been in college now. What did we talk about? People who drank too much. We drank instant coffee, tons of it, always on diets. Once in a while we'd go for a run. Our bond continued to be something about improvement. We'd run the quarter mile at Spy Pond Field, wheezing animal noises coming out of our throats and lungs. Then Mary would pull a wrinkled pack of Salems out of her running shorts. Here, let's sit down. We'd smoke slowly, looking at the trees and the track.

It was an utter necessity, no matter how I felt, to find something I was excited about and tell Mary, to dazzle her. We had these reunions. It was something I had to do.

The worst was when I graduated from college. It seemed I wasn't a kid anymore, and I couldn't imagine what I could be. I wasn't anything. I got a waitressing job. I needed money to go to Europe in the fall. Mary had another year in school. She majored in Nursing. She wouldn't be like me. She came to my house that afternoon I began the waitressing job. I had a white uniform and a hair net in my pocket. I didn't want to go to work. I had just graduated. She brought a couple of bottles of Guinness Stout. I got a little drunk. I was so depressed. I was scared. What if I am a waitress Mary. What if this is it. The

look in her face was worse than mine. It had to be. I was crack-
ing. I was falling. I was a shattered piece of junk lying around
the pedestal we had built for me. Oh, it was a terrible sight.

Then I saw her at a wedding a few years later. I told her I
was going to New York. Soon. To be a writer. I was leaving
town fast. Oh Eileen aren't you ever going to grow up. She had
one of her big glommy boyfriends in tow. I had come with a
girl. I thought that was cool. It was her cousin's wedding. The
one she was always jealous of. I never saw her again. I heard
her father was dying of liver cancer in a rest home in Nahant
and she took care of him until the end. I heard she married
a neurosurgeon from South America who speaks seven lan-
guages and plays oh I don't know seven musical instruments.
I heard she lives on Comm. Ave. I heard she has twins. I heard
oh you know Mary she's always the same. I heard her husband's name is Jose Paris.

POPPONESSET

I guess I was about 18 and I was in a car driving down the Southeast Expressway towards Cape Cod. We had just had our Biology exam and I was immensely relieved. The sky was a pale blue like it is in late afternoon. I had a tall can of beer in my hand and it seems I see me in profile. How strange. I was riding in Louise's car, a black Mustang. She was a short athletic constantly tanned girl. I had a strange feeling of excitement around Louise which compelled me to fulfill her idea of me. It didn't seem too bad. She saw me as intelligent, I think, and she laughed at me in a way that implied I was a riot. I didn't know for a fact that she thought I was good looking, but here I was in a carload of girls heading down the Cape to a party at Louise's family's house in Popponesset. We were going for the express purpose of meeting other friends of hers, guys. Ones she had gone to high school with and she described them as hunks, or something like that and it was perfect in her mind that they meet me and Anne who we also knew from school. And being from Lexington they already knew Sally and Diane and we were going to have fun. I felt extremely passive about it, exhausted from the exam and sort of apprehensive at the idea of meeting them. It seemed destined that they wouldn't like me, there seemed to be something missing. I often thought different guys to be quite beautiful and I would watch the way they walked and moved their hands and leaned and held things and looked around.

We got down to Louise's house and we brought our huge amounts of beer in from the car and our small amounts of clothes. We had big bags of doritos and stuff. Bunches of cigarettes. We threw ourselves down in the soft family beach furniture and proceeded to talk, just us girls in the fading light. I wasn't intending to smoke, was off them for several months now and had been through the hard part, which was gaining weight, and now that I had done a little of that, everything tasted good and I could breathe pretty well and so it was a big mistake to begin now.

I watched the smoke curl up in the air through the windows of the beach house and I grew immensely intelligent and witty as I tended to in a group of girls, not being afraid after a couple of drinks that anyone would be embarrassed by my intensity. They were intense too. It was a big secret to everyone and we hid it well and let it out now and then when we were drunk, that we were smart and cared and thought about many things. Diane had long dark hair and she also held court I noticed and she held her cigarette like an older woman when she spoke and I figured she was probably turning into her mother or someone else.

They're here, shrieked Louise. "Dave," she yelled strutting out and it was apparent Louise was quite drunk. Everyone was. I remember being quiet for a couple of minutes like someone told me to shut up, no let me be frank I barely remember a thing. I was walking on the beach with Kit, Kit Anderson was his name and he had on a red sweater and we had been talking maybe a little bit inside and I had no feeling he liked me at all, in fact he was holding me up and I felt burdensome and he felt like the boys from Arlington only I didn't know this guy at all and he was a big blond. I remember we were trying to make out, but that was boring and pointless because I was so drunk plus we didn't care about each other at all. He was probably drunk too but I don't know. I went into the bedroom with Kit and then it began. I don't know. Just a rhythm of many guys, I seem to remember all of them in there at once but that may have been a blur and then precisely Dave sitting down, a therapist's son, Dave Margolis something like that and he was dark haired and he was sitting on the other bed saying you are disgusting, you are a slut. It was like being drugged in the dentist's office. I felt fat, I remember loathing my body. It went on and on, people on top of me, feeling scared, feeling turned on. Am I dreaming? Rape was the first sex I ever heard of. Some girl tied to a telephone pole down by Spy Pond. It seemed to always happen in nature. Choking. I had a lot of cocks shoved in my mouth. Hoots. Getting fucked with cold hot dogs. There was pancake batter all over the place. I remember my wool plaid pants being off. Being white. It was cold.

Dave was talking to me like it was my fault. I was trying to talk, but my tongue was so thick. That underwater feel. You're an asshole. Um not. The door was slightly open into the kitchen and light was flooding in through a crack. Louise's brother was on top of me and I could see a little smile on his face and he was sucking my tit. He's happy. How weird. He was hurting me and it felt pretty good. He had his glasses off. I pretended I was asleep.

In the morning everyone girls were sleeping in clumps all over the house. I had my own bedroom it seemed. I was alone. So sick. Tried to make some coffee. Gave up and walked down to the beach. There were these polyps, pink and translucently fleshy, scattered all over the little tan beach. I sat on the side of an old row boat. I felt like the inside of my head had been scooped out. I was painfully numb. I had been raped, right? Even if I don't know exactly what happened. That's how I feel. A bunch of good-looking suburban guys, 18 or 19, same as me, who all owned cars, trashed me for two reasons: I was drunk, they didn't know me. I wrote my name on the sand with my toe. EILEEN MYLES. Yes, that's who I am. I rubbed it out with my foot.

How are you feeling, Leena. I was standing in the kitchen trying to make some coffee. Louise explained that she thought I liked it, that's why she didn't interfere. Sally had passed out. "Those guys are assholes, Leena." Anne just said she was scared. She didn't know them either. Diane went out for pizza with, I can't remember his name. I wasn't ever going to drink again, but I felt safe at the card party that night. The beers helped me relax. People were kind of taking care of me then. But Eddy, Louise's brother, just killed me. So righteous about what a bunch of little pricks they were. I went out with him a few times after that—we saw Vanilla Fudge. I wanted to see if his story would ever crack. Louise must've known he fucked me too. Once she pulled into a gas station in Lexington where Dave worked. She didn't warn me. *Louise.* Hi Dave. *Hey Louise.* He can't see you. I'm sure he doesn't even remember. Hey Dave! She got out of the car.

MARSHFIELD

Marshfield is on the south shore of Massachusetts about half way between Boston and the Bourne Bridge. A small section of it is known as Brant Rock—Brant Rock, Mass., and that's where my family would rent a place each summer for a couple of weeks or a month. We'd get this big old place on Hancock Street off Ocean Ave., which was right on the water. The giant sea-wall protected us from the waves. At night in bed I could hear the ocean beating against the sea-wall, also foghorns.

We rented the house on Hancock Street from a couple named the Lemmes, pronounced, "Limmy." Helen Lemme was the business man who had a hilarious habit of saying "Surely" to absolutely anything anyone said. Well, we'll have to think about it, my mother would say when Helen had informed her she'd raised the rent. "Shirley!" she'd go. She said it with the outside corners of her mouth. "Oh, Shirley," she said, no matter what you said. Her eyebrows were incredibly darkened with eyepencil and her hair was black like a character in a comic book. "Mom, is her hair really that color?" I'd ask, riding home from Brant Rock, the deal finally closed.

"Oh, come on," said my mother, amazed that even kids were so stupid.

Most of the house was knotty pine, cozy-looking, and the art was marvelous. Big prints of comical hoboes cooking their dinners against a night sky alongside the railroad tracks. "That's the depression," my uncle said. The house smelled great when we came in, usually the first tenants of the summer. Musty like only wildly floral, slightly damp old couches could smell. Striped canvas beach furniture out on the front porch and rougey old pillows, small ones, thrown around, dusty salmon rose, brown-stained. The porch was screened in and freshly painted every few years that dark green color and if you sat in a rocking chair you could spend hours observing how the paint filled some holes in the screen entirely, others were okay, or partial, blobby drips had dried running down the screen. I'd get a common pin when no one was around, trying to straighten out the filled-in portions.

The base of the house under the front porch was cement embedded with stones about twice the size of your fist, stones from the ocean, round and smooth. A cement walk led out from the front door, with grass on either side—the dryest, sharpest grass your feet had ever stepped on. At the end of the walk were two posts, square, but like our lions. They were cement and round rock and the top was flat and smooth. If you were in a rush to get to the beach but had to wait for someone to bring their towel or something, you could sit on one of the columns.

There was no light in my room so I had to sit at the top of the stairs and write in my diary. My uncle Tim used to watch teevee, drinking beer, eating graham crackers and baloney. I used to run down and get a few from him, and return to my staircase. In later years, Brian, Tim's son, watched Johnny Carson, drinking beers, and smoking Marlboros, and I'd come in, around 13, and smoke one with him.

There was a big bathtub in the house which no one used. The joke was that no one took a bath all summer. There was a shower on the side of the house, strictly cold, and the thing to do was to wash the salt off yourself there, occasionally bringing some shampoo in, Prell, I remember, since it didn't break, nor did Johnson's Baby Shampoo. We had a nice square backyard with soft green grass, where we'd play wiffle ball a lot, and the Red Sox were always on my uncle's transistor. He sat there all summer in a chaise lounge, with a year's worth of *Reader's Digest* piled up beside him and the ball game always on.

The kitchen faced the backyard. There was a window over the sink and it would take me hours to do dishes, doing them perfectly, looking at the old stone church just beyond our yard and there was a clothes line in our yard and clothes swayed on it all summer. All the boys' floral and plaid trunks, jock straps, our bathing suits, paisley, with little skirts, half-ripped off, or older stretch ones, turquoise with a bra inside, my mother and aunt's with tucks in the front, and big zippers down the backs. All the big striped towels, and the cool one my family had: a Confederate flag. "What's that," everyone would say. "The Confederate flag. You know the South used to be a *country*."

MY FATHER'S ALCOHOLISM

All through my childhood I was a devotee of the dark-haired man. There was Tyrone Power, there were endless boys in comic books: Super Boy, Reggie, Walter in Little Lulu. Obscure brunet boys who I based my fantasy life on. They were beautiful and they were perfect. The enhancing frame of the comic book, approximately 2½ by 2½, facilitated a world of inked-in colors, bound by the fineness of a cartoonist's pen, forever non-blurry, and when the artist got to the head, the hair, they could color it in. Black. Crowned with a head of blue-black hair in a world in which darkness was cop, the system of order—my boys had power, black ruled.

No cartoonist could resist having at least one black-haired character. After the Archies, the Iggies with small spikey lines as code for hair, their crew-cuts—eventually they'd come along. My father's name was Terrence. He had black hair. There was a clear line from him to my dream world and back. My father insisted from the get go that he was in the same frame as me. He elbowed his way into my consciousness. That's Eileen, That's Eileen. As if the world were a school about me. Relatives participated in the plot. One of them, my father's white-haired brother, Ed, gave us a story book about a little girl with braids, who loved to play with kittens, and as if I were an idiot my father showed the book to me and said That's Eileen. I mean yeah, I had braids and a cat. But was I cute? As a picture in a book. Childhood is wide and impersonal. Something that was not me, but showed me the world on its way, is gazing down at a bowl of milk with rice crispies glistening in the morning sun. Breakfast. So beautiful I didn't want to eat it.

The darkest part of my house was the stairs. You had to come down so the day could begin. My father went to work very early. He was a mailman. Weekends, however, he would hold court in the parlor. Atmosphere would be pumped out on 78s all day. Nelson Eddy & Jeanette MacDonald, Bing. Danny Kaye singing those boisterous, eerie tunes: Oh Thumbaleena don't be dumb—tum, tum, tum. My mother's participation in the weekend music festival was evidence that they loved each other. The occasional dance through the house, my mother's sighs at the appropriate song, as she worked. That this was going on all the time was a fact of life and the weekend, like my Dad. One morning moving down through the darkness from the kid's world, a song came on downstairs and with its opening bars my father yelled out: This is Eileen's song. Gordon MacRae was belting out: Oh what a beautiful morning, Oh what a beautiful day. I've got a wonderful fee-ling, everything's going my way. The singer went on to describe how the cows were doing, and the beauty of the fields. He was this big happy farmer. I must have expressed appreciation of the tune at some point. That had to be it. But I never wanted to hear it every weekend when I came down the stairs. Even today it's accompanied by reluctant floods of light. You didn't want to be thought about that much, before you even knew "you" were there. I can remember a time when my name was for other people, before I even knew it was mine. The anonymous quality of its vowels—"Ei" being a word you heard a lot. Later I would know it was a pronoun, but before I could write, before anything had established that different contexts for sounds, words, meant different things, the "Ei" I heard a lot when people spoke seemed to mean "you." Sometimes they talked about themselves and said "Ei" but if they looked at me, or said it loudly, it mean "you." Then "Leen," that part. It sounded like meat. Roast beef. It had something to do with that. Usually what was going to happen was contained in the second part of what they called me. The "Ei" got my attention. The "Leen" either went really high which meant I was in trouble or slow and soft, the part when the tongue hit the roof of their mouth meant something nice. I was good. If they hit the first part with the second part really fast I was bad or in danger.

As I was travelling down the stairs from the bright kid world, through the dark soft tunnel with carpets towards the place where my parents would move me around, before I really knew I was anybody at all just that movement, never really awake, but very wide, hearing and feeling everything, I heard my name, that thing that made me know that something was going to happen, that woke me up. Now something my father was playing was also mine and I had to remember what I had done the first time I heard this song in front of him, that was the shock of the first time I heard "This is Eileen's song." After that, everytime I heard the song wherever I was in the house I knew that he was sitting in the parlor thinking about me and I was supposed to do something, probably go look at him. If I pretended I hadn't heard it my mother would get in on the act. She'd move her head in his direction. Go see what he wants. Sometimes I'd scream, "I'm eating." That was always a good excuse. If I was in the middle of something good, drawing, I would carry what I was doing. I'd walk into the doorway of the parlor, with my large pad of drawing paper and my charcoal pencil in my fingers and I would stand there, looking at him to show him I was mad. He'd be sitting there on the couch in his big baggy pants, cross-legged in his white socks with a cigarette momentarily held to his lips. He'd smile up at me like I was a surprise. He was dreaming. He'd forgotten he'd called my name. It was like I was a note he had sung in a moment that had passed.

We went on errands with my father on his days off. My mother would ask him to pick something up. Take the kids, Ted, she'd say and we'd go trudging out with him. Inevitably these errands brought him to Cambridge or Somerville where liquor was sold. He would pull into a parking place at some point in the journey and he would introduce his departure with a very quick—Back in a moment, Back in a Flash, Gotta take a whizz, Gotta get a Bromo. My father always talked in slang and frequently we just didn't understand him. We'd sit in the car for interminable periods of time, thinking of the sound of his last word: Flash, Bromo. We would look at the signs over the stores that weighed ever so heavy in our eyesight. Was that Bromo. Was all this time "Flash." Other time words, ten minutes, a second were often used in these breaks from us my father would make and I would try to remember if the last time we had stopped was a moment or a second. I would pull the button on the car door up and down. Don't do that said my brother. Why I'd ask. Dad wouldn't like that. The roof of the car was covered with all rough fuzzy stuff. A light sat in the middle of it and it looked like a big piece of candy. We weren't allowed to turn it on because it hurt the car. There was a tear on the side of the roof and inside of the tear, Look Terry said, revealing it to me, a St. Christopher medal. We would always be safe in this car. You could look out its windows slightly spotty from rain and dirt and first pretend the world looked like that, then remove it and let it be the window. I liked making the world spotted. The world got the shape of the car windows and that was good for a while. There were little round handles like stirrups on the walls of the car and I would hold on to one and pretend to be a horse, Ker Klop, Ker Klop I would yell and chug in my seat until Terry would yell stop you are driving my crazy. Terry never moved. He climbed behind the steering wheel as soon as Daddy left. He would sit there looking straight ahead like an adult. Once we saw Aunt Nora walking along the sidewalk. Look Terry, Look—Aunt Nora. You shut up. Terry she likes us. It's Aunt Nora. Shut up Eileen. He acted like we were doing something bad. Once Daddy had a day off during the week so when we parked Terry got to put nickels in the meter. He let me come out and watch. What are those lines, I asked pointing at the meter.

That's how long Daddy's gone. When it's red I put another nickel in. And then he comes? *No,* he said.

Once we had stayed a really long time in Inman Square. It always reminded me of M&M Square. I would think about that when we sat in the car—looking for something that had to do with M&Ms. Back in a Flash, M&Ms. My father always reminded me of comic books. That's why I was always looking for him in them. He came out really happy with a friend that time. Uncle Joe's inside he said. Why don't you kids come in. It's really late, Dad, Terry said. It was getting dark. And we hadn't gone to the A & P which is where we were supposed to go. Party pooper he said which made me laugh. The word poop always made me laugh. Inside was not like a store. It was more like a home where you bought drinks and potato chips. It was kind of stinky and smokey and it was all men. Uncle Joe was sitting in a booth. Hi kids he said. It was sort of like a soda fountain but it was all dark wood like houses in Somerville. The radio was really loud, a woman was singing. And there was a green parrot in a cage. It was all men and it was like a pirate place and I began to understand that my father was like a pirate and that's where he would go and come back different.

Everything was different when we got back home. Hello my father would yell from the foot of the stairs. It was like we were all kids now and we were in trouble. Terry and I were holding a big potted plant, a red chrysanthemum. My father had a finger to his lips, almost laughing. Go ahead he said giving us a light shove up the stairs. Surprise Terry and I yelled when she saw us holding the chrysanthemum. Shit on you Ted my mother said to my father who was standing in back of us and then it got really sickening. She didn't make us not eat but we were sent upstairs really fast. My brother and I both had stuffed rabbits we slept with. It was how we talked late at night. If we didn't want to be alone we had our rabbits talk to each other because they couldn't be heard. I knew Terry was crying. He didn't want to carry the flower when my father told him about it. Do you want to have a bunny talk, Terry. No, he screamed and he got up and slammed his door.

Once he took us to the fireworks and he left us there. By now he had joined the American Legion which was right on the other side of the park. Now you kids stay right here, don't move, I'll be right back. Pretty soon the fireworks were over and everyone left. Kids asked us if we wanted to go home with them. We're okay, we smiled. We told our father we'd meet him here. Maybe you should just come home with us—we can give you a ride. Finally when we were the only people left on the bleachers and even the fire department had left down in the field—then we just knew we had to go home. We were in bed when my father came in that night—there were some other voices down there with him—it sounded like his friends had given him a ride. Fireworks still make me kind of anxious. Once I took some acid and watched them through binoculars on the roof. It was perfect.

My father's work day ended before I came in from school. He had to be the source of the gifts that appeared for me on the table when I got home. A harmonica sitting there, a Hohner, not a toy. It was like he was reading my mind. Slides for my microscope—the most amazing one being egg of silkworm—a hot pink sphere with a small slice removed so it appeared to be biting something. A clear tiny bubble had escaped, was drifting away from its pink insides. Sometimes I'd run to the parlor where he was invariably sleeping on the couch. I'd run in, jump on his stomach and jounce until he woke up. I'm up, I'm up, I'm up.

Dinner was often a scene. There were times when my mother would force him to the table from the bedroom. He couldn't walk. He couldn't sit up. She'd put food on his plate and his face would fall in it. She would pick his head up by his hair. His face would be covered in cabbage and potato and the juice from the corned beef. Nobody wanted to eat after that. He looked like a baby crying. His expression just sagged. I remember her screaming but I don't remember a word that she said. Because she was always angry and he was always sad it's easy to think of my mother as mean in those days. He finally fell off his chair and implored us all on his hands and his knees: I'm sorry, I'm sorry. There was still food on his face. Then he got mad and turned to the kitchen door, all glass and slammed his fists through it—I'll show you something he blubbered crying like a baby and a man.

I had this game with my sister, called Dirty Kids and Clean Kids. We would make real hobo sloppy boy kids, bums with filthy clothes. Despite my sister's entreaties I would only draw boys for this game. I didn't know how to draw girls. It made me feel funny plus I didn't have the same feelings about wanting to see them go from bad to good. Anyhow the bad kids would go through a factory I had also drawn. Once they came out the other side all beautiful and fresh with new clothes we knew that things were better and it made us feel good. It was our favorite game for a while. Just the fact of my sister's existence makes me think this game was fairly late in my father's alcoholism. I would say Bridget want to play Dirty Kids and Clean Kids? We would rush upstairs. More than once my mother remarked that this game must be pretty great the way we were so excited about it. Maybe we could sell it and make some money.

One Halloween he took us out trick or treating. Not just Terry and me, but Bridgie too and all the kids on the street. My father wore some big black old dress and he put a mop on his head and he had some kind of tall witch hat and he put red stuff on his nose. I think he looked like from the Wizard of Oz, more like the scarecrow, but he was a witch. He just sort of trailed behind us, watching out. I was a cat that year. My father painted whiskers on my face. It's funny to remember being so little that someone taking you places meant you could go. My father wasn't like a parent. He was like an older brother. Kind of, when he was good. Some punks tried to take our candy on Lombard Terrace and my father asked them why they were bothering his friends and the punks ran away. My father let us stay out so late our bags were all breaking and we couldn't carry them. It was great.

At home some nights it was hard to tell if he was good or bad. My father would put on a show. He had a skimpy little muscle man bathing suit. He would slick his hair back and come out in that and lift his arms and flex his muscles. I felt like I didn't get it. My mother seemed to be very happy and was laughing a lot. Then he ran into the bedroom and came out again. He wore his big army coat and he had a toothbrush, a black one under his nose and clicked his heels together. He was Hitler. Hitler always reminded me of the Devil. It was scarey. Oh Ted, my mother would exclaim. Then he would come out as a woman. That was the worst. I remember a big pink coat that may have been my mother's, and a tight little scarf around his head. I don't remember any makeup, maybe some rouge on his cheeks. It was like he was doing Grandma, his mother who was in a mental hospital. The woman part was really the scariest. My mother was really happy I think because she could keep an eye on him when he was acting funny and making us watch. He was her boy. But I wasn't so sure he was being good—the house felt hot, it was manic and scarey.

Late at night my mother would scream Oh Ted you've done it again. He had wet the bed. She could have left him. She could have thrown him out.

He had many car accidents and then he couldn't drive anymore. People always gave him a break. I can tell he's a nice guy said some woman who drove him home—so I'm not going to turn him in. I made him promise me he wouldn't drink and drive again.

On Friday nights my mother would go to the priest. It was dark out after supper. She was going to discuss my father's alcoholism. The priest's name sounded something like corn, like corn chowder on Friday nights. My father and I would sit in the den and watch teevee. It must've been before supper which makes no sense, but that's when war movies were. My father was in the Air Force in World War II. He was in a part of the Air Force called the red ball line. Men drove all over

Europe in trucks. Jeeps I guess because the Germans would string these thin pieces of wire across the road and my father would make that clucking sound as his fingers pointed across his throat—the guys in the jeep would get their heads cut off. My father was always interested in suicide. He told me about the Kamikaze pilots on the Japanese side who died for the Emperor and rode their planes right into the same building and died. My father loved to talk about hari kiri. He always wore a white teeshirt around the house and would demonstrate how these other Japanese guys with swords would stick their swords in one side of their stomach and pull it across. My mother and father were fighting in the kitchen once and my father grabbed the big butcher knife and stuck it in my mother's hand. He pulled his teeshirt up: C'mon, Gen, do it to me. Don't tempt me, Ted, she said.

My father was really sad that he didn't get to be a pilot in the war. He failed an eye exam. He washed out.

We sat on the couch and looked at the black 'n white movies about the war. My mother was out talking with the priest. The movie was about a club of men who went out on flying missions and some of them never came back. They were British. My father had been in England during the war. He loved the English countryside my mother said. The letters he wrote, *uh*. She groaned at their beauty. Apparently, she had thrown them out.

Each time a man didn't come back from a mission the men in the club turned over his mug on the mantle piece. My father loved it. He started crying. He had been really quiet up to there. He was being good. That's what I hope they'll do when

I die. Here's to Ted Myles, never hurt anyone but himself. With that he picked up a green bottle of beer from the side of the couch. It was the most interesting bottle of beer I had ever seen in my life. It was magic. It was like he had invented that bottle. He lifted the beer to his lips. It had a horse on its label. Daddy! Oh I'm sorry he said. He was surprised he was drinking too.

A few minutes later he vanished into the kitchen. He was too quiet. He was standing by the sink holding a glass of whiskey. I'd never seen my father drink before. Before he lost his license I heard he'd pull over at the top of Route 2 before coming home and knock back a pint of Old Thompson. Rye. He was standing in the kitchen with his cup of gold. Did he call me one of those names I hated? Princess. Kiddo. Eileeny-Beanie-my Queenie. I became my mother. I grabbed the glass out of his hand and dumped it down the sink. He fell down on his knees, apologizing, repeating again and again. I'm sorry I'm sorry I'm sorry. The light in the kitchen was neon, incredibly bright.

My mother got her license. I'd go with her after school to pick up my father at the post office. He worked on Mt. Auburn Street in Harvard Square. He delivered mail in Harvard Yard. We sort of felt like Harvard was ours, so many members of my family worked there. Aunt Anne cleaned rooms. Toilets, she insisted. My cousin Brian worked in the cafeteria. So did my brother, briefly. My uncle's uncle owned a drugstore in Harvard Square. Harvard was the best college in America so it was nice that we lived near it. Sometimes my father would talk in his sleep. He'd be calling his route from the couch: Dunster, Adams, Leverett. I was standing outside a building one night with a boy I met at a mixer. What's that I pointed. Leverett House. Wow.

Often my father would take us to see the museums. I liked the dinosaurs and all the rocks. He liked the glass flowers. Everyone does, I guess. They remind me of death. Glass flowers make no sense to a child. Actually Harvard just seemed really old. It reminded me of a big bank. Our hi-fi came from Harvard. It cost 85 bucks. The students at Harvard were rich. They were always leaving and selling things. A whole collection of records came with the stereo—Ornette Coleman, Gerry Mulligan, John Coltrane. They had a dense musty smell. I listened to this Harvard music in college. A Love Supreme, A Love Supreme. My father's clothes came from Harvard: Burberry coats, London Fog. My father liked to look like F. Scott Fitzgerald, that was the idea, an Irish Ivy Leaguer

There was a drawing pad, Aqua-bee, he gave me, with charcoal pens. It was half drawn on. They just used it for doodling, this big expensive pad and then they threw it out. There was a little pen and ink drawing: the lines were really shakey and sort of scribbled over, but it looked cool, like modern art, the person wasn't working hard but they were smart. It was a man's face with sort of a hat on: Don't be such a Philistine it said. I didn't get it. Wasn't Goliath a Philistine? It meant something else. I asked my mother. Isn't it from the Bible? My brother laughed. I hated it when he knew something and wouldn't tell me.

There was a drawing that came from Harvard, rolled up, with an elastic around it, I believe. It was drawn in blue and black, soft pencils, with lines and shading. It was a man's face, long and thin and he wore a turban and his nose was pointed and his lips were curled into a sneer. I looked at it and closed it quickly. It was evil. I would hide it and look for it again and again. It was like someone's secret, it was something I didn't want to know. It was insidious.

So we'd park on Mt. Auburn Street and wait for my father. He'd come to a window, the head, he said, and wave and come out in a few minutes. I don't think my father ever came out of work drunk so it was a good time. Then we headed over to Aunt Anne's who still lived in Somerville. Once my father met us there and he had just had all his teeth pulled out. He was forty. I guess my father always had bad teeth. Oh your father was always self-conscious about his teeth. That's why he doesn't smile in pictures. He made friends with Mrs. Matheson who also had false teeth. Be true to your teeth or they'll be false to you, he'd say when he took them out.

And later there was something wrong with his ass, hemorrhoids. I guess Mrs. Matheson also had that. It was a joke. And so did Aunt Anne. They all went to the same doctor. They called him the Rear Admiral. Then my father had to sit on this black balloon—it looked like an innertube. I tried it once. It was like a toilet seat. My mother seemed to like my father getting sick because it kept him home and there were more jokes and we could take care of him. Things were under control. And he had ulcers too. It all seemed normal, all these things in his body going wrong. It was about being an adult, being a man. He was falling apart.

In the summer my family took a trip to New Hampshire. My father drove even though he didn't have a license. It was okay if she was with him. My father seemed very quiet and sad. He wasn't drinking. And that was good. We were going to this place called the Polar Caves in the White Mountains. I thought of bears. There's a black and white photograph of this trip. My sister and my mother and I are standing by an outside bathroom. It's labeled squaws. My sister always looked upset in pictures, my mother looks, nervous—I have a tan and am good looking. My father took the picture. We all have kerchiefs on. And sweaters. It was an overcast day.

When we got to the caves my father decided not to go in. You okay, Ted, my mother inquired. I don't know if it's another photograph or a memory of my dad. He's standing outside there with a cigarette to his lips. He's a grown man, an adult but he looks extremely vulnerable out there, smoking, worrying. You really did want to take care of him. He had that. Inside it was all these boulders pushed together by nature, by the Ice Age. There were little tunnels you could push your way through. They were tight. You had alternatives, though, and I had heard about these. There was the lemon peel and the orange squeeze. One was tighter than the other, easier for kids to get through. I was getting older so it was important to get through the smaller kid one. My mother even had a hard time with the lemon peel in which you only had to crouch. The orange squeeze you had to climb and then slip through. There were little lamps on all the walls. *Good* thing your father didn't come said my mother. We all got cokes and went back to the motel. Our motel had postcards free at the front desk. It was called the Mar-Jon and it had a pool. Too bad the sun never came out.

Ted, my mother screamed. He was down on the floor. His legs were kicking a little bit and there was some spit forming around his lips. He was just lying there on the tile floor between the kitchen and the room you sat in. What did we do? I can't remember. He was just there. It was like the biggest thing I ever saw. It was like the world stopped. He had on this plaid cotton shirt, black and white with maybe some red. It looked pink. He had the sleeves rolled up, to mid-forearm. He had his watch on. And then it stopped. He sat up. What happened. Ted, you were out like a light. I think we went home early on our trip.

One Christmas, I don't know when, we went over to Aunt Anne's. She had a tiny house and her sons, my cousins Brian and Gerald had tiny rooms. She was on the first floor of a three-family house. They had even less of a backyard than we did. It was cement. You could rollerskate on it. And everywhere you looked there was another house. The fences between them were more like bars. Rusty metal ballet bars you could put your leg up on. My cousin Brian was an athlete. His room had catcher's mitts. There were pictures of baseball players on the wall. Gerald was a deejay, liked electronics, was mean. He saved things. There was a big jar of pennies on his bureau. There were bottles of booze. There were millions of comic books to read which was lucky. Everytime we ate at Aunt Anne's we had to wait for hours to eat while the adults laughed and drank. Ted had a beer my mother said proudly when she meant he'd been good. Gerald was crazy about Elvis Presley. The sad part was he wanted the adults to think Elvis was good. It was weird. So everytime we listened to a Johnny

Mathis or a Bing or a Mario Lanza, then Elvis had to come on and show that he could do that too, whatever it was. My father had brought a Danny Kaye record to the party. It was a Christmas Party. I guess he wanted to entertain. To tell you the truth I bet he wanted to do a Danny Kaye imitation. He knew the record by heart. Everytime they changed the record my father would start, Hey Gerald, I—Okay Uncle Ted Gerald would go like a wise-guy, but just let me play Aunt Genny a song I know she will like. This went on many times and then my father vanished. There weren't many places to go in that tiny house. Where's Ted, Aunt Genny finally said. That was my mother. In the bathroom Gerald said putting down another platter. She got up. She knocked on the door. Ted? He sheepishly slipped out of the bathroom. You okay she said. Fine, Mum, he said. Uh-oh. He tried his record one more time and Gerald ignored him. It was so stupid. He had been gone. It meant something. He got up. Suddenly he was roaring drunk. He was white. He was red. He smashed the hard little 78 on the corner of the hi-fi. Don't play the Goddamn record, see if I care. He was screaming and he was crying. It was like the inside of our house was at Aunt Anne's house. Everybody wanted to throw up. Too huge, too big.

The worst part was after dinner. Gerald vanished and then he put my father's record on. He had glued it. It went Cara mia, up. Cara mia, up. Stop it Gerald said my Aunt Anne. It was making everybody sick.

We found bottles all over the house after my father died. In the toilet tank, in our comic book box. He used to come home from church on Sunday and my mother would make him open his coat. She'd find all these little nips and hide them. She said she started to forget whose bottles she was finding. We always thought it was because we had been born. It was our fault. There's a picture of me and Terry in those Pilgrim stocks—you know, heads and wrists poking through holes. It was some day we went to Plymouth or Salem. My father's standing behind us. We're laughing, he looks worse, a prisoner. All the pictures look like that after a point. Me and Terry goofing around in front of an old car, my father in the square of the driver's seat, looking sad, looking trapped.

I think he was gay, said my brother. Was he? Certainly not says my mother. He liked sex, she insisted. He was oversexed. There was a letter she received after his death from a woman who was on his route. Such a wonderful man, she expressed. Now, why would you do that, asked my mother. I think there was something going on there. Once my father wrote a story. He wanted to write my mother said as if that was the problem. He always read books on the nights he was good. Big fat historical novels. It was part of the writer pose: dark-haired man in a soft chair with pipe in his mouth, reading a book. He wrote this story and she sat him down. Your father wants to read you his story. She stood behind him, wanting us to be serious. His story was terrible. And naturally he was drunk.

21, 22, 23 . . .

Something happened this morning. The sweetest little baby cat came meowing at my window and woke me up to the soft shades of about 9:30 A.M. rather than vampirish 5 o'clock that I've been getting used to waking up to which is why I've got this purplish night eye hanging on my head right now—running out around, drunk, late at night like it was the middle of the day since I'm so sad and there's nothing to get up for. I got up and took a slug of milk myself since I wasn't going to feed the baby but had started talking madly to her like I always have. I know the second your feet hit the pavement of this city I'll try to stop smoking or something silly like that, representing youth representing change and I'll start telling stories like the oldest woman ever born. Remember how I turned you on to soft-boiled eggs? It was one of my rituals that made you feel so safe—it was the oldest egg timer in the world, yellowed from cooking and time, from the 30s or the 40s, older than even me and you smashed it in a fit of rage once when you were breaking everything in sight since I had done something outrageous, I'll tell you about that later, but we'd get up in the morning and scramble around for change and go out to the bread store (I'd get you to go out in the morning and you'd go to a different store, the rolls were different) and get a couple of rolls and I'd time the eggs scientifically with my timer and that's how and when I turned you on to them and we'd drink gallons of that strong coffee and start smoking millions of cigarettes immediately and start talking and talking which was freedom in this soft morning light though it was winter then and the light was harsher. And you looked like the greediest 21-year-old cat, your eyes all lit up and horny for everything which turned me into the oldest woman in the world, talking and talking really hitting my stride at about the third cup of coffee. You always said I turned you on to breakfast but it was talking in the morning or anytime that it was all about. I've always had a friend, all my best friends were of this sort who were one slice more adventurous than me and they said, "Let's . . ." and I'd go, "Sure, I'll do that." Always being the coward or not an initiator but always ready to go on an adventurous ride. I could've been 8 years old and I'd do the same thing. Once we were on our way and we were secretly thinking Oh no we're really doing this, or what if . . . that's when my old part would come on and I'd talk about fucking anything, how I liked my eggs, some halloween in 1955 when my father dressed up like a witch or look how that cat turned its head in the sunlight. We'd be walking down the train tracks, we'd be eating the stolen candy behind the store but I knew that just because I couldn't say let's do it, but you could, my job was to make it cool and start spiralling away from the situation distracting us from where we've been, going on to another place like what I'm doing this morning, done with myself this morning because a cat just woke me up and she wanted to come in. I've always thought the tender trap was not a cunt but a comfortable place where all the stories in the world live. I think I was born in a mental asylum to have known this—that time is so short or so long that exchanging cigarettes, listening to the birds, watching the light you must talk and talk so you won't be scared by the length or the shortness of it or even its ferocious speed. You caught me at an odd time, full of rituals. You thought the Shaklee one was so alcoholic, quarts of milk and this powdered stuff so I'd never starve—a weird powdery glass of this chocolatey stuff and then the coffee and then the talk. I insisted that you drink it because it was protein and it was healthy and we talked for hours before you went out and got the job. I loved the way you looked sitting in the brown chair gleaming like you had sat there all your life sitting in my life and I couldn't stop talking I was so happy just to have you sitting there. You always had that crazy look in your eye—at night about 4 or more beers along—it was like something clicked and hell was going to break loose now and you were going to have an idea which I've never had. I think the world is made up of people like you and me. You're more like the hero and I'm the one who'll walk us through. Danger comes to me but some people are born full of it. That's what that cat reminded me of this morning when I wouldn't let her in. Heroes must be tamed or something—I've seen several walk in here and look around like they could stay for a while. Hmmm, this is nice, you got something to eat—tell me something.

Though it's good to be waking up inside of my own life for

a change, at least I'm alive and waiting for my hero to come instead of sleeping through the knock or the moving shadow to come along. It's so easy to give up—to live in dreams with yourself instead of in stories with a friend. I distrust dreams. It's just your brain re-stirring information uselessly, fending for itself in another dimension, making movies of its own fears and you wake up horrified or calmed by something that never happened or dissatisfied and you go back down for more which is all you get. Dreaming is like getting drunk alone, the less you live the more you dream, the more fantastic and outrageous the dreams get. I bet that's all that dead people do, dream endlessly, and dreams are death in training. It would be different say when you wake up terrified and there's someone there and you tell them the bad one. Dreams in movies and dreams in books are cheats—either made up ones where the writer is too cowardly to tell the story she means or else she has had this dream and thinks it is important to tell everyone about it when really the only person who really cares is one lying next to you in bed.

I probably sound like the oldest woman in the world by now. I'm not, I'm only 32 but for once in a very stupid dreaming while have woke up in the morning and have all these new thoughts and no one to tell them to and was just remembering when you were around. I've developed the habit of living alone and I think a habit is particularly comforting to others, especially those who haven't had the time to develop habits. A woman stayed here last spring for a while and she liked everything, the lights the sheets strong coffee in bed, my cigarettes in my mouth before I had even begun to breathe. She wanted to hang out all day she didn't want anything to stop but I was very wary because she reminded me of the other one and how I let her in and she changed everything so she could have habits too and when she left I was entirely alone. She was even the same age as the other one and I was 4 years older by now so I thought well maybe there's only one age for me. She said you know it's funny you talk like you're a musician you know you don't stop talking which is what she was and I noticed she didn't stop talking either and I didn't think but really felt I was in for it this time. Do they think of me as an older woman? They must, but I am only 32. Even last weekend there was another one. We did it at night she was lying on my couch and thought it was great that you could stay in on Saturday night and just lie around talking. She brought me the Sunday *New York Times* which made me wonder whether she thought I was a family or I needed a job. She was also 21. I didn't explain that I always go out and generally only talk like this in the morning but I had done a lot of drugs for the past three days which is another one of my habits which I do when I can't get my habits together when I can't stand being alone so I take a lot of drugs and talk to myself viciously, getting things done. She was this new type of 21-year-old, the last one was too, the optimistic kind so you don't brag about the drugs you've done or how many people you've slept with or the sad parts of your life. You talk about what you believe about life and the things you're planning to do, and you really do them. It's kind of abstract for me, but refreshing. I've always liked 21 for some reason. They still like to spend a lot of time talking which is where I'm at. I don't even have coffee today I'm so broke and I've got this black eye so I think maybe I'll call my friend and ask him to bring some. We can talk about my black eye for starters. He's only a friend and won't plan to stay.

QUIETUDE

There was a summer after I graduated from college during which I waitressed so much that I couldn't do anything else, it always looked like it would interfere with the likelihood or the quality of my next shift. I worked in the Pewter Pot in Harvard Square. This was in 1971. I suppose the high point of the summer was the morning Daniel Ellsberg came in; lemon tea, blueberry muffin. I had a tiny affair with the cook. One of the other waitresses was his girlfriend, so our "affair" was just for one night. Let me put that incident off until later, it's really not the point of this story, it's the quality of the time I'm getting at. It's intense, packed and tightly controlled waves. An emotional density resembling childhood. Today I cannot participate. If there is something I will always carry in my heart it is this earnest unwillingness to be part of the bunch, the whole horrible let's do it generation to which I belonged. A catholic hand was raised to life.

I suppose it resembled purpose, this unwillingness. Not an immediate purpose, but one that slowly evolved, would become known and recognized. Despite the fact that the world was made of something going fast I knew that I was something slow.

One night I went to the Casablanca with my friends and had a beer, a Heinecken. I had one and decided to go home. You see I was saving my money to go to Europe. Though fall came and there was a month, one month in my life when I knew I was doing something different, something wrong something new. Harvard Square was filled with legions of college students going back, the leaves were crinkling and shaking, the air was getting cold. Traffic was thicker in the impossible square, but I was someplace different, no longer a student and I was going very very slow. Europe would never be as slow as the month of September was in Boston. I felt invisible in the morning looking out the windows of the Pewter Pot, no longer angry at the rich and privileged kids from all over America who came to Cambridge to go to school. It was as if I were going to die, going to Europe. I constantly thought about being an American. Surrounded by something totally other. Already I felt strange and separate by my difference, like a clog in the traffic of the days I was watching pass in the street. There was some celebratory feeling about getting out of college that I would miss all my life. Or think about missing. I watched other people graduate in the style of Dustin Hoffman and be confused about how to grow up. I had decided to go away slow. Europe probably wouldn't do it. And I was right. Europe was old. So old that nothing mattered at all. Nothing could happen. For a long time I would be living under water and would be unable to come up. Until I could breathe.

Incredible things happened in Harvard Square over the years. It was shaped like a circle. You would walk really slow. I knew a girl who used to work in the same store as I did in high school. Sally, she was very sexy and very smart. She was known as a slut, but I liked her and we used to laugh a lot. Then I heard she had a girlfriend in New York. I got this kind of filthy feeling I used to fight all the time. Generally I got it alone in bed at night or once as Kim Novak died at the end of *Of Human Bondage*. I associated this feeling with ruin, later as pleasure.

One day soon after I had learned about the woman in New York I was rounding Brattle St. and reflected in the window of Brine's was Sally, then in Bailey's window, then Reading International, Cardell's, Billings & Stover—Sally's face followed me like a crime and I could not turn to greet her which would be tantamount to embracing the crime, I ceased to know her, whose face had broken into panels which became the slow sickening merry-go-round of Harvard Square.

If I didn't participate at all I wouldn't get stuck, if I didn't let anyone know I was alive. In my room as a child, a room I was now living in for the last time, I would spend hours gazing at the peace of my bookcase, all the books I had read and the pit of my stomach would drop in the midst of the peace. Spatters of black ink grazed the bindings of several volumes, *Tales from Greece and Rome,* to name one and then at the foot of the book case a nearly scrubbed-away patch of black india ink forever marked the hardwood floors. But now I could gaze at that marred perfection, those completed books and that summer I would just go to bed, get up like the very rhythm itself would propel me into a future where I would be allowed to live.

The cook didn't eat, that was one thing about him. He ate cottage cheese and catsup, he wore big baggy pants, rimless glasses, long hair in a pony tail. His name was John, he was from New York, came from a rich family, his father was a judge. But he got his high school girlfriend pregnant and he had to leave town—he wanted to marry her but they wouldn't let him.

John was an alcoholic. All he did was drink, I heard, and read comic books. So I went to his and the waitress's funky Cambridge apartment one night—it was a crack in my scheme, some other woman invited me, I forget her name she was maybe five years older than us and the younger you are the greater meaning small differences in age possess. So her invitation was less threatening than say John or his girlfriend asking me over so I walked in with a brown bag full of beers and John yelled what are you doing here. He sounded mad, he looked happy. His girlfriend was friendly, I got the picture that she was a nice girl—at work I had only gathered that she was a hip girl, blonde hair and then lived with John, had quit school, didn't come from here.

Their crummy Cambridge apartment didn't fascinate me, it depressed me. Everything described as Bohemia is just someplace you fall. I neither understood having a nice apartment with a good shower and a loud cotton couch and a fluffy rug or a dump filled with old shit like this place. It was only more likely if you didn't know what to do with your life. But I just couldn't see how they could take the risk. I assumed that most of the kids who dropped out of college were rich. I never wanted to know what was out there. I felt pushed out of college like being pushed out of my mother's body had trapped me in life.

John and his girlfriend were having a fight. She was in the bedroom, he kept going in and coming out. She's got her period he said at some point. Then John and I went out and got more beer. I really didn't want more but I just felt carried by the experience. This is exactly why I always clipped things off early. I was down by the Charles with John making out and then he told me that I was fat. I felt a little fat. He was right. He was unique in that when I came to work the next day he was friendly and I think he may even have wanted to go get drunk with me again. She's not my girlfriend he said of the woman who stayed in the bedroom most of the night. Once when he was loudly pissing in the bathroom she came out. John's being a jerk, I don't know, I guess I'm in a bad mood she had explained.

Actually I enjoyed the experience in that it helped me close off the possibility of being open that summer more completely. I had to work. I always had to work. That's all I can remember. But more than a worker I was a prisoner. I was a prisoner in high school too. I didn't know why I should want to go to a hockey game but I couldn't anyhow. I was ringing up cigarettes at the tobacco counter at the Harvard Coop on Saturdays. I was eating candy and I was getting fat. I was stealing twenties from my register and buying records across the street in the annex of the store. I bought the Doors album. I would lie on the couch in my mother's house and dream about getting on the Crystal Ship and going away.

ROBERT MAPPLETHORPE PICTURE

Fear of not being understood is the greatest fear I thought
lying on the bathroom floor at 11 p.m. Worse than not pleasing
people, worse than anything else I can think of. Worse than
being cold or alone. Worse than getting old. There used to be a
club called the 80s I announced walking back into the kitchen.
Did you know that. Right in the beginning of the 80s when
that was a new thing. I went there one night with Ybette. We
saw a band, Walter was in it, that guy we had been shooting
dope with, the night I OD'd, I was thirty. Right there with
the decade. Ybette's breasts were so lovely and large, her sheets
smelled sweet, I loved sleeping with her but Ybette was cruel.
She would taunt me for not knowing how to make love to her,
though she had pursued me right up to the point of the bed
and then I was supposed to perform as the dyke though by all
evidence I was undeniably femme. At least with Ybette. But I
loved holding her, lying on her couch when we were high. She
listened to classical music and the stones some girls. Doo doo
doo doo doo-doo, oh I miss you girl. At the 80s we took speed
did quaaludes when we got home. Having failed her again in
bed I had to get up at 10 to go to Bond Street so I could have

my picture taken by Robert Mapplethorpe. Things like this made me welcome in her bed. But I woke up at quarter of 11. I called and according to Robert Mapplethorpe it was fine. No problem he said. See you at noon. He showed me pictures of Lisa Lyons, incredibly worked out. I looked at pictures of black men, gorgeous men, a penis lying like a turd on a stool. Lisa's fingers lifted, one from each hand—the feminine way to thrust your muscles out. She was big. We smoked a joint, I drank a ginger ale, said no to beer. I guess we talked about John Giorno who had set this thing up. I said I was a poet. You got a band he said. No. How come he asked. I just write poems. He didn't get it. I felt like I was being lazy. It wasn't true. I worked hard. You don't know how hard it is to be a lesbian. I think at the time I worked at a hospital taping electrodes to people's jaws and heads so we could watch their dreams. Ybette got me that job, and then she would give me speed so I could stay up and then she mocked me all night because I was a clod. I came to work all nervous with my hair wet in a pink shirt. Thank god I was sexy. I couldn't work with my head. I was always too confused. Robert Mapplethorpe was cute. The kind of boy I really like, slightly evil-looking with black curly hair. Motown music played all along. That was how you could tell he was a fag. I mean the shots of the black men could've been about the time which was still loaded with speed and minimalism. Everything was a good idea. A girl with big muscles. We'll try it. Turn your head. Look at me. Look away. Turn your chin. Slightly. Good. Front. Look down. Great. That's it. I'll have prints in about a week. Call me if you want one.

I came back—sorry, "we" did, with Christine, my "real"

girlfriend. It was a nightmare, life with her. Finally I had forced her to move out in May but I let her come back in June because I felt sorry for her plus I was broke. Then I met Ybette. At the time I was housesitting for Pat, the art writer who was always trying to make me respectable. Write about art, that's what poets do he said. Him and his wife would always have me over for drinks. He'd look at his watch, "Company's coming!" He'd look at me. Time to toddle off. If I was an art writer I probably could stay. So Chris was staying in my shack on Third Street. Ybette and me slept in Pat's palatial mansion on St. Mark's Place with framed droppings on the wall from DeKooning's plate. I had not improved in bed, always passed out, but now thanks to Pat, again Ybette was impressed. Chris came to the door one night begging for booze. I passed a bottle of wine out the door—now you promised you'd leave me alone. Who is it Ybette yelled. Just the landlady I smiled climbing back into bed to smell her great smell. A pussy too sweet.

Christine went with me to Robert Mapplethorpe's and like I said she was either a monster or an insane lamb. She was wearing a peach colored V-neck sweater in the middle of the summer. I don't know what she looked like. Robert was coming down the street with Lisa Lyons and we went up and smoked a joint. He showed me this fabulous picture of me. I looked like a statue—all glowing stone. My eyes look cruel and suspicious. I thanked him for his rendition. I wanted to apologize for bringing Chris—I felt I had blown my opportunity to be whipped and fucked by famous people. I don't know, the occasion was all wrong. I walked home with this woman who was ruining my life, had been doing so for a while.

I come from Boston. My mother has a wall in her home
that was reserved for nephews, nieces, grandchildren happy
cookouts aunt and uncles, my brother my sister, my step-
father, everyone but me. Things didn't last long with Ybette.
For example one night I had money so we weren't in the usual
situation of her taking me out, paying for my drinks and telling me I was a drunk. She buying the late night pastrami
sandwich, paying for the cab, the quaaludes, the coke everything. But me having money, that was much worse. And I
wasn't good at it. Actually I was cheap. We approached some
club. Manhattan, a woman's bar and there was a big line so I
told the woman at the door I was a reporter for some paper,
maybe the *East Village Eye* that I thought I could be writing for. I was writing an article about women's bars in New
York. Nice the tough woman at the door said, returning to a
conversation with a friend. You want to wait I asked Ybette.
She nodded no. Walking through Washington Square Park
I was crying. I don't know why. She said I was sensitive, and
so was my girlfriend and we were both too crazy for her. We
were at some party and some woman was flirting with me so
I stole her hat and we left and finally I was leaving Ybette's
wearing the hat, drinking a beer walking down 9th Avenue
crying and I never saw her again. And that's in ten years. It's
nearly the nineties—

I thought of my mother's portrait wall. I had showed
Ybette the picture that Robert Mapplethorpe had taken of
me. That's why I had a crush on you she said. That's who you
looked like to me. But you're not like that. My mother had
this wall in Boston. I went home at the end of that summer,

1980. I said Mom, a famous photographer took this picture of me why don't you put it on the wall. I don't know if I have a frame to fit it she said, nervous. Momma you can get one at Woolworth's. Well I suppose you're right. She sighed. Put it on the teevee for now. I did. And before I left I wrote on the back in pencil "photo taken by Robert Mapplethorpe NYC 8/80." This was my favorite kind of art, a dirty secret. my mother had no idea who Robert Mapplethorpe, Patti Smith's boyfriend was and no one who ever walked into our house would know either. Years from now someone would find the picture of me among the effects of my family and think what a perverse and egoless writer I was to leave such an important documentation of my existence in a humble house in Arlington, Mass. There would be such a future because something would happen to me. Soon. I was sure of that.

In 1988 I drove to Manchester, Mass. with my girlfriend Sara to meet my mother and my sister and spend a weekend with them. I was determined to find a way to get into her house in Arlington and get that Robert Mapplethorpe picture off the wall fast. I needed it. Mom, we were thinking we were going to pass through Boston so since we've got Sara's car I was thinking it would be a good opportunity for me to take that trunk of my stuff that you're always trying to get me—

"No way." My mother has a way of being emphatic. Of being inhuman and cold. "Uh-uh, I don't want you in my house when I'm not there. Who will the neighbors think you are—when they see *New York* plates. They don't know who you are. Sorry."

Later I brought this up with my sister who lived in Cambridge. She was studying massage so Sara and I were letting her practice on our bodies. "Of course she wouldn't let you in her house when she's not there. She doesn't trust *you*."

My therapist was really great and acknowledged that my family treats me cruelly. That's probably the reason I got involved with women like Ybette and later Robin. Luckily Sara is not like that at all. Well there was one little thing she said about me at the table but mostly she's not like that.

Go take it, my mother said the next time I came home and then she got up and she took it herself right off the wall. Get yourself a frame, ooh she sighed as she slid the ruthless portrait of me out of the cheap black frame and underneath my stepbrother and wife and five kids were sitting on their front porch. It was like discovering a Rembrandt under an old Norman Rockwell clipped out of the *Post,* something junky like that. Wonderful she said replacing icy me with an entire warm family. I haven't seen that one for quite a while. She sat back down to look at it, smiling.

Sara says I do look quite a bit younger and points out that my nose was not yet broken and is smaller. Your eyes are glassy. You can tell you were fucked up. I was I said. I was really fucked up. I was even late—she gives me that look: "You've told me before."

Tom says I look much better now. But he always looks at the soul.

I could put it in the bathroom. That would be kind of cool. While you're shitting here's a picture of me ten years ago. Robert Mapplethorpe took it. The hair's a mess, did you cut your own hair. Of course. Didn't everyone. Well, all my friend got really good haircuts then. I didn't know you went there. I used to go to the 80s all the time. It wasn't open long.

Paul says he had the same problem. And him and Robert were very close. File it away he says, getting up to go. That's all you can do. It's been great seeing you dear.

I tell people how cool he was when he took my picture. How cute he was and how comfortable he made me feel. Oh that must've been before Robert went bad. PCP. Coke. Yep. That was the end of that Robert. He was great.

It's true. My eyes are glassy. Shallow. My hair's dirty too. The jersey was green. Dark green. I had a tan. What kind of frame would make it okay for me to hang it. I could put a vase of white flowers next to it like it was a shrine to the past. You've got to come over and see it sometime. It's kind of scarey. I don't understand who she was at all. But that's all right. It's the past.

LESLIE

I stood in her little kitchen in San Francisco, much bigger than mine or even yours. I stood:

"She lifted her arms like this." And it was triumphant. It was victory. The hands and arms lifted over her head like you know, the most incredible Olympic diver. She was like a statue in that moment. Lifted them. And dove.

Now this is the Hudson. Really cold. In January. I know, it's incredibly dirty. Full of disease. Little head bobbing. Calling my name. Help. Help. She woke up. It reminded me of a painting in my friend's house. Of a drowning man.

Oh before that. Everything. Down the street. Throwing herself into puddles. In front of a car. Guys pouring out of bars and she would tear into them pounding. I was trying to restrain her. Once or twice in a storefront I had her arms pinned but she kept turning on me. And then she broke and ran down to the river.

It was so beautiful and I couldn't jump in. She could swim. I couldn't. It was separation. I would drown.

Leslie. Leslie. Imagine it. Your name calling you to your death. I didn't go. One of those little houses. You know like on construction sites. The kind of house you would dream of living in when you were a kid. Little light. Guy gets paid to sit there all night. Well they came running. A couple of those guys.

I was still standing up explaining in Leslie's kitchen. No by now I was sitting down. At the table. She was across from me. It was a big kitchen. Much bigger than mine. About the size of yours. This is a late night conversation. So the world was as big as the night. Two speakers.

One lowers the other one down. He puts his hands over the water and she grabs on. It all seemed like it was supposed to happen so it wasn't a shock. A little house got placed in the head of your childhood so two men could save a little shrimp. That's what she looked like. Once they pulled her up she curled up. There was a black cotton blazer involved but it didn't get wet. She took it off neat and hung it on a wooden piling. One of those poles. Then she dove. It was performance. Absolutely. That's what this was all about.

Lying there in a simple sweater and boots, work boots. Some dark-colored jeans. Very dark when wet and under the sky of January night about 2 A.M.

That night was filling this night. Leslie's house was bright.

Take me to the hospital. Lock me up put me away. Please. Please. Do you have a phone I asked the guys. Sure. The little house had a phone. So where should I bring her? St. Vincent's he said. I'll meet you there. Sitting in the lobby chairs smoking with him. This is incredible, Leslie. He had a very nasal voice. He said my name. Old friend. We used to ride his bike on Staten Island. Years ago. It's a very cool place. Weird. This is probably the best for her, he said. And it's true. It's like salvation.

I get this phone call in about a week. I have this black jacket a man's voice says. You go get it she asks me. I can't do that. I felt like she should, you know? It was my jacket so I had it back.

So I started drinking an incredible amount. Martinis. Leslie I can't stop. Now you've asked the big question. It's like sitting in heaven after I died. Did I?

She came over to my apartment one afternoon in the spring. Did you ever feel like spring is this sap, this slow-moving stuff. I was so depressed. Almost summer. Her eyes came in first when she entered my home. My place is little. I love your apartment, Leslie. It's great that you've got so much space. She had moved in with someone else but she wasn't happy. We went down the street and we got a slice of pizza. Something. Something.

On eighth street the one that faces the street. So you sit there with your triangle wagging in your mouth. I was just sort of counting things and fitting the cars in with the sidewalks and how people dressed and whether they're old men or young girls. I could make this moment be enough if I slowed down everything, but I couldn't work that on her.

And I couldn't keep her out. I mean she was in my life. She had moved out, but she was in there. If we never drink together again I think I'll be safe. It wasn't true. I was never safe from her. I think she wanted to kill me.

"Fuck this. I'm getting a beer."

I followed her to seventh street. Always following disasters.

Even when I was a kid. Long stories, believe me. Several steps behind damage. When a mother says keep your eyes on them and she goes on dumping potatoes in the water she probably doesn't know you will go on watching them for the rest of your life. As if you could make anything stop.

There were some concrete steps to the Polish bar, a metal railing that was warm, not cold in the late afternoon. I was murmuring something deep down inside like prayers. I just happened to know that I hadn't had a drink in a number of days which was running through my head as we walked into the old bar. We sat in a booth. Do you want one.

Time staggered. Something different. Green bottle on a wooden table. It was as if I were an eagle on a cliff looking over a valley and a little green teeny lake was way down there. I with my sharp eye could see it. Even as I dove with my mouth to the lip of it, a bottle of beer I kind of thought maybe I wasn't really there and I wasn't, time was slow. For me this was alcoholism.

Leslie you are a doctor. You have just asked a question and a world revolves around it. Why did you stop drinking. Well there were beautiful moments. Her dive into the cold. My mouth lunging down towards the simple nipple of the beer so that everything on either side of first ave could get big and I could be good again, young and looking slowly at the world as it was. Not judging so much.

Leslie I want to tell you this story. My freedom is this. Winding along on either side of first avenue with booze and my girl who I was born to drink with, not seven steps behind disaster but with it. Its friend.

She was full of complaint. I was now the happiest woman in the world and rued those recent days of terrible dryness and confusion. Life mellowed. The dark walls of the Park View Inn were like the sweet thick amber ale that flowed down my throat. I hate this jukebox you clattered with your mug on the plastic table. Everything was good.

Another place had old birdy men. Didn't their faces look kind of distorted and incredibly old. I was prepared to look at damage now. They were fish in this fluid of darkness and artificial light and we were nibbling on a fruit that sustained us and we were away from life. Such secret rooms. You wailed.

Leslie, have you ever been in love. The hands of something huge like an animal lick your face and hands. This is mine. Sport that straddles all natures and awaits me like a pool, we dampen our pages we dip our books in it. We tell it our stories. Booze is like death, but slower now. Death is our friend. It wants me alone. Even as I sit with the human race in church. Everyone can sit with me now when death holds my hand.

"I have really fucked up." She felt ashamed of breaking some promise that she made, but I have never had a bad drunk and didn't understand. I had my death back and I was amused by everything except her discomfort but I didn't care. Unfortunately we were drinking on her money.

I picked out a brown quart of beer from the freezer, and a bottle of Guinness to mix. I pulled out my bed, a brown couch. She lay there complaining next to me. Oh shut up. You're going to finish it aren't you? You know you don't have to she screamed. Oh shut up. I put my bottle away. I knew I had a friend.

My home is kind of dirty. Alcohol casts a kindly light on poverty and the wealth of slaughtered words falling into my notebook. Lay around in the morning drinking coffee celebrating the return of comic dissolution. Oh fuck forget everything fix nothing. I am invisible.

Leslie something happened a little later on. My place is pretty small. I felt dread. It's the opposite of religion. Sex without the trembling, it's just dirty, something fierce keeps coming closer, you can almost smell it and it's the monster of your childhood the thing you dreamt about. Turning a little too fast all of a sudden. Someone behind me kept laughing. I felt very very wrong. I was in trouble. What could I do. Thoughts came fast.

The phone rang. It was her. Where are you. I'm in a bar. She kind of giggled. I'm drinking a Heinecken. This can't be true. This is the person who was so sorry she drank last night. What happened to her. Where are you? I'm—

It got cut off. "That's amazing," said Leslie.

It's true. A giant red phone on the floor. I'm looking at it. I can hang around and it will ring again. Or I can get out of here. I can do that. Just go.

I did. And I never drank again. By now I was standing in the middle of the floor. I had to do that to put myself in relation to the phone and the exit which I pretended was right there, but it just leads to Leslie's pantry.

"That's an incredible story," she said. Yeah, I know, I said. That's why I don't drink anymore. Her kitchen was so bright.

I felt . . . just kind of hollow. She looked at her watch. "Well, it's three. I've got to go to work tomorrow." She took a different exit, down into the dark hall. Thanks for listening, Leslie, I yelled. "Thank *you*," she said from the bathroom. "Help yourself if you want some tea or something." I was sitting alone in that big kitchen. No. I'm fine.

EPILOGUE

I threw myself down on the orange chair. My play was complete. It was a Saturday in March. My desk across the room was loaded with red and green and yellow candles. A method of inspiration not unlike Schiller's rotting apples or anyone else's cigarettes. On the chair I was calculating how much I really needed to live on. Amazingly I figured even $250 a week would get me through. I have pretty small bills. *The phone rang.* Miss Myles? Is this Miss Myles? Miss Eileen Myles. Miss Myles, I'm a photographer, my name is Jack Ross. I was given your name by a young lady who does some modeling for me. She seemed to think you'd be looking for work, that you might need some money. No, I am not at liberty to reveal the young lady's name. You must understand she does not want her friends to know she is doing this kind of work—she was simply interested in doing her friend a favor. She thought you might be needing some money, Miss Myles. If I haven't made myself clear Miss Myles, let me be more direct. These are photographs of a sexual nature. Does this sound like something you might be interested in. Because I don't want to go on. I don't want to waste my time or *yours*, Miss Myles. You *do* want to hear.

Good. Good. Now, let me tell you a little bit about what I do. Remember, you can just tell me to stop if it begins to sound like something you don't want to hear. What I'm offering you Miss Myles is an opportunity to make big bucks. And the further you are willing to go, the more you make. Do you understand, Miss Myles. Good, good. The first thing we do, the simplest and the most basic is the nude posed photo. This is the kind of thing that would be sold in Men's bookstores—let me ask you Miss Myles—how tall are you? And how much do you weigh? Well, okay. I'm asking you these questions because I don't know if I'm going to be able to use you, Miss Myles. We're both taking a chance here, a risk. You might wind up coming in one day and I'll find I can't use you. You might not be right. There are no guarantees here, your friend said you might be needing a little bit of money. Now let me ask you right now, have you ever done this kind of work. Okay, so you *are* used to having your clothes off in front of people. This is not art, I am making myself clear. These are photographs of a sexual nature. Now, like I said, the basic nude photo is the lowest paying thing we do. If you're willing to go further, the rewards are greater. We also do film work. Are you interested in film work Miss Myles. You are. Good, good, very good. Again, no guarantees. You might come into the studio and we'll both feel this is not working. Now, let me ask you a question Miss Myles. Before we talk about film work which is more lucrative than the nude posing—I want to ask you about any hesitations or doubts you might be experiencing. If you have any doubts— let me ask you this . . . are they because you don't want your friends to see, or because your head can't handle it. You don't want your friends to see. Because we can do things about that. One of the film things we do is something called a loop. We might be interested in doing a dominance loop. Sado masochism Miss Myles, are you into it? Do you have any curiosity in this area. It's very popular and you can make big bucks here. Very lucrative if you like this kind of thing. If your concern is you don't want your friends to see, then we can put you in a fall, Miss Myles, or we can use some very heavy makeup, or we can shoot you mostly from behind, that's also a possibility. You'd be working with a man and a whip. Maybe high heels, there'd be a costume. You think your head could handle it, Miss Myles. You sound like you have some hesitation. Can you explain that hesitation to me Miss Myles. Do you or do you not need the money. It sounds like something you might have done when you were younger—just for kicks, am I getting you right, Miss Myles. This is very different. This is not art, like I said, and this is not for fun. This is business and I am offering you an opportunity to make *a lot of money*. That is the only reason for doing this. Do you need money or don't you Miss Myles. You don't know. Are you waiting for something or can you tell me what kind of situation you find yourself in. Well, when will you know? A month. I can. I can give you a month Miss Myles. That's what you want. Are you sure. I can give you more time or less time. Let me recap your situation so we know we're both talking about the same thing. You're interested, you do think your head can handle it, but you don't know if you need the money, Miss Myles, and you will know in a month. I look forward to speaking with you again. And I beg you to think it over very carefully, this is not a joke.

JEALOUSY

I had heard about a women's SM bar down by the river. It was someplace that was for men most nights and for women just one. Being really anxious not to miss it I managed to organize a bunch of my friends into going. Christine came of course. Even Lucy who wasn't gay showed up. She brought her friend Tina who was "sort of a lesbian," Lucy said. I think I had to go home early and work that night. It was just an exciting thing I had to at least touch, to verify its existence in the world. We got there and it really stunk. We heard it had been good last week. There was a video playing of men giving each other blow jobs. They weren't taking our presence very seriously at all. The air was thick with the smell of tobacco, beer and semen. There were a couple of slings up, and a whipping post. A really stupid looking woman sat up on the bar against a brick column with a black leather outfit covered with studs. It was so depressing. I guess I wanted to see women swinging from the ceiling with their fists up each other's cunts and strips of flesh on the floor. I figured if I really liked it I could come back alone.

Instead, it was dark, cavernous and empty. On the door

was a plastic ass. The place's man name was ASS-TRICKS and tonight it was called MS. ASS-TRICKS.

Do you play soccer, Tina asks. She was watered-down cute-looking, maybe a little old and alcoholic-looking. I felt complimented, naturally, since it meant I didn't look a wreck. 32 was very much borderline year. I was either an older woman or an old woman. I was delighted I might look like a healthy kid.

Actually, it was a set-up. Lucy wanted Tina and I to get together because she was appalled at both of our situations. Ever since Chris has been back in town, a week or two now, she had tried to make every single one of our friends. I assured them that it was okay, that our living situation was a temporary one, but still they all politely shot her down. She was usually pretty drunk, plus everyone except maybe me knew I was still obsessed with her.

Tina was having an affair with this tall woman, Rebecca, who lived with a man. We don't know how much there is of this in the world. At one point he found out, about five years ago I guess, and everyone was upset and then after a few months Tina and the tall woman resumed their affair except now they "weren't" having one. Often Tina, the tall woman and the guy would get drunk together on weekends like nice well-mannered New York intellectuals. He doesn't know, Tina would insist to Lucy.

So after a couple of drinks I left MS. ASS-TRICKS. I had to go home and proofread. I knew there was a pill and a couple of Heineckens at home. It turned out to be one of the worst nights of my life since I couldn't find the pill and I was sure it wound up on the floor so I spent a good amount of time between midnight and 6 A.M. crawling on my hands and knees around the refrigerator and under the bathtub and sink.

Lucy and Tina and Chris went to Lucy's apartment and Chris fell in love with Tina and tried to ask her out. I'm sure she was high on my pill. The report went that Tina did think Chris was cute but she was such a baby and seemed like she drank too much. Everybody says that about everybody else, the drinking part. I think Christine stayed over or something because I recall being alone all night. When she came home she announced she had a crush, I said alright, now I can go out with other people too. And also I know I won't have to share my money. You know, if we're independent like that.

Then I met Mane. She was kind of beautiful in a gross European way. You know, spoiled, and a little too well-fed. And demanding. She looked like a very couth version of my friend Susan from Maine which is how we all wound up there a couple of summers ago. Well, Mane was into spoiling me. I picked her up and brought her home one night from the Bar on 4th Street. She bought me steaks and bloody marys. I couldn't believe my incredible luck to easily seduce this interesting woman until I got to know her better. Mane was crazy. She had a husband, and a mother-in-law who she was staying with on Washington Square South so she had very direct sex with me and got dressed and went home. It was the best of all worlds, I could be alone because Chris was off on her first date with Tina so I was laid, fed, and writing in my notebook by 2 A.M. The nights in my life that make me feel famous.

Mane had an incredible scar over her eye. I thought it made her nuts. She was always insinuating that there was a lot of intrigue in her life, she was a smuggler or something. I don't know, maybe it was a language problem. She was Angolan and had some incredible story about the revolution. The Africans running down the streets with guns and torches, holding their dead up on pallets. She was a little European girl looking out her window, fascinated and terrified. Once she went out on the street in the middle of it and her family were nearly out of their minds with panic.

Then she left. Mane left New York, I mean. That's when the drama arose. Chris had no urge to stop seeing Tina. One night when she was "making the money" I threw tomatoes all over the apartment because I had bought them to make a nice salad as I had been instructed during the day and now she was strutting out to make a phone call around dinner time. Thought maybe she'd have a drink, didn't feel much like dinner. I was drinking wine to calm down and taking more and more valium. I was maybe on the first day of not smoking, always a sign I was losing control of my life. Boom Boom Boom big tomatoes, oh yeah eggs too all over the ceiling and walls. No one's going to make a little wife out of me.

Next day I stopped drinking. Not really, it was just intended to corral Chris and stop her from seeing Tina. My new sweetness would draw her in. I don't know when the ploy, or the actual desire to see other women failed in me. I was hanging with Lucy, who wasn't even a lesbian.

Chris was going to do a performance, a kind of anti-performance art statement and it would happen at Prescott's where

Tina and Lucy worked and naturally I drank for free. Christine had a white lab coat and a great 12-inch single with all these jungle sounds shrieking and cooing from inside the leafy green. It was the background, she was the foreground with FUCK ME written in big letters on the back of her lab coat. She had a kind of pretty poem dedicated to Tina which she would read at some point in the anti-performance. It was all kind of charismatic and dream-like. I incredibly believed in her—but she was scared out of her mind which caused her to make ever more complicated plans. I couldn't understand why she didn't just do a poetry reading but I am a great fan of the complicated which was her.

There was a Friday, early January, where we had gone off to Queens to get the necessary blue pills from my diet doctor and with that fervor we gathered our materials, the record, and we taped it someplace and we were busy the entire day gathering and Christine kept saying she was so afraid of making an asshole of herself. No way, I insisted.

How was it we would up at Prescott's late that night. And all the major participants were present: Lucy, Tina, Chris, me, and even their boss who owned the bar. I think Christine was working there by now, during the day, picking up beer bottles and sweeping the floor. Ogling Tina I suppose. Why is it that people are always so withholding towards those who adore them meanwhile adoring someone else. Chris and Tina were "dating" but it was not a match made in heaven. It makes the world go round, this distracted energy. It makes it so I cannot sleep.

Chris went off right away. Tina leaned over to me and said

you know I've always had a crush on you. I didn't know at all how I felt toward her because I didn't know her. This is not just playing innocent. But I knew the devil when she spoke to me. I said I've always had a crush on *you*. Who cared? Hadn't Christine already taken her shirt off and splashed beer all over herself. Wasn't it already on its way to being a horrendous night? She would get fired by her boss who looked at this point *at least* embarrassed. What's happening to my girls?

Boom she was out the door. I guess I'm not needed here or you two can go fuck yourselves. She was out on the street running up towards Puffy's sporadically throwing herself into mud puddles and beating up men who seemed destined to turn around and kill her but they didn't. A car almost hit her and she would pummel me brutally when I attempted to control her, restrain her from wreaking havoc on the next cluster of men leaving Puffy's. I've always thought Tribeca was such a sick neighborhood. It's not a neighborhood, that's what's wrong with it.

Then she turned and ran like a deer. This I could handle. A good clear run. A run towards the river. It was the middle of January and it was an awful night. I don't think she had a jacket on. I never thought she'd do it. Here she goes. She got to the edge, the wooden ledge you look down at the Hudson from. She lifted her arms in a pure Isadora Duncan type pose and Zip dove right in. I ran to the edge right after her. I felt an urgent voice that seemed to come from my feet. If you jump in you won't get out. You can't swim. You'll drown. I can't swim, it's true. Help, Help Chris yelled. You could tell that the second she hit the water she realized it was not a good idea. Speed and booze is not a good combination. If someone asked me if that was what this was all about rather than human emotion, jealousy, I'd say yes, exactly that—just speed and booze. They tell their own tale. So does icy cold January water. So does self-preservation. I bet I'd be dead if I jumped. So what'll I do. Just down there, maybe a hundred feet away was one of those small cabins night watchmen hang out in on construction sites. Luckily there was one of those. What's going on he yelled running over. One guy lowered another. He got his friend and they pulled Christine up out of the water. At the risk of pissing her off for all time because we are friends again she looked like a shrimp curled up there on the wooden ledge, she looked like a fetus, a wet fetus crying. Take me to a hospital, I don't want to live she sobbed. I couldn't get over her energy. She wanted *something* for sure.

We—me and the two guys, or was it one now that I think of it, took her to St. Vincent's. It was so good to smoke cigarettes inside of the hospital. Just remembering it makes me want one now. I had called Richard who works in an emergency ward on Staten Island, he was our guide through the mysteries of how one puts one's friend inside. This did seem to be what Christine wanted. She seemed calm as soon as we got to the hospital and they started asking her questions. It was hard to leave her there. I'm okay she said.

The next day she called me. She asked me to call Tina and tell her she was there. She asked me if I would read the poem she had dedicated to Tina, if I would read it in her place at Prescott's on Sunday. I said I would. And I did, only I took the dedication off.

I wish I could remember how the days went. I feel like I'm looking through a window at my own past, and if I could just trace it with my fingertips or my breath on it I could see where I've been. I was requested to call Tina and tell her where Christine was. It turned into a meeting between me Tina and Lucy. We were in Lucy's little padded apartment where I had been so many times. It seemed padded against echoes and outside. It was a very Aquarian apartment, a love of history and androgyny prevailed. Usually high on speed I could see why I was her friend. Tina seemed like a little princess in Lucy's apartment. She was small and had curly hair and it seemed so utterly evil and obvious to sleep with her that night. Let me roll back this sleepy weekend. I did go and see Christine in the hospital one of those days, it must have been Saturday. I showed her the book I brought her—*Stop-Time* by Frank Conroy. She gasped.

She asked me not to sleep with Tina. I said I won't. Though it seemed like the easiest thing in the world to do. Tina all sitting there like a little poodle in Lucy's padded apartment. No actually she looked butch. And when she went to see Christine in the hospital she also gave her a copy of *Stop-Time*. That must've been when she gasped. It's a beautiful and mean-spirited book. I read it about three years later after I met the man in a professional context. He was a monster. It's a book about control. About institutionalization.

The next day when I woke up at Tina's it was very difficult. I remember she was kissing my back which I love. Staying in the apartment of someone you know well's lover, spending a night where someone you know has been having an affair, being in their affair and having one too is a gorgeous grey feeling. The phone rings and rings and you know it's your girlfriend in the hospital. She's probably going to kill herself and it's your fault. No it's not. I liked drinking Martel right out of the bottle, a small pint bottle she kept on her kitchen shelf. It became part of my secret about her that I drank that. She eventually answered the phone and it was Christine and no, she hadn't seen Eileen, though she saw her at Lucy's last night. Was Chris trying to control the world from the hospital? Tina laughed.

When I finally got home and got a call from Christine I sighed pathetically and said I had been walking the streets all night. I don't know I felt really fucked up. I said it in the most broad way possible, pretending to be pretending that my aimless walking was not about her. Poor _____, she called me, a pet name. That really hurt, it hurts now, the moment of pulling one over on someone you love. Being loved for your deception.

It didn't last. Life is just like a movie. I mean I see it like a movie, that's how things look and they work that way. Chris worked in the morning at Prescott's and Tina came in around noon so they had to begin speaking. I called one day after Tina and I had spent our night together. She wanted to repeat the experience and so did I but in another realm. I already knew that I had lived, and had done what I wanted. I never saw these things, affairs, as having any kind of process. It was about stealing, lust, sexuality. Do you know how many women steal underpants? I once got caught stealing men's socks. So I was restraining myself which was rewarding, being wanted but being good. It was tension and I had no way of ever keeping the picture together without tension.

So I called Chris at Prescott's one day and Tina answered. I could hear a smile in her voice—at me, and she said Yeah, she's here and I knew that Christine saw that smile and I knew that she knew that instant.

What do you say? I'm sorry? Christine threatened to jump in the river again, she said she wished she was still in the hospital. I feel like I'm losing my mind she shrieked. I just sat there and looked at the broken glass on the floor and the pale purple tulip wet and scrambled among the broken glass. As soon as she went out the door I called Tina and warned her that Chris might be coming her way. Christine knew it the instant she saw Tina smile. She got on the phone and said Eileen what's going on? I said I was calling to see if you wanted to go to the movies after work. Tina seemed happy that Chris knew and I was too in a way because there's nothing as nerve-wracking as peace. I just sat there and looked at the wet tulip on the floor. I cried and I cried when she left. After I got off the phone with Tina.

I don't want to tell you every detail now. I knew that something had to give since Chris kept saying "Some part of me just can't help wanting revenge." I bumped into Mark in the West Village one day. I was trying to distribute copies of *A Fresh Young Voice from the Plains* to those mean bitches in Three Lives. They are so dedicated to literature they hate it. It was such a cold day in January. I think I had some grease on my face but still it was stinging. I felt reckless and sexy and potentially uprooted. Mark was telling me that him and his wife were going to Arizona for the month of February but they could not find anyone to take care of their house in East Hampton. God! Chris had been continuously saying she needed a way to get out of the city for weekends. I could be alone during the week to write. It sounded perfect. I suggested myself to Mark, we went and had a couple of glasses of wine at Blazing Salads where his friend worked and I gave him a copy of my book to show him I had changed. We dated my first year in the city. It was pretty perverse. If I was in a blackout we would spend the night together. If not I would say goodnight and walk down into the subway, wait a minute, walk up and go to the Duchess. It was my imitation lesbian year. I stood like a little tin soldier with my bottle of Heinecken's—look at all the immense bulldykes and femmes with bouffants. Lesbians sure looked funny in 1974. We've really advanced.

I called Christine instantly. She didn't sound so enthused. Do you have any money? Nine dollars and sixty cents. I think I'm getting my period. I feel depressed. Do you want to get some food? I got chili and cheese. Probably some onions too.

It was a real love affair that month of February. Chris and I watched a documentary on Santa Lucia one cold night out in the Springs. It was our vacation. The beautiful colorful island on teevee. I don't mean to make this so sad. Our phone bill was a fortune that month. I had a lot of visitors. I read a lot of books. There was a major grant I did not receive, the Ingram Merrill grant, and it meant that I had been borrowing like a fool for months against nothing. I went up to my local bar and fucked my local artists, drunks really because I needed to get drunk and feel young and popular which was extremely easy in February in East Hampton.

Christine remained on the wagon. She called me on Valentine's Day and I wrote her a love letter, and felt loved and secure, not to be so corny.

So Lucy said, How do you feel about Chris and Tina seeing each other? A bell-shaped sound formed in my heart but it didn't ring. God everything went blackness inside. I cried and cried. Maybe it's not such a big thing, Lucy said, but they did leave together after the reading Sunday. You would've liked it, Richard was real good. Great.

I wonder what anybody thinks about using your own life, the actual words people say to you in the secrecy of love, or separation, or the oblivious moments when they've simply torn off an insult and flung it at you and you're the one who remembers every little word, at least the ones I use and I fling it back in their faces, if not there, then here, sooner or later and they say, "Oh, I can't believe I said that." Tina told me that every time Chris saw that I used her in another story she would get really upset. She hates it Tina said. Last summer, I mean the summer before last I wrote about Chris and Judy mostly because I thought I would never see Christine again and in a few weeks there she was one Sunday night on the other end when I picked up the phone and it didn't even ring. I always think it's such a secret story, this one, I just need to tell this story for me or else I will burst. It's lonely to be alive and never know the whole story. Everyone must walk with that thought. I would like to tell everything once, just my part, because this is my life, not yours.

CHELSEA GIRLS

The waitress *was* cute. If you passed by that restaurant on a summer night you'd see all those tiny white Christmas lights in the trees in their backyard where we liked to eat. She was cute in an utterly conventional way—dark hair, very fair skin. No one ever really looks like Snow White but that's what I'm thinking of. And to go out even further on that limb—the reason Snow White is so unreal and gorgeous for me comes from that description of her my mother used to read before I fell asleep: eyelashes black as black window frames. Imagine eyelashes that dark. No one has them, but my mother gave me women to love.

I was sitting in that twinkling summer restaurant with my girlfriend Chris who was always trouble, but nights when I had money were okay. We were both sitting in that restaurant and I was writing poems on napkins: "like a fascist. Your/beauty, . . . our drinks . . ." Christine's mind was wandering, so was mine. I had a shirt of hers on—I worked, but she had new clothes. It didn't seem right but it was absolutely right that I wear them. It was just that when she had money she knew what to do. Mary, the waitress had blue eyes inside the powerful black celtic eye-

lashes. She set our drinks, vodka tonics, down with authority and no fuss. Having both waitressed, we knew we were
making her night better. Oh this couple I really loved came
in. Drinking a lot, kind of bored looking. Chris was tanning
that summer and planning our next play. I was writing my
poems on napkins and making our living in a way I would
never forget, cooking French toast for Jimmy Schuyler. Then
sitting down and reading the books I would pick up off the
floor of his messy beautiful room in the Chelsea Hotel. I lived
for nights like the one I was about to have with Mary Turner.
Actually the Mary Turner nights sparkled best in the morning
recitation of events for the amusement of Jimmy Schuyler.

She *is* cute said Chris—she was preppy-looking, athletic. She wore a white alligator shirt, without the alligator I
think—small tan, not too much, mostly the kind of tan you
get from sunbathing on the roof of the gym across the street
from the Chelsea where I later learned she went. She had that
fresh sort of sparkling all-American look which gets subtly
wild once you pick up that she's a lesbian because then the
strong all-American girl eats pussy which makes her bad, and
everything that's good be bad, and in cahoots as she's putting
your drink down on the round table with an umbrella in the
center and with her big blue eyes she goes I want you too.
It was swift, fast, the check, rrip. Christine saw it all. Why
don't you get her number. Tsk, I went, quietly. The tsk carried
everything: disapproval, I wouldn't do that, are you kidding,
who cares? My tsk was as tough and private as every one of
Mary's solid little gestures that led me towards being someone
slightly drunker who would sleep with her that night.

We walked down Bleecker Street, I smoked. Kept the stubby blue pack of Gauloise in the pocket of the dark blue cotton shirt that was Chris's. Sometimes I could forgive her for buying clothes because I thought in reality she was buying me clothes. I felt like mother. I paid the bills. She was the teenager and oddly enough she dressed me. Let's go to the Duchess I said lighting another one. I slid my yellow bic into the small pocket of my orange painter pants. I had such faith in things. I had a little notebook in my back pocket where men carried their wallets. Firstly I was a woman, then I rolled my cash and I put it in my pocket. It was impossible to carry two square things. If you wanted anyone to see your ass. And I did but I didn't.

What—so you can see your waitress? She won't be there. Was she there? I keep seeing her in the second bar when I was further along the glowing cord of drunkenness and sex. I saw her in the Duchess and it was electric. I saw her among the sea of leaning and dark bodies—just a peek. I put the information away instantly. I was owing Christine one—making me support her—being volatile so I had to be reliable, being young so I had to be old. Look who's here Chris said. I know I said. I didn't want it turned into a mockery. Christine was the boy in our relationship. Not the butch. No Chris was the pain in the neck little teasing boy—guess who's here means Eileen likes a girl. You know it was like we were in the 5th grade and I was doing something really finky. There was something very sick about our relationship and to her credit Chris always pushed it to the surface as quickly as possible. Could we possibly be two boys out cruising women together. But then why was I living with Chris? What did it mean. Was I that desperate. Chris was beautiful. I thought. But at this moment standing there in the Duchess around quarter of one in the summer holding a cold can of beer in my hand Christine's beauty was less than a fact.

Well go talk to her then! You must really like her. You are really weird. I wasn't. Not if I was planning to do something, to go after the waitress. Was I planning to do that. No I couldn't do that. I was the good one, here and everywhere. It was a private universe I assure you but there I was—sort of a lamb of god or something. I secretly thought even my poetry was a sign of my goodness. Wet words on soft limp paper. Holy Holy Holy. All of my pants had a little black circle, a mark that hit just above the patch jean pocket of my ass. My life was a network of private signs. Leaking pens. Stuff that stayed in place as I moved along. There was lots of trouble but I didn't ask for it. I moved slow across the dance floor towards Mary Turner who held her beer close to her shirt and looked up at me unsurprised and said hello.

What a surprise I said, sounding tremendously stupid but also picking up instantly that what I said didn't matter at all. Where's your friend she asked. Chris, I informed. She's over there I said waving my hand. Can I get you a drink she asked her tone ironically still implying she was still my waitress. Yeah I would love one of those pointing to the Bud Light she held against her breast. We both slightly twitched at the suggestion that I would like one of her breasts and the embarrassment loaded her brisk departure and she smiled be right back with that wonderful natural toughness.

I think it gets learned in Catholic schools. Once a sado-masochistic nun banished myself and four of my twelve-year-old girlfriends to half an hour in the paper closet where we awaited the smell of her soapy body middle-aged teeth bad breath. It always seemed like nuns ate really strange food. Our crime had been giggling uncontrollably at her tales about martyrdom. It seems the Romans thought of nothing all day but how to torture Christians and Sister Ednata did justice to that obsession with her ecstatic tales told with her big lips of naked Christians tied up and left on the silvery blue ice in ancient Rome. Women's tits were cut off and served symbolically on plates, there were endless spankings, rape, tearful pleas by virgins like St. Agnes that their chastity be preserved and naturally it was not. They were violated and then they were killed and all these people who had suffered so much were now in heaven and hearing their trials just made us laugh and we'd go make eyes at each other in class and cough into our handkerchiefs such code words as *ah-slut* which stood for us. Little whores who would go to hell. Waiting for Sister Ednata in the paper room I could smell girlfriends and Donna Murphy burped and Debbie Considine's stomach was growling and we were laughing so hard we were almost peeing and the nun flung the door open and we sobered up. I don't remember any punishment. I remember the riches of the piles and piles of unmarked paper, a heaven of sorts. I remember the shiny wood of the incredibly old lemony-smelling wood shelves. St. Agnes School was a huge old-fashioned box for sex and paper and prospective temptations. It made girls like me and Mary Turner and for that I am grateful.

I raced back over to Chris, being good. What do you want she said, leaning against a pole. I was wondering what *you* were doing, trying to take on the role of a mild accuser. Really and what's your friend's name? I don't know. I was just telling her what a good waitress she was. Would you like another beer? I asked, shaking her can. Chris smiled. Up at the bar I ran into Mary Turner. Couldn't wait, she asked. Uh, I said. Everything we said went two ways. No I'm getting a drink for Chris. Well here's yours she smiled, giving me a beer and her back, turning to a friend. I looked back at Christine who had missed the whole thing, bent over the jukebox, undoubtedly looking for that song by Air Supply. She had the weirdest taste in music. She was like a red neck boy from the midwest who looks like a god. He wore red lipstick. We were fags. These bands she liked told me all that. She should have stayed home and bought a truck. So what's her name, Chris asked.

God I groaned. I was sort of praying now. Nothing had happened so maybe I should just ignore the whole thing. We stood there in that nook next to the jukebox facing the bar. I was looking at that blonde bartender that Irene Young was all excited about. She was cute too. God I was bored. Mary Turner walked up with her blonde friend from the bar. Hi she gleamed, aiming at Chris. I'm Christine, this is Eileen. Sometimes she had excellent manners—it always shocked me. She was so competitive. I'm Mary Turner and this is Beth. Beth nodded and couldn't have been more bored. Maybe we'll see you girls later. We're going to The Club.

Streets were so dark that year and it was really the hottest summer. I should have been drinking vodka all night, but I was drinking beer. The smell of bread from the bakery on Carmine Street spilled over to Bleecker as we were walking by. I don't know why I was hungry. The sidewalks looked like it had momentarily rained. Proprietors trying to cool their sidewalks off and oil in the gutters that made those teeny rainbows. Urban nothing—I liked it so much. Pizza shops, all those dangerous boys roaming the streets who were always trying to get into women's bars. There were tourists too. Across the street was a bicycle shop where I would buy a bike next year. Got a cigarette? I didn't bother to question Christine who'd been preaching that never again was she going to smoke. I displayed my pack. I'll wait she said. That's right I thought. She hates Gauloises. There was a diagonal brass bar on the big wooden door. We pushed it. The summer of three dyke bars in the West Village. We were rich. This one looked like a Chinese restaurant. Several stars were twinkling outside. The bartender waved. I owed her money. We went downstairs.

You know we don't have to stay together tonight said Chris. Well sure I said. Do you want some money. Come and get me when you want to go home. Give me five bucks. I mean we don't even have to go home together. And walked off. How can you punish someone who's pushing you into doing something bad. She was Protestant. If anything. She was like an animal that could sniff out my state before I had even worked up the question of what I could or couldn't do. I went up and got a vodka. Hello said Mary Turner. She was sitting there alone. Where's Beth I nervously asked. Is Christine your lover asked Mary Turner. She's my roommate I said pushing my hair out of my eyes. Between my words and my gesture it was probably clear that Chris and I were having a fight. The best I could ever figure out about talking to people especially other lesbians was that we were mostly acting. Mary Turner put her hand on my shoulder. She was playing with my hair. This was unbelievable. How did you like your food, she asked. I liked it. Are you ummm. I was making conversation. I used to be in a program for physical therapy but I dropped out, she replied. I'm a poet I said. She looked at me. I was standing there thinking I'm 29. I wonder how old she is. I sipped my beer. Let me buy you a drink, okay she asked. I nodded. Well what do you like she asked. Vodka tonic? That's what you were drinking at the restaurant. I was standing there praying I would get really drunk really fast. Out of the corner of my eye I saw Chris strolling by. She looked okay. Do you like Stolly she asked. Sure I said. It's really better for you. Really do you think that way about booze. I don't drink much she said moving her glass around the bar, spreading the circles. I pulled out a cigarette. And I don't smoke. I do. I said. I love cigarettes. Finally I said something intelligent.

Chris stood about three feet away from us. I turned feeling someone looking. She beckoned me with her index finger. God! You okay I asked. Was there a crisis? I didn't know. I didn't know how to be. I was wondering if you would loan me a couple more bucks. She looked a little sad and vulnerable and the word loan implied she had forgotten that we lived together.

The floors in my apartment are nice old wood. There's a tree outside the window and in summer its shaking green leafiness acted like curtains that softened the hungover mornings and allowed the darts of light in the later afternoon to illuminate my place. Sometimes in the afternoon friends would come by and we'd drink red drinks, hot ones. By the fall the leaves were down and I began to think of my apartment as blue. It's warmer now, everything having gone around twice. Chris used to live here. For a couple of years. There's a character now called Eileen's apartment and perhaps she remembers everything I don't.

Well where are you going. Home. Well I'll see you in a little bit. What about your girlfriend. We're just talking. Maybe I'll get another beer. Oh God this was so awful. And what was on the jukebox. This place actually had one of those rotating balls. Mary waved from the bar. Christine marched over towards her. Oh God. Oh no. Hi Eileen. The woman I began talking to had big bags under her eyes, was skinny but kind of powerful. Having a good time, Eileen? She always treated me like I was drunk. Was she flirting? Years later I learned she had a crush on me, at least that's what she said, but at that moment I thought she was laughing at what an asshole I was. I guess flirting often looks like sarcasm.

Looking up I saw Chris drink her new beer and Mary laughing and smiling. She did not have her arm on Christine's shoulder. Excuse me I said to the flirt, walking over. They ignored me for at least three minutes. Can you imagine? And I'm facing the bartender I owe fifteen dollars to, my back is to the flirt. So I went to the bathroom. Then they looked up and I kept walking. In the bathroom I leaned against the cool tiles and looked at the flooded bathroom floor. Two women were giggling in the stall. I smelled pot. It's broken they yelled and broke into gales of laughter. I thought of the paper closet. I should turn out the light and fling open the door and I should be and am Sister Ednata. I looked into the mirror at the dark blue shirt.

Chris was outside talking to the flirt. I approached but veered away at the last minute. Actually some really big woman in a cap was moving at the same diagonal as me so I chose to surrender. One of these really flowery femmy songs was on the jukebox. One woman's humble voice reinvented and reflected one million times. Eileen Chris yelled. It was marshmallow music. I am going to leave now she confided but I think you should go home with her. Maybe she has a girlfriend I suggested. Just a roommate . . . Chris. Don't do me any favors, Eileen. *I'm* going home. The ball turned a few times and I went back to Mary. She's nice, she said. Listen do you have a girlfriend? I live with my ex-lover. She's a go-go dancer. And we have a male roommate. He cleans house. She smiled. Do you want another drink. Can you handle it she said kissing my neck. I nodded.

We were going up Eighth Avenue in a cab. You know where we were going? We were going to the Chelsea Hotel. I loved the moment when Mary said should we go to a hotel. She kind of snickered like a dirty girl. I was glad I was not with a complete sophisticate. I was with another Catholic. This was unique. It seemed I never met them, or got this close. Well, I have ten I said. Keep it. I'll get it. She was only giving me profile now but it probably did bother her. They probably gave us the tiniest room in the Chelsea. We were on eight.

Because of my job with Jimmy Schuyler I was very familiar with the place, its smells and sounds and the degree of dilapidation, the ugly art in the lobby that wasn't distractingly exotic or worthy of note at all. It was normal. It was like fucking at home. You know, like your mother's home. Mary lived nearby and had the cab stop at 21st so she could run up and get a bottle of champagne. It was corny of course, but I had only been corny like this with men, men that I didn't like. To be with a woman who had such a mundane mind about what was sleazy or hot was really great. We opened the door and it was small. The bed a small one was immediately to the right of the door. Mary put the bottle on the night table and immediately began to strip down. She was a sport. She had an athletic body, she wasn't skinny at all, but she wasn't fat. She had a body basically like the women in my family. Most of the women I'm lovers with have bodies like my sister. Not Chris, but I'm talking from the future now. Her athleticism made me shy and besides I didn't go to the gym and was really kind of scared to take off my clothes. I was drunk and was just more comfortable being dressed. So we rolled around the bed that way for a while, this crazy part of me shocked that I was making out with a naked woman and keeping my clothes on for a while made me a man, my big dick cunt. Please she finally said as if it were something we'd been discussing for a while and she began to unbutton Christine's blue shirt and kiss my breasts which sort of looked like hers. Then it seemed that every time a woman kissed me and touched was like something that had never happened before. Still it's like that. Kind of a shock.

I pulled my own orange pants off. My sneakers I kicked

on the floor. I reached for my cigarettes. She said no. We were kneeling on the thin bed at the Chelsea Hotel just kind of facing each other. I kissed her mouth. I looked into her eyes. The pale blue light flooded in from the back. She had very round nipples. She would suck mine, I would suck hers it was kind of like we had both just gotten this toy. She'd take a sip of the champagne. Eventually she let me smoke. She smoked too. Eventually she did everything. We rubbed our bodies and breasts against each other till we couldn't stand it anymore. She was so pretty. She was very strong. We rolled around. We held each other down. Then we fucked.

I had never been fucked by a woman before. It's scarey. You want to do something for so long. Anne Clarke had black framed eyes. In high school in front of Brighams she was dancing in front of everyone to a car radio blasting "Girl I want to be with you in the day time," except she would go Beep Beep-Beep Beep Beep-Beep-Beep-Beep and wag her knees and sway her arms slightly bent just for the absolute delight of everyone standing there 16 17 18 sipping their cokes, watching this girl called Clarksey. It's like having a boy around. And everyone laughed. We were twelve and Donna was showing her padded bra in her basement to all the girls and I was afraid to come in too close because I thought so much about Donna Murphy and how beautiful she was and now I would see her nipples. She couldn't handle it either. We just couldn't handle that I was a lesbian though no one knew it yet. I was like a boy, that's all.

The first time I was in bed with a woman it was also in morning light and so was the first time Christine had her head between my legs. I was running my tongue along the lips of the cunt of the first woman I had ever had my clothes off with and this is what love felt like. One thing, not two. That was it. With a woman I felt whole, not different. For instance if I wanted to put a finger inside her vagina and she said not that, then I knew that maybe the new room wasn't as big as it felt and it went on from there, being diminished though never ultimately losing its glamour but being bound nonetheless by what each woman told me lesbians don't do. So Mary started fucking me. One finger two fingers three fingers. And her face all that strong part coming out, dissolving her prettiness and pale freckles and celtic distance into force. I had really liked the thrusting presence of a man's dick inside of me. What I didn't know what to do with was men. Who would rub their beards against my cunt and up and down my clit for hours and I wondered what was wrong with me it was such a dirty thing. I couldn't get off. Only once or twice. The last man being such a pig that I couldn't believe I was letting him eat my pussy. I had a tremendous orgasm. He laughed. The first woman put her head between my legs and the complete sin, the absolute moment of sex came back and I was all in one piece coming apart. I was willing to sacrifice all for that moment. Even I guess my vagina, that jar. I thought I had to give that up but there was nothing like that at all.

I've gotta go to work. What are you talking about? She was holding my head on her chest. I told you this man I take care of who lives here.

Ten o'clock. I came into the world of 625. I was squinting. Hello Dear boomed Jimmy. O shit I forgot the papers. I see.

I'll go down. It's okay you can get them later when you go out. Are you sure? I'm quite alright. Jimmy was so big. He was like an enormous sunflower lying on the bed of his long skinny room with French windows that opened onto clanging noisy twenty-third street. It was a street I knew nothing about till I worked for Jimmy. The Chelsea was a myth loaded with old denizens, Europeans from the 60s, rock bands and then Jimmy and Virgil Thomson. He was so skinny when I met him and now he was so fat. You look a little weathered dear. I do! Well, I put the pan of water onto the stove. I've got a girl upstairs. A friend staying in the hotel. No we're having sex, I met her last night. I was with Chris in this bar, she kind of forced me into it. I'm sure she did. Actually standing in Jimmy's kitchen such a regular thing felt strange in a way that fucking in the Chelsea didn't. Now I felt I was doing the wrong thing. Well, maybe you want to get back up there. Well, she's waiting but I'll make you some french toast. That would be fine. I could still taste champagne while the buttery smell of french toast filled the pantry. I opened the apple sauce and examined the dry stuck apple sauce coating the rim of the glass. I was wanting normal now and normal was tawdry. What's her name, your friend upstairs. Mary. She was our waitress. Whose? Me and Chris. You girls lead quite an exciting life. Yeah well I'm sure she's home breaking every glass in the house or selling my books. Oh I don't think Chris would act that way. I'm sure she'd do something better than that. Right. The light flooded in through the windows as I placed the dish down next to Jimmy on his bed. There was a little chair, salmon colored, next to his bed with several packs of Export "A"s, old coffee and rings on the orange seat from other coffee cups. There were pennies, two prescription bottles of pills. Oh god I forgot the pills. Now this really was bad. I was standing in his room on the old green rug. The floor was covered with books: Firbank, Virginia Woolf's diaries, John Ashbery, *As We Know*. He was like a music box. As you flashed each to him he was bound to respond in his type of quip: He's writing in columns now. It's pretty good. Oh she's much too interested in typesetting to really chase pussy. The phone rings. Hello Dear. I think that would be very nice. He has big lips. His lips are like some kind of fruit he squeezes his words out from. I wonder if the drugs do it. Make him slow and careful. The silences here in the room, the spaces that linger and fill the air when we speak are what I know about Jimmy more than the things he says. The room is yellow. I come in babbling every morning—Oh God what a night. But I must take care of him first. Once I do—he's finished eating, when he's lying on his bed with the soles of his bare feet facing me and I'm sitting in my chair by the window reading a book I found on the floor—I wait for a break—Christine's really mad at me because—I would throw her out, he advised solemnly. You would? Read my new poem, Dear. It's on the desk. If you like. Jimmy was gay. He went to dyke bars in the Village in the forties. The butches would rise and bow when the femmes came in. The first day I stood facing him, a thin man with long curly hair rigidly lying on his bed I blurted out I love your poems. He said thank you. His friends, a painter and a dealer were standing nearby. They needed someone to spend some time with him and give him his drugs. Say your favorite poet in the world is lying there. Who you've always been told is unmeetable, has nervous breakdowns, is a recluse into SM. Just out of a hospital, almost killed himself. Jimmy Schuyler was my new job. Slowly I moved his possessions to the Chelsea from an 8th Avenue flophouse where on the final day among the dry cleaned clothes still in plastic bags, charred bits of poetry on papers, art prints books—I masturbated because it was a filthy and interesting place and he found out because I told one person who told someone else. It's all right dear I don't need anything. Go have fun.

From his bed he ran the show. It's a talent a few people I know have, mostly Scorpios which he was. You'd be hesitatingly starting your story, or like a cartoon character running right in when you realized the long wharf you were taking a short run on, his attention was not there. It was hopeless. The yellow in his room became brighter, the air became crinkly your throat became parched—you felt you had simply become a jerk. The presence of his attention was so strong, so deeply passive—such a thing to bathe your tiny desperate words in that when it was gone you had to stop and hover in the silence again. Then he might begin, or perhaps you could come up with something else once the brittleness, the void passed. You had to stay silent for a very long time some days. He was like music, Jimmy was, and you had to be like music too to be with him, but understand in his room he was conductor. He directed the yellow air in room 625. It was marvelous to be around. It was huge and impassive. What emerged in the silence was a strong picture, more akin to a child or a beautiful animal.

Hello Dear. Sometimes I came in and he was sitting on his chair by the bright window. He got up early. He told me that, but I could also surmise it from the number of cigarettes in the ashtray which he never dumped, and how much spilled Taster's Choice was on the kitchen counter. (*John* says Taster's Choice is the best. The emphasis on John meant both that it was a funny thing to have an opinion on and a useful tip that one should take.) I saw his dick a lot. Probably more than any other man's in my life. It wasn't small, it was kind of large. As I would narrate my nightly voyage he would tell me about all his affairs in the forties and fifties and invariably these often very famous men who were practically myths now would be rated: He was like sleeping with a reptile. Really icky. Edwin. He had a lovely dick. I'd be standing over him holding a dirty dish and figured to leave the silence alone. Well yours looks pretty good I might say as it nudged out of his boxer shorts.

I ran up the two brown staircases to Mary. The firehoses were there. The Europeans were coming in and out of their rooms. I crawled back into the blue bed with her. She was slightly asleep. Not entirely. I don't love you I thought. I kissed her. I kissed her again. I thought of the big sunflower man downstairs. He was not sex. It was something else. I hugged her. She was everything else. It was blue. She was Mary the mother of god. Till check out time I sucked on her tit.

I returned around 3 with his pills. I knocked. Jimmy I yelled. I had the key. He was sound asleep. I put the pills on the chair.

Here's your paper I said to no one. He'd been up making coffee. The kitchen was a mess. I stuck his change between his glasses and this morning's coffee cup. I kept 3 bucks. I stuffed the bills into my orange pants and I felt something damp. It was the poem I wrote on a napkin last night. The ink was kind of smeared but I could read it. Want to hear my new poem, Jimmy. I wrote it last night. It's called "Under My Umbrella."

                    the old are very ugly.
            You know what I mean?
            When you see them
            smoking a cigarette, it's
            like the tip of the iceberg.
            And their boozy wrinkles
            under their eyes. You
            know I like this evening.
            I really deserve the leaves
            in the trees
            around this restaurant. I'm
            kind of overwhelmed by
            the beauty of things
            like a fascist. Your
            beauty, mine,
            our drinks, I wonder
            if I should catch
            up, you're drinking
            faster than me, Oh
            I guess I'll get
            another vodka tonic

and see how the evening
goes. Clink-Clink.

He woke for a second. Nodded. I'm leaving now. Did
you have a good time? Oh it was alright. Bye Jimmy. Then I
opened the door and stepped back out to the hall which I've
mentioned was brown. It was a hot summer day in 1979.

ACKNOWLEDGMENTS

Thanks forever to John Martin of Black Sparrow Press for the original publication of *Chelsea Girls*. And to Jack Pierson, great friend, whose wise advice and portrait of CG in '90s remain the muse for this new edition.

"Bath, Maine," "Merry Christmas, Dr. Beagle," "Light Warrior," "Bread and Water," "Everybody Would Go Play Cards at Eddie and Nonie's," "21, 22, 23 . . ." and "1969" were first published in *Bread and Water* and *1969*, respectively, by Hanuman Books.

Many thanks to the editors of the publications in which some of these stories have lately and initially appeared: *25 for 25: Outstanding Contemporary LGBT Authors and Those They Inspired* (Lambda ebook), *The Nightboat Anthology of New Narrative Writing, Warhol & Mapplethorpe: Guise & Dolls, AMLIT, Avenue E, Bomb, City Lights Anthology, Dear World, Discontents, Fictions South/Fictions North, Gas, Longshot, VLS, Woman on Woman II,* and *The World*.

For inspiration and help at crucial moments I'd like to thank my mother. And my brother and sister, Terry and Ann, whom I love. I also thank Ruth Novaczek, Tom Whitridge and Nathan Kernan, Leopoldine Core, Tom Bair, Nick Flynn, Emma Smith, Kevin Killian, Dodie Bellamy, Dale Peck, Bob Gluck, Jennifer Montgomery, Sarah Schulman, Tim Dlugos, Rene Ricard, Benjamin Weissman, Laurie Weeks, David Rattray, Laurie Stone, Elinor Nauen, Joe Westmoreland, Megan Adams and Angie Romagnoli, Myra Mniewski, Tom Carey, Faye Hirsch, Tom Clark, the MacDowell Colony, the country of Mexico, the Indian subcontinent, and Helen and Brice Marden.

Also thanks to Paul Weitz for the great pleasure of seeing the first line from "21, 22, 23 . . ." at the front of his feature film *Grandma*.

EILEEN MYLES has published twenty books of poetry, art journalism, and fiction and libretti. She's a Guggenheim Fellow, has received the Shelley Prize from the Poetry Society of America and a Lambda Award for lesbian fiction, and was named to the Whiting/Slate Second Novel List. She also received an arts writers grant from Creative Capital/the Warhol Foundation and a Foundation for Contemporary Arts grant. She lives in Marfa, Texas, and New York.